Dear Reader,

Is there a baby in th[...]
lives are going to cha[...] [...] [...] [...] [...]
for the three heroines in this brand-new collection
of stories, *Baby and All*.

USA TODAY bestselling author Candace Camp
brings you an emotional story of a woman who
believed she'd never be a mother yet finds herself
bringing up baby with the help of her handsome
neighbor in "Somebody Else's Baby."

"The Baby Bombshell" is the infant who lands in
the lap of a career-driven beauty who doesn't know
the first thing about parenting. Fortunately for her,
she's about to get some fast—and passionate—
lessons in love and babies from the sexy single
dad next door in this heartwarming tale by reader
favorite Victoria Pade.

When a PR executive finds herself playing
mommy for the camera with her sexy boss, it's
"Lights, Camera...Baby!" in this fresh and fun
story from award-winning author Myrna Mackenzie.

Happy reading!

The Editors
Silhouette Books

CANDACE CAMP,

a *USA TODAY* bestselling author and former attorney, is married to a Texan, and they have a daughter who has been bitten by the acting bug. Her family and her writing keep her busy, but when she does have free time, she loves to read. In addition to her contemporary romances, she has written a number of historicals, which are currently being published by MIRA Books.

VICTORIA PADE

is a bestselling author of both historical and contemporary romance fiction, and the mother of two energetic daughters, Cori and Erin. Although she enjoys her chosen career as a novelist, she occasionally laments that she has never traveled farther from her Colorado home than Disneyland, instead spending all her spare time plugging away at her computer. She takes breaks from writing by indulging in her favorite hobby—eating chocolate.

MYRNA MACKENZIE,

winner of the Holt Medallion honoring outstanding literary talent, loves to write about the unsung heroes and heroines of the world, and after many years of writing she is still thrilled to be able to say that she makes her living daydreaming. Myrna lives in the Chicago suburbs with her husband and two sons. Readers may write to her at P.O. Box 225, LaGrange, IL 60525 or visit her online at www.myrnamackenzie.com.

candace
camp
victoria
pade
myrna
mackenzie

baby and all

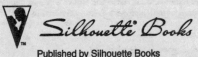

Silhouette Books

Published by Silhouette Books

America's Publisher of Contemporary Romance

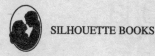 **SILHOUETTE BOOKS**

BABY AND ALL

Copyright © 2003 by Harlequin Books S.A.

ISBN 0-373-21808-7

The publisher acknowledges the copyright holders of the individual works as follows:

SOMEBODY ELSE'S BABY
Copyright © 2003 by Candace Camp

THE BABY BOMBSHELL
Copyright © 2003 by Victoria Pade

LIGHTS, CAMERA...BABY!
Copyright © 2003 by Myrna Topol

This edition published by arrangement with Harlequin Books S.A.

® and TM are trademarks of Harlequin Books S.A., used under license. Trademarks indicated with ® are registered in the United States Patent and Trademark Office, the Canadian Trade Marks Office and in other countries.

Visit Silhouette at www.eHarlequin.com

Printed in U.S.A.

CONTENTS

SOMEBODY ELSE'S BABY   9
Candace Camp

THE BABY BOMBSHELL   135
Victoria Pade

LIGHTS, CAMERA...BABY!   245
Myrna Mackenzie

SOMEBODY ELSE'S BABY

Candace Camp

Dear Reader,

When my editor at Silhouette asked me to contribute to *Baby and All*, I knew immediately that I wanted to present the way a baby can interrupt one's life in a delightful way—by pulling one out of the bleakness of grief. There is nothing like a baby to shove a person right back into the world of life and love.

My own daughter was born only a month before my mother died unexpectedly. It caused me great sorrow that my daughter and mother never got to know one another, but I also realized God's infinite wisdom in what happened, for I'm not sure I could have made it through that terrible time if I hadn't had the joy of my baby's presence.

Nothing warms the heart and soul like holding a baby close. I hope that reading "Somebody Else's Baby" brings you a little of that very special joy.

Best always,

Candace Camp

Chapter 1

That man was on her doorstep again.

Cassandra was tempted to turn around and not answer the door. But she was coming to learn that he was annoyingly persistent, and she feared that he would just keep coming back until she talked to him. And since he had already disturbed the peace of her afternoon, she supposed she might as well get it over with.

Fixing an implacable expression on her face, she opened the front door and moved into the doorway, crossing her arms over her chest and looking at him in a way she hoped conveyed the idea that she would never in this lifetime agree to his offer.

He smiled at her, as he had the other two times he had presented his offer, but this time, she noted, there was a certain forced quality to his smile. She hoped that meant he would stop bothering her soon.

"Mr. Buchanan, my answer is the same as it has been the other times," she said firmly. "I have no intention of selling any part of my land."

She would, she thought, as soon sell a part of herself, just whack off a toe or foot and take cash for it, as give up even one piece of this place. It was Philip's. He had died here.

"Now, Ms. Weeks, if you would just hear me out…" he began, again flashing the smile she was sure a great number of women found charming.

He had the kind of looks many women liked, a sort of rugged, outdoorsy handsomeness: thick dark brown hair, golden-brown eyes that lit with humor when he smiled, tanned skin marked with laugh lines and squint lines around his eyes from years spent in the sun. Cassie was glad she was impervious to that sort of appeal. Since Philip had died, she hadn't felt a flutter of interest in any man.

"Mr. Buchanan, I heard you out the last two times, and I see no reason why I would feel any differently this time."

"What I'm asking for isn't unreasonable," he said earnestly, moving fractionally closer and bending down a little to look her in the eye.

"Perhaps not—if you consider it reasonable to expect another person to sell you something of theirs simply because you want it," Cassie retorted. "Personally, I don't. There is absolutely no reason why I should give you part of my property because you bought your lot without taking the disadvantages of it into account.''

''I took the disadvantages into account,'' Sam Buchanan snapped back. ''Building houses is my profession. I'm a contractor.''

He was not sure why this woman was so determined to be unpleasant, but, frankly, she was beginning to irritate the hell out of him.

She was pretty, even something close to beautiful, a few years younger than himself, with a face of classic lines, eyes bluer than the lake that lay beyond the house and trees, and blond hair that tumbled in a soft riot of curls almost to her shoulders. But she did little with herself, catching her hair back in a simple ponytail, no makeup on her face, her clothes obviously expensive but plain. She wore no jewelry other than a watch and a wedding band. She seemed to want to keep her personality just as spare and unadorned, even prickly. Every time he had seen her, she had assumed the same sort of attitude—crisp and defensive, as if he were there to hurt her.

He knew she was a widow; Lew Mickleson, the man from whom he had bought the property, had told him that. He wondered if sorrow had soured her personality, or if she had always been remote and defensive.

''I knew the shoreline was shorter than I would like,'' he told her, trying to get back to a calm and friendly tone. ''And rather rocky, too. But its advantages outweighed the disadvantages. That lot was one of the few pieces of property of this size left on the lake. It was exactly the setting I was looking for. And the house had potential. I was able to renovate it to what I wanted.''

"Yes, I heard the workmen," Cassie said dryly, then regretted her words. They sounded disagreeable. Of course, that was how she felt about this man and the property next door. Even before he started harassing her about selling him some of her shorefront, his workmen had disturbed her peace for several months last year, working on Mr. Buchanan's house. Still, she sounded like a grouchy old woman, even to herself, and she hated to think that was what she had turned into.

Cassie sighed. "Look, Mr. Buchanan, I understand that you think I'm being unreasonable by not selling you this property. But I like my shorefront exactly the way it is. That was one of the features of the place that attracted Philip and me to it. The curve of the shore, with that outcropping on the east and the big rocks on the left, makes it very private and secluded."

Seclusion was what Philip had been looking for when they'd first bought the property seven years ago—a quiet place where he could relax and unwind from the pressures of his fast-paced life in L.A. And then, four years ago, when they had moved here permanently, the peace had soothed them, wrapped around them and eased their pain and sorrow at the illness they could not fight.

"I appreciate that. I really do. I don't want to disturb your peace. I just want a small strip on the other side of the rocks, enough to put a boathouse and dock.

It will be hidden from your house by the trees. I've considered the sightline. You won't even see it.''

"I would see it when I walked down to the shore," Cassie pointed out sharply. "It would be sitting right there."

"It would be very unobtrusive," he told her. "Let me show you my design for it. It would fit the landscape. I'm talking about leaving a lot of the trees, and the boathouse would be built out—"

"No!" Cassie was a little startled at how loud and sharp her voice came out. The word had popped out of her instinctively, everything in her rising up against the intrusion. "Don't you understand? I don't want it there!"

His jaw tightened. "But you haven't even let me explain it to you properly. You'll hardly know it's there, and I'm offering more than a fair price."

"No amount of money is going to make me sell! Now, please, go away and stop bothering me about this."

Cassie stepped back inside quickly and shut the door, turning the lock with a sharp click. She was almost shaking, her heart beating faster. The rage had sprung up in her so swiftly, so unexpectedly, that it had taken her by surprise.

She walked away from the door, going deeper into the house, as if by getting away from him she could escape the anger that had seized her. She wasn't sure exactly why she had felt so suddenly and fiercely angry.

It had been like the time right after Philip died. For

the first few months she was alone, she had often felt
that quick uprush of anger. It hadn't taken anything
to make it flare up inside her, hot and urgent, as if
she had to defend herself from some attack. She had
known then that it had to do with Philip's death, that
there was a huge pool of rage inside her because he
had been taken from her so arbitrarily and so awfully.

"You're angry at God," her friend Amanda had
told her, and she supposed Amanda was right. Her
pain, her fear of living the rest of her life without
him, the sheer unfairness of a man as young and as
healthy as Philip dying, boiled and twisted inside her,
bursting out at unexpected moments.

Cassie stopped at the hallway. It lay in the center
of the house, dark, quiet. The doors on the right side
all stood closed. At the end was the darkroom Philip
had had installed for her; she never used it anymore.
The next room was his office, and the nearest one
was the den, which they had converted to his bedroom
when he could no longer go up the stairs to the second
floor.

She leaned against the doorframe, resting her head
on the cool wood of the door. Inside, she knew, were
all the things Philip had used, the contraptions that
had made his illness more bearable—the hospital bed,
the wheelchair, the breathing equipment. She had put
them away in there and closed the door, unable to
part with them, equally unable to look at them.

After a long moment, she turned and walked into
the large family room. It was floored in warm golden
oak, and across the room the wall was set with plate-

glass windows centered by a wide stone fireplace. It was the center of the house, which was cool in the green shade of the trees in the summer, in the winter warm and cozy with a roaring fire in the hearth.

She went down two shallow steps to the couch, made of butter-soft leather in a deep wine shade. Like all the house, the room showed the signs of having been renovated to accommodate a wheelchair—a ramp that took up part of the steps. Cassie sat down on the couch, curling her legs up under her and leaned her head back against it, waiting for the peace and beauty of the lake landscape to soothe her frazzled nerves.

It had been over two years since Philip had died; days occasionally went by now when she did not even think about him. But for some reason, the argument with her next-door neighbor had left her thinking about Philip.

She had met him almost ten years earlier. She had been twenty-six and was beginning to establish herself as a photographer in Los Angeles. She had done publicity photos for an up-and-coming singer and, as a consequence, had been invited to an enormous party kicking off the release of the singer's first album. Cassie had gone somewhat reluctantly, thinking it would be a tiring bore but too good an opportunity to get her name out to pass up. Philip Weeks had been there, and that had changed the rest of her life.

She had seen him standing talking with a group of men, slim and sophisticated, his blond hair silvered at the temples, his gray eyes piercingly intelligent.

Unused as she was to the upper echelons of power at that time, she had not known who he was, and even when he strolled over to where she stood and introduced himself, she still had not realized that she was speaking to the president of the very recording company that was throwing the party. It was only later, when she was ecstatically describing her conversation with him to Trilly, her roommate, that Trilly had explained to her who Philip Weeks was.

He was fourteen years older than she was, almost forty, a fact that had bothered her parents and some of her friends but had not seemed like a problem to her at all. His age simply was not a part of his personality. He was bright and well-read and full of energy. No one could be around him without feeling the force of his charisma. Cassandra knew she was in love with him by their fourth date, and by the time they had been dating two months, he asked her to marry him. She was more certain of their love than she had ever been of anything, but to please her parents, she had agreed to wait another six months before she married him.

She had never for a moment regretted her decision. There had been times during their marriage when she had cried, times when she had cursed his busy life for keeping them apart, times when she had struggled to adjust to a husband and even more so to a stepdaughter, but none of those things had ever hurt or shaken her enough to make her question her love.

The fact of the matter was that her married life had been, on the whole, almost idyllic. She loved her husband. She also had a career she loved, and being married to Philip had only made that career easier. Given his wealth, she no longer had to worry about making money but could concentrate on developing her art. And, she knew, as Philip Weeks's wife, doors opened to her that would have taken her years to open on her own. Thrust into a world full of celebrities, she had ample opportunity to exercise her photographic skills, and her edgy, unusual photographs of singers and movie stars soon brought her acclaim.

In retrospect, she thought, she should have known that her life was too perfect, that nothing so good could continue for long. They had been married for five years when Philip had fallen. The only injury had been a bruise on his cheek that he had made jokes about, but the fall had worried both of them because there had been no reason for it. They became even more worried a few weeks later when it happened again. He had gone to the doctor, and, after a number of tests, they had received the news that had caused their world to cave in: Philip was diagnosed with ALS.

A fatal disease, the doctors had said, the number of years he had left not certain. It would progressively destroy him, striking first his ability to walk, then talk, until finally he would no longer be able even to breathe on his own, and eventually he would die. Cassie and Philip refused to accept it at first. Philip had consulted other doctors, then read everything he could find on the disease, looking for some loophole, some way out, some way to fight the disease.

It had taken months for the news to really sink in. Philip, being Philip, had had to fight, although he had come to realize that it was a battle only to prolong his time, to delay the inevitable end. He had resigned from the recording company, and they had sold their elegant Beverly Hills home. They had moved to their vacation home on Crescent Lake in the San Bernardino Mountains, a two hour drive from Los Angeles. It was close enough to L.A. for his regular doctor's appointments, but secluded and peaceful enough for the refuge he sought.

They renovated the house, installing rails to aid him in walking and adding ramps for the wheelchair they knew he would have to use before too long. They read about and tried every innovative form of treatment they could find, from exercise and nutrition to acupuncture to esoteric "healing" practitioners. If anything worked, they had no way of knowing it, for the doctors had told them the disease progressed differently in different people.

Cassie had cried; she had railed against fate. There had been times when she had had to go down to the shoreline, far from the house, and scream or beat a tree branch to pieces against the rocks. She had felt as if every day was a battle against the disease. But slowly, inevitably, the disease had won. Philip had gone from a cane to a walker to a wheelchair, then to a communication device and finally to breathing equipment. With each move, he slipped farther from the world.

She had watched him go, and it had been an agony

for her, although she had been determined that he not see her own struggle. But despite the pain, it had also been a time of quiet, peaceful intimacy. They had spent all of each day together. Initially he had maintained an interest in the music business, reading the trade papers, but he had eventually lost enthusiasm. He had urged Cassie to keep up with her photography, but she had stopped after a few months. It seemed so unimportant compared to his life-and-death struggle. People had come to visit at first—friends, Philip's daughter. But the visits had grown fewer and fewer as Philip got worse. Gradually their world had narrowed down to this house, with the two of them its only inhabitants. And in that time, Cassie thought, she had come to love him even more.

He had died two and a half years ago, and she had been left alone in the private little world they had made together. Cassie had remained in the house, unable to leave the place where she and Philip had shared the last years of his life. Los Angeles held no appeal for her any longer. Indeed, almost nothing did.

Cassie sighed, blinking the moisture out of her eyes. She did not know why the argument with that annoying Sam Buchanan had brought back memories of Philip and his death. It had been long enough that the pain was no longer fresh and searing. That was the good side of it, she supposed. The bad side was that she rarely felt happy, either. The best that her life offered her anymore was a more or less even keel— except, of course, when someone like her next-door neighbor interfered.

She would like to keep it even. It was a big improvement on the aching emptiness she had felt right after Philip died. The pain then had seemed almost unbearable.

She kept herself mostly busy. There was the house to keep straight and her financial statements to look over. She ordered DVDs and books online by the dozens. She went to Phoenix to visit her parents two or three times a year, and she talked to them on the phone in between. One or two of her friends in Los Angeles kept in touch with her. Sometimes, she drove into L.A. and just went to the new Galleria or some other mall and strolled around, looking into stores, looking at people. But those times were rare, and she found the noise and traffic too much to put up with.

Cassie knew she would never move back there. She had grown to love the peace and quiet; she could think of no reason to return to the hustle and noise of the city. And Philip was here. She had buried him in the small cemetery in the village of Crescent Lake, and she visited his grave often. But more than that, this house held her last memories of him, and she could not move away from this final small remainder of his presence.

The telephone rang, startling her from her reverie, and Cassie got up to answer it. She immediately recognized the brisk, hearty voice of her agent booming over the phone. "Cassie! How are you?"

"Hello, Meredith," she replied, smiling. "I'm fine. How are you?"

"Busy, busy, as always. When are you moving back to L.A.?"

It was Meredith's usual query. City-born and bred, she could not imagine preferring a quiet life on a lake to the noise and bustle of Los Angeles.

"Never," Cassie responded, as she usually did. "I told you."

"I know. I just keep thinking you'll come to your senses sometime." She paused, then went on. "Elizabeth Portwell called me today."

It was the name of the editor of the two books of Cassie's collected photos. Cassie had finished the second book around the time Philip had gotten sick. It had been published a year later and, like the first one, had done well. Periodically since then, Elizabeth had urged Cassie to do another one.

"Meredith, I don't have anything for another book. I don't even have enough photos to do a showing. You know that."

"I know. I told her you didn't have anything ready yet. She's willing to go to contract, though, on the basis of an idea. She'd love to look at a proposal, maybe a few examples of photographs."

"I haven't taken any pictures in years, Meredith. I don't have any examples. I don't even have any ideas for photos."

"There's no rush," Meredith said soothingly. "I just thought you could think about it. Maybe go out and shoot a few pictures…"

Cassie sighed. "Meredith, I'm sorry. I know you

want me to get back into the swing of things. I know you're concerned about me."

"I am," Meredith agreed. "I hate to see you wasting away up there."

Cassie chuckled. "I'm really not wasting away. I've gained five pounds the last year."

"Good. You needed to. I was beginning to worry about you."

"I know. And I appreciate it," Cassie told her. "I really do. But I'm doing all right. I just…I'm not interested in taking pictures anymore."

"Don't say that, sweetie," Meredith protested. "This is just temporary. You'll feel better. It takes time. Really."

"Perhaps you're right," Cassie replied noncommittally. It was easier not to argue with Meredith, who made her living persuading people to buy other people's works. Far better to slide out of the argument.

"Of course I'm right. You just wait. One morning you're going to wake up and want to get out the camera. I know it. When are you coming to L.A. again? Call me—we'll do lunch. There's a great new restaurant not far from my office. Very trendy."

"I'll call you next time I'm coming to L.A.," Cassie promised. It was an easy promise to make, since her visits to Los Angeles were few and far between.

After she hung up, she walked down to the lake. She sat for a while on the bench she and Philip had set in the best spot for viewing the water. The lake was, as always, calming and beautiful, blue, with diamond-sparkling light dancing on it, the dark green pine trees framing it and beyond, like a backdrop, the scrubby peaks of the San Bernardino Mountains.

She walked for a while, turning purposely in the opposite direction from Sam Buchanan's property. She walked until she was tired and the light was starting to fade, then she returned home. Supper was salad and a hearty soup she had made the night before, and she ate it on the sun porch, watching darkness descend on her land.

Later, after she had washed up the dishes, she went on her customary tour of the downstairs, making sure all windows and doors were locked and the alarm system was on. Then she took a book and started upstairs to her bedroom. She had turned one of the second floor rooms into her den; it was where she usually read or watched TV at night, cozier than the big family room downstairs, with its bank of windows.

She was almost to the top of the stairs when the doorbell rang. She stopped and turned around, astonished. *Surely that man didn't have the audacity to return this late in the evening!* Cassie started to ignore the sound and continue climbing the stairs, but curiosity won out finally, and she turned and went back down to the front door.

She looked out the peephole, then stepped back, astonished. Quickly she reached out and unlocked the door, then swung it open. "Michelle!"

Philip's daughter stood on the doorstep. Cassie hadn't seen her since a few weeks after Philip's funeral. In fact, she hadn't even talked to her in almost a year. Michelle never called Cassie, and she seemed to resent it when Cassie called her. Finally Cassie had more or less given up, realizing that she and Michelle were not destined to help each other through their grief.

But now, with no word of warning, here she was at Cassie's door. And even more astounding—in one arm she carried a baby.

Chapter 2

"Michelle!" Cassie wasn't sure whether or not she should step forward and hug her. It would be a little awkward with her holding the baby, and besides, Michelle had always been prickly about any gesture of affection.

So she settled for smiling and stepping back, holding the door open wide. "Come in."

Cassie led her into the family room, saying, "This is wonderful. It's such a surprise. You're looking good."

She had a feeling she was babbling. She often did with Michelle, as though if she talked fast enough and long enough, she could keep the situation from disintegrating.

"Thank you. You, too," Michelle said, giving her a smile.

Michelle did look much better than the last time
Cassie had seen her. She had had an unhealthy
bloated look to her face then, and her eyes had been
vague. Cassie had been sure she was strung out on
something.

Michelle had been fifteen when Cassie married
Philip, and she had been the prototypical rich, troubled L.A. teenager. Her parents' divorce two years
before seemed to have sent her into a downward spiral
from which she never completely recovered. She was
moody and rebellious, and in the years of Cassie's
marriage to Philip she had spent much of her time in
and out of drug rehab centers. Cassie had tried to
befriend her, but Michelle had resented her, and their
relationship had never been easy.

"You've gone back to blond," Cassie said, her
eyes straying curiously to the baby in Michelle's
arms. *Who was this baby? Could it possibly be Michelle's? Had it been that long that they had been
out of contact?*

"Yeah." Michelle shifted the baby a little, and it
stirred. It had been asleep this whole time, its dark
lashes casting shadows on its plump pink-tinged
cheeks.

"Who is the baby?" Cassie asked carefully. Conversations with Michelle tended to contain a number
of landmines, so one had to choose one's words carefully.

Michelle looked a little embarrassed. "Mine."

"Really?" Cassie grinned and leaned forward for

a better look. "I didn't even know you were pregnant."

Michelle shrugged. "I, well, I don't know. At first I wasn't sure I was going to keep it, and then..." She shrugged again and looked at Cassie with a faintly defiant expression. "I knew you would lecture me."

Cassie started to deny her statement, but on a moment's reflection, she had to admit that she probably would have pointed out that Michelle was too young, too unsettled, to care for a child.

So she said honestly, "You're probably right. I'm sorry. I guess I forget sometimes that you're grown now. I would have been happy to help you, though, if I could have. But then...I guess the baby's father..."

That area, too, could be touchy, Cassie realized. Michelle's relationships tended to end badly. Apparently this one had, too, for Michelle shook her head and grimaced.

"Nah, not him. He was long gone by the time she was born." She shrugged again, Michelle's favorite gesture. "He'd'a been a lousy father anyway." Suddenly tears welled in her eyes. "Not like Dad."

"Oh, sweetheart..." Cassie could feel tears coming into her eyes, too, and there was a sharp pain in her chest. "Philip would have loved her. I wish he could have seen her."

"Yeah, well..." Michelle set her jaw and shrugged, blinking away tears. "Anyway, my mother let me move back in with her until the baby was born.

And my friend Rachel was my coach. So, you know..."

Her voice trailed off. Cassie noticed that Michelle had said that her mother had let her stay only until the birth, and she suspected that there was some sort of story there. But Cassie did not want to ask her about the matter, for she imagined that it would only be hurtful to Michelle. So Cassie quickly changed the subject, asking, "What is her name?"

"Sydney. It's pretty, don't you think? Sydney Weeks."

"Yes. It's very pretty. And so is she." Cassie stood and bent over her, gazing at the baby. There was nothing as pretty as a sleeping baby, she thought.

This was Philip's grandchild. It was really hard to conceive of the idea. She tried to look for some resemblance—the blond hair, she supposed. But the face was too babyish and unformed for her to see anything of Philip in it. Still, just the thought stirred something in her chest.

"How old is she?" Cassie asked.

"Three months."

Sydney squirmed again, screwing up her little features. Her eyes popped open, and she stared up at Cassie with bright blue eyes. Then her face twisted, and she opened her mouth and let out a little mewing cry.

"She's probably wet," Michelle said and sighed a little. "She's always wet."

"That's the way they are, I hear," Cassie answered

lightly. "Do you need anything from the car so you can change her?"

"Yeah. I'll go get the diaper bag. Here, will you hold her?"

"Sure." Cassie felt less sure than she sounded. She had held a baby a few times during her life, but she was not very confident in doing it.

She liked babies and had always planned to have them one day, but by the time she was beginning to think about starting a family, Philip had gotten sick, and after that, she had put it completely out of her mind. Few of her friends had had babies. Many of the couples they had been friends with were more Philip's age than hers, and their children were older. Cassie was an only child, so she had had no nieces and nephews to practice on.

Michelle handed Sydney to Cassie, who took the baby gingerly in her arms, cradling the baby's head in the crook of her elbow. Sydney was still squirming and emitting little intermittent noises of distress. Her face was screwed up and had turned red now, and her eyes were squeezed shut. She opened her mouth wider, letting out a louder noise and showing the full extent of her gums. Her arms flailed around, and her legs were kicking, too, knocking aside the light receiving blanket wrapped around her.

She was working up to a full-fledged cry, and Cassie was frankly relieved when Michelle came back in, carrying a large yellow bag on one shoulder. She changed the baby's diaper and after that fed her a bottle of formula that she warmed up in the kitchen.

Cassie held Sydney again while Michelle did that, and this time Sydney did not fuss, just regarded Cassie solemnly while she flailed her arms and legs about jerkily.

It was, Cassie thought, an astounding thing to look at this little scrap of flesh and to think that she was connected to Philip, that his genes lay in her. She watched her move, smiling a little, and thinking that perhaps she might just like being a stepgrandmother. *What a thought at 36!* But she thought it might be fun to go out and buy some clothes for this little girl—dresses and caps and embroidered little booties.

"Have you come to visit for a while?" Cassie asked when Michelle returned and sat down to feed Sydney.

"Oh, not long. I just thought you might like to see the baby." Michelle did not look at her as she spoke, and Cassie suspected that she felt a little guilty about coming so briefly.

"Yes, I'm very glad you brought her. And if you'd like to stay longer or come again, that would be nice, too." Michelle offered no comment, and Cassie went on a little hesitantly, "If you'd like to, we could go to Philip's grave tomorrow. Or you could go by yourself, if you'd rather," she added hastily. She did not want to intrude on Michelle's grief. Michelle had never liked for anyone to witness her emotions, good or bad. Anger was typically the only thing she allowed to spill out.

Michelle shook her head. "I don't want to see it."

She raised her head and looked at Cassie shamefacedly. "You think I'm terrible, don't you?"

"No, not at all," Cassie assured her. "You don't need to visit the graveside if you don't want to. I don't think there's any right or wrong about it. It just depends on what you feel."

"I don't like to think of him there," Michelle said, her expression stony. She looked back down at the baby, saying in a lower voice, "I hated seeing him sick, too."

"I know you did. So did Philip. He understood why you stayed away. He didn't want you to feel guilty."

"Do you think so?" Michelle looked up at her, the expression on her face almost pleading. Obviously she did feel guilty about not coming to visit Philip more, Cassie thought.

"Yes, I do," Cassie replied honestly. She knew it had made Philip sad that Michelle had stopped coming to see him, but she also knew he also had understood the fragility of Michelle's personality. "All Philip wanted was for you to be happy. That's all he ever wanted."

Her words seemed to relieve Michelle's anxiety some, for she smiled a little, and her brow relaxed.

After Michelle had fed the baby, she laid her down on her blanket on the floor and let her wiggle and kick, cooing at the ceiling and her own hands. Cassie put together a salad and sandwich for Michelle, and she ate it in the family room as they talked and watched the baby wriggle on the floor.

Their conversation was the sort they usually had—not quite strangers, not quite friends, not quite relatives, they found that they had little to talk about once they had gone over the particulars of the baby's name and birth. Michelle was customarily vague about where she was living, though she did go so far as to say that it was somewhere in Hollywood. She wasn't going to school; she had finally given up on higher education, she told Cassie. She didn't have a job; the trust fund Philip had set up for her ensured that she would never have to work.

Michelle seemed a little happier than she normally was—and much more so than she had been since Philip's death. At first Cassie put it down to the presence of her baby, but as Michelle talked, Cassie noticed a number of references to someone named Kyle, often accompanied with a smile.

"Now who is this Kyle?" Cassie asked teasingly, and Michelle let out a smug little laugh.

"He's a guy," Michelle replied; then, as if she could not hold it back any longer, she rushed on. "I'm crazy about him, Cassie. He's just the best! I mean, he's cute and fun and just so—perfect. I've never been with any guy like him. I can't believe sometimes that he would choose me. He could have any girl he wanted. I thought he was an actor when I met him. He's that good-looking, you know?"

"He's not?" Cassie asked. This was one of the many areas of Michelle's life where she resented questions. Cassie tried to keep from prying, but given

Michelle's history with men, it was hard not to be concerned about her. "What does he do?"

"He's a musician. He's so talented. I wish Dad could have heard him play. He's not playing right now. His old band fell apart—you know, ego and all that. So he's trying to get another band together. But it's hard, you know?"

Cassie nodded. It sounded like Michelle's usual sort of love affair. Everyone but Michelle was able to see that her relationships were invariably train wrecks. Michelle seemed to have the ability to throw herself wholeheartedly into love time after time, each time believing that this one was different, that this man would last, be loyal, really love her.

Financially, at least, Cassie knew that Michelle was protected by the ironclad trust that Philip and his attorney, Mike Goldman, had set up for her. Emotionally, Cassie did not know of any way to protect Michelle. Only Michelle could do that. Until that happened, Cassie knew of nothing to do except try to support her and be there when she needed a shoulder to cry on. For most of her adolescence, Philip and Cassie had tried arguing Michelle out of her crushes, but it always had the opposite effect of making her more misguidedly loyal to the man she had chosen.

Michelle waxed enthusiastic for a few more minutes about Kyle, but after that the baby began to fuss again, so she made more formula, then went through the routine of diapering the baby and dressing her in footed pajamas.

Cassie fixed up a pallet on the floor in the room

where Michelle usually stayed, folding up two comforters into a soft bed. Michelle rocked the baby in one of the chairs downstairs until Sydney went to sleep, but it took three tries before she was able to lay her down on the pallet without the baby waking up and crying again. By the time she got the baby successfully down, Michelle looked as if she might start crying, too.

"You okay?" Cassie asked when Michelle came back downstairs.

"Yeah," Michelle answered unconvincingly. "Sometimes it's just kind of hard, you know. I get tired."

"Of course you do," Cassie sympathized. "Maybe you should hire some help."

"I had somebody at first, while I was at Mother's house. But Mother was all…you know, 'Michelle, the baby's crying hurts my head.' Only it wasn't that, really. It was because this stupid guy she's dating said, 'Wow, Trish, I can't believe you're, like, a grandmother.'"

"Oh, dear." Cassie could well imagine how such a comment would have affected Michelle's mother. Trish, a starlet when she had married Philip, had always been very vain and prided herself on looking far younger than her age.

"Yeah." Michelle shrugged. "She just laughed and acted like it was some big joke. But I could tell she was mad. And after that she started talking all the time about how Sydney cried too much, and she couldn't sleep and her head hurt and all that. And finally, I said, 'Well, maybe I should just leave,' and she said, 'Yeah, maybe you should.'"

"Oh, Michelle!" Cassie's heart ached with sympathy, and she was filled with the old familiar anger against Michelle's mother. Granted, Michelle had always been difficult, but Cassie was certain that a large number of her problems could be traced straight back to Trish. She had always been much more concerned with herself and her looks and whatever young man she was interested in at the moment than she had been in her daughter. "I'm so sorry."

"I shoulda known better," Michelle said, her voice rough with unshed tears. "I don't know why I thought she'd like her granddaughter any better than she liked her daughter."

"Oh, sweetie..." Cassie laid her hand on Michelle's arm, wishing, not for the first time, that Michelle would accept a hug.

Michelle grimaced. "It doesn't matter. It's not like we ever got along. But then Rosa—that's the woman that helped me with Sydney—didn't like so much taking care of the baby at my apartment. I mean, she didn't have a bedroom like she did at Mother's, and she had to travel, you know, and—oh, I don't know, I think she didn't like Kyle. You know? Like she was always making little comments and stuff. And finally she quit a couple of weeks ago. So I figured I could do it by myself."

Michelle tried to smile, but the effort wasn't entirely successful.

"I'm sure it's very hard," Cassie said. She could

see that Michelle's nerves were frazzled, and she worried whether Michelle was really up to taking care of a baby full-time. "Perhaps you ought to hire somebody else."

"Yeah, I guess." Michelle looked away. "It's just such a hassle."

"Well, now you're here, and I'll help you. You can relax a little. We can even look into getting you some good help. How does that sound? You just sit here for a while and take it easy. I'll get you something to drink, if you want. Water? A soda? Or maybe something soothing—I have herbal tea or hot chocolate."

"No. That's okay. I think I'll just go out and sit on the back deck for a while. Chill out."

"Sure. Well…if you don't mind, I'll go on to bed. Will you lock up?" She suspected that Michelle would like some time alone to soothe her baby-worn nerves.

Michelle nodded, giving her a quick smile, and Cassie went upstairs to her room, moving quietly for fear of waking the baby. She undressed and went to bed, then, as was her custom, picked up a book and began to read. But she found it difficult to concentrate on what she was reading. Her thoughts kept going back to Michelle. She wondered when Michelle planned to leave. Surely she would remain here a day, at least. Cassie found that she wanted to hold Sydney; she wanted to play with her and just look at her. She also could not keep from worrying about how Michelle would fare with a baby. She was not the most stable of people—and God only knew what this musician boyfriend was like.

Michelle had seemed awfully tense tonight. Cassie thought that her tension had communicated its presence to Sydney and made it more difficult for the baby to sleep. Of course, Michelle was probably tired from the strain of driving, and maybe she was nervous about Cassie's reaction to her showing up with a baby. But, given Michelle's history, Cassie could not help but wonder if it was drugs making her tense and jumpy. Admittedly, that wasn't the way Michelle usually acted when she was on drugs; in the past she had been giddy and inanely happy, or sunk into some zoned-out state. Still, Cassie was not naive enough to think that her stepdaughter couldn't have moved on to some other drug that affected her differently.

She knew so little about her or what she had been doing for the past year. Cassie felt a pang of guilt, knowing that she should have made more effort to keep in contact with Michelle. It was not an adequate excuse that Michelle had made no effort to keep in touch with her, either—nor that Michelle had acted as if she never wanted to see Cassie again. Michelle had always been prickly and stand-offish. Cassie couldn't help but feel that she had let Philip down by not pursuing a closer relationship with his daughter.

Finally, her brain still buzzing with such thoughts, Cassie fell asleep.

At first Cassie wasn't sure what had awakened her. She opened her eyes and blinked. The light coming in around the curtains was still pale. She had become accustomed, over the past two years, to staying up late at night, reading. It was always so difficult to turn out the light and lie down without Philip beside her. When he had had to sleep downstairs because he could no longer climb the stairs, she had moved a twin bed downstairs, so she could sleep in the same room with him. She had even managed to adjust to the noise made by his breathing equipment in the last stages of his illness. It was far harder to adjust to his not being there at all at night.

As a result, she usually woke up later than this in the morning. She lay there for a moment, wondering what had awakened her and considering whether she could go back to sleep. She realized that there was a noise somewhere in the house, an insistent whine.

Curious, she got out of bed and padded across the floor to open the door. The noise was a great deal louder in the hall, and she recognized it now—the baby was crying.

"Michelle?" Cassie called and went down the hall to Michelle's room, her steps quickening the nearer she got to the noise.

She pulled open the door. Sydney lay on her back on the makeshift pallet. Her arms and legs were waving frantically, and her face was tomato-red and scrunched up tight, eyes shut and mouth wide-open. And she was emitting a piercing, nerve-shredding cry.

"Oh, honey!" Cassie cried out sympathetically and rushed over to pick her up.

It was immediately apparent as soon as she touched

the baby what the problem was: Sydney was wet, her pajamas soaked through, along with the comforter on which she lay.

"Oh, poor thing," Cassie cooed, and knelt on the floor beside her, quickly unsnapping the pajamas and pulling them off her, followed by the sodden diaper.

She glanced around the room and spotted a plastic sack of disposable diapers sitting beside the diaper bag. She pulled one out, then realized she really needed to wash the baby off. She was a little unsure what to do, but she looked into the diaper bag for a cloth and found a pop-up container of disposable baby-wipes. She pulled one out, feeling very efficient, and wiped the baby off, marveling at the amount of creases and folds in her chubby little legs.

Then she took a diaper and unfolded it. She had never put one on before, but she reasoned that it couldn't be too hard. She unfolded it, decided which was the back, then lifted the baby's legs and slid the diaper under her. It was a little awkward; one or the other kicking leg kept sliding from her grasp until she took a firmer grasp of them. She folded the diaper up over her front, fastened one tape, then the other.

She took a critical look at the finished product. Well, it wasn't the neatest thing ever, she thought. It was definitely lopsided, with one tape coming farther forward, but at least it was on there. She dug through the bag and came up with a plain little cotton top. That was more difficult to put on, for she was uneasy about lifting up the baby, and Sydney's arms were also flailing wildly.

The baby's crying had toned down a little when she took off the diaper, but as Cassie struggled to get her into the top, Sydney's cries turned up a notch. Well, that was the best she could do, Cassie thought, carefully sliding her hand behind Sydney's neck and back and lifting her up to her shoulder, then standing. Michelle would have to handle the rest of it.

She walked down the stairs, calling Michelle's name, but she didn't have much hope of her answering. She figured her stepdaughter must have gone outside or else she would have heard the baby's cries by now. Cassie walked through the house and out onto the back deck, calling Michelle's name. She hoped Michelle hadn't decided to go for a long walk along the lakeshore.

Turning around, she went back through the house to the front door. Sydney's arms and legs were moving as hard as they could, and she was screaming at full pitch. Cassie was discovering what she had done wrong in putting on the diapers. Between her fear of hurting Sydney and the baby's squirming, she had not fastened it tightly enough, and it was slipping lower and lower with each kick.

Cassie opened the front door and walked out onto the porch, looking around and calling, ''Michelle!''

There was no answer, and she went back inside, through the hallway into the kitchen and over to the window to look out the side of the house. It took her a moment to register that the parking area in front of the garage was empty. Michelle's car was not there!

Her heart began to slam in her chest. Suddenly she

had a very bad feeling about this. She stood frozen, staring at the empty driveway and telling herself that Michelle had not just run off. *She had probably realized she needed something and had decided to run into the village to get it. That was all.*

She whirled around, looking wildly around the kitchen. *What was she going to do?* Her pulse was pounding, and the incessant shrieking in her ear wasn't helping her nerves any. *How could something so small make so much noise?* It scared her to look at the baby's face, so red it seemed as if any moment she might explode. Surely that couldn't be healthy!

It was then that she saw the white envelope sitting in the middle of the kitchen table. She couldn't imagine why she hadn't noticed it before. There was something so ominous about it that she felt as if she might stop breathing. She had to force herself to go to the table and pick it up.

"Cassie" was written on the front in Michelle's looping handwriting. Cassie knew, without even opening the letter, that Michelle had fled, leaving the baby with her. Jiggling the baby in the vain hope that Sydney's cries would die down, she tore open the envelope and pulled out the paper inside, shaking it open.

Her eyes ran down the page, the sick feeling in her stomach growing. "…I feel as if I can't breathe… know you'll understand…some time to myself…just to be with Kyle."

Cassie dropped the letter from her nerveless fingers. She stood for a moment, mindlessly bouncing the baby. All right, she told herself, just think—you have to do something. The baby had to eat. And obviously it was up to her to feed it.

She opened the refrigerator, hoping that Cassie would have left some bottles of formula made up. No such luck. Nor was there any sign of formula. Cassie started toward the stairs, shifting the baby to the other arm. As she did so, the too-big diaper slipped halfway off the baby's bottom. Cassie grabbed it in the back and tugged it up. She would have to take care of that later. Right now she needed to make the formula, whatever that involved. She hurried up the stairs, jiggling the baby and humming to her, wishing she could remember more than a few bars of any song. Sydney was impervious to such feeble efforts, continuing to scream full blast.

In Michelle's room, Cassie looked around, hoping against hope that Michelle's suitcase would still be there, but clearly one of the bags she had brought in last night was gone; only the diaper bag and one suitcase were still standing there. She looked into the diaper bag and spotted the formula can and several bottles there, so she slung the bag over her other shoulder and started back down the stairs.

As she reached the bottom of the stairs, the doorbell rang, cutting through the baby's screams. Cassie swung around, her heart rising. *Michelle had come back!* As she whirled around, the diaper slipped again, and as she hurried to the door, Sydney's kicking legs sent it lower and lower. Cassie yanked open the door.

Sam Buchanan was standing on the porch, a long,

rolled-up paper in one hand. His eyebrows flew up in surprise as Cassie appeared in the doorway, shrieking baby in hand.

"You!" Cassie stared at him for a long moment, her face falling in disappointment. She started to turn back, and at that moment, the diaper fell the rest of the way off. Cassie groaned. She looked down at the diaper, then back up at Sam Buchanan.

"Here!" she barked, handing him the baby.

Chapter 3

Astonished, Sam's hands closed automatically around the child.

Cassie turned and hurried back into the house, calling over her shoulder, "I've got to get another diaper."

Holding the half-naked, screaming baby, Sam watched Cassie run up the stairs. Whatever he had expected coming over here this morning, it certainly was not this. He also could not help noticing that she looked damned good in the short faded blue sleepshirt she was wearing.

He looked back down warily at the baby in his hands. A baby without diapers was a disaster waiting to happen. With a sigh, he dropped the rolled-up drawing on the floor and cradled the baby in his left arm. He hummed a vague tune, patting the baby firmly on the back while he bounced up and down. The yells decreased in tone and began to take on the rhythm of the bouncing. Sam dug in his pocket and pulled out his car keys and jangled them. The baby rubbed her face against his shoulder, then gulped and snuffled and glanced at the keys.

When Cassie came running back down the stairs with a diaper from the pack upstairs, she found her obnoxious neighbor standing in the entryway, bobbing up and down and emitting a low, *mm mm mm* sound, all the while jangling keys in front of Sydney's face.

Sydney, one fist jammed in her mouth, was watching the keys, her eyes moving now and then to Sam's face, and her wails had been reduced to a muffled noise that seemed to match his weird hum. Cassie came closer.

He turned and saw her and smiled. "Good. A diaper."

"Yeah." Cassie had to smile. "If I can get it on right this time." She added hesitantly, "You seem to know what you're doing."

He grinned. "I used to do this a lot. But my daughter's thirteen now, so it's been a while. Here, you want me to do it?"

"Tempting," Cassie said, "but I guess I better learn."

She took the baby and sat down on the floor with her. Sydney looked at her, her fist still jammed in her mouth, her lashes in starry wet clumps, still emitting pitiful little noises. Cassie's heart melted at the sight.

She laid her down on the floor and slid the diaper under her, more efficiently this time. Sydney started wailing again at the imposition of a diaper, and Sam bent over them, jangling his keys like crazy.

"I think this kid's hungry," he commented.

"Yeah. Now, if I can just manage to get her formula made, we'll be all right."

"Here, I'll hold her." He picked up the freshly rediapered Sydney. "You fix the formula."

"Okay." Cassie led him into the kitchen, where she took out the formula can, read the directions, and set about mixing the formula and heating the bottle. "How does anyone manage a baby by themselves?"

Sam shrugged. "It *is* easier with two people. But, as I remember, you get some experience and it works better. Hope that bottle's coming up soon," he added. "She's tuning up again. I think the key trick has gotten old."

Sydney's low-level grumbling was definitely turning once more into sobs. Cassie dripped a little of the warm formula on the inside of her wrist, as she had seen people do countless times in movies. It would be better, she thought, if she knew how it was supposed to feel. Since it was neither scalding nor cold, she decided to take a chance and handed Sam the bottle.

He stuck the bottle in the baby's open mouth, and suddenly, blissfully, there was silence.

"Oh, my God." Cassie sank down into one of the chairs at the kitchen table and rested her head on her forearms.

"Sounds like you've had a rough morning," Sam commented, sitting down, too.

Cassie nodded. She would never have guessed how good it would feel to hear a baby greedily gulping down a bottle.

"Who is this little tiger?" he asked conversationally.

"Sydney Weeks. She's my stepdaughter's baby."

"I see. You baby-sitting?"

"You might say that. I got up this morning, and my stepdaughter was gone."

"What?" He stared. "You mean she just left?"

Cassie sighed. "Yes. She left me a note." She picked up the letter from the table, where she had dropped it earlier. Unfolding it, she read through it again, more slowly this time. "It seems her new boyfriend thinks they would do better without a baby around. And Michelle wants 'some time to herself' and she can't 'cope with a baby right now.'"

There was a long silence. Finally he said, "Wow."

"Yeah. Michelle was always good at delivering bombshells." She looked over at him and smiled faintly. "Thanks. I was pretty freaked out."

He chuckled. "Babies can do that to you. I remember when Jana was a baby. She'd get colic, and my ex-wife and I would be up half the night with her, rocking and bouncing. I knew a couple that used to drive around every night to put the baby to sleep because she always went out like a light in the car."

Cassie smiled. She glanced down, and suddenly she realized she was still wearing her old cotton sleepshirt, faded and shrunk by many washings to a dingy blue and stopping several inches above her knees.

"Oh, my." She could feel a blush rising in her face. "I'm sorry. I must look a fright." Her hand went instinctively to her hair—*she hadn't even brushed it!*

"You look fine," he assured her.

But Cassie was scarcely listening. She felt guilty that she had been rude to this man yesterday and here, today, he had helped her out without a quibble—and, embarrassingly, she had been sitting there chatting with him in only her nightgown.

"I, uh, I'll just run upstairs and get dressed." Cassie turned and fled from the room.

She ran up to her bedroom. One look in the mirror confirmed that her hair was indeed a mess, and her sleep shirt showed more of her legs than any woman her age should show. Mortified, she ripped off the sleepshirt and went to her closet. Instinctively she reached for a staid outfit to offset the impression of her old nightshirt. She pulled out beige silk pants and a matching blouse, but a moment later she realized that it was ridiculous to put on silk when she would be caring for a messy baby.

Cassie pulled out some jeans and yanked them on, then dithered over the choice of tops before she told herself that she was acting like an idiot. *He would start thinking that she, too, had run off.* Irritated, she grabbed a plain blue button-front shirt and put it on, then tried to straighten out the tangle of her curls.

Hurrying back into the kitchen a few minutes later,

she found Sam still sitting at the table, a dishcloth over his shoulder, with Sydney tucked up against him while he patted her back. Just as Cassie walked in, the baby let out a burp so enormous that it seemed unbelievable it could have come from something her size. The sound startled a laugh out of Cassie, and Sam smiled back at her, his brown eyes twinkling. Cassie felt her awkward embarrassment melt away.

"Thank you so much," she said sincerely. "Why don't I make us some coffee?"

"Coffee'd be great," he accepted.

Cassie got out the coffee and filters and set up the machine. "Would you like something to eat? I have some bagels, I think."

"I've already eaten, thanks. But you go ahead. I imagine you've had quite a workout this morning. You probably need some fortification."

"You're telling me." Cassie cut a bagel and put it in to toast, then walked back to the table and sat down.

Sam had turned the baby and was holding her in the crook of his arm so that she could look around, which Sydney was doing with great interest. Cassie leaned down, looking into her big blue eyes. Sydney returned the stare, then broke into a big toothless smile that made Cassie laugh with delight.

"She's beautiful, isn't she?" she asked.

"Yep." He looked up at her. "Must run in the family."

Cassie cast him a look. "She's my *step*-grand-daughter."

He chuckled. "Oh, yeah, that's right. Well, you look as if you could be mother and daughter."

Cassie reached down and ran her fingers gently over the baby's head. The baby *was* blond and blue-eyed, like her. "I guess her eyes will change to gray, like Michelle's. Do you suppose she knows her mother's gone? That she's here with strangers?"

"She doesn't seem scared. I can't remember too well when they get scared of strangers. It was thirteen years ago that Jana was a baby. Now she's more into CDs and arguing over tube tops." He paused, then asked tentatively, "Do you think her mother will come back soon?"

"I have no idea." Cassie sighed and walked over to the counter to take out her bagel and spread cream cheese over it. "Michelle's unpredictable. Obviously."

"What are you going to do?"

"I don't know that, either." She brought her plate and both coffee mugs to the table. "Sugar? Milk?"

"Whatever. I'll drink coffee pretty much any way it comes."

She poured their coffee and sat down. "I haven't even thought about what I'm going to do. I just woke up and the baby was crying, and it took me a while to even find the note."

"What about Michelle's mother? Maybe you could take the baby to her?"

"Trish?" Cassie hesitated. The idea of turning the whole problem over to someone else was tempting. She sighed and shook her head. "No. I'm sure she wouldn't want Sydney. Michelle told me last night that her mother made her leave her house as soon as she didn't like being a grandmother. Besides, I couldn't turn a baby over to Trish. She was a terrible mother. Philip even thought about suing for custody, but he was afraid that would have made it harder on Michelle. It would have been a horrible media circus. And the way it was, at least Trish let Michelle stay with us a lot. She didn't stick to the letter of the divorce decree.''

He nodded. "Yeah. I get along with my ex-wife pretty well, but still…you never want to rock the boat too much. It's a lot easier on the kid if your seeing them doesn't cause problems.''

"Exactly.'' Cassie nodded, glad he understood. Some of her friends had been adamant that she and Philip should have sued for custody of Michelle. They were usually, Cassie had noticed, either not divorced or didn't have children. "Still…I worry that we did the wrong thing with Michelle. Everything was always such a problem.''

She picked at the edge of her bagel, frowning. "I've always felt guilty about her.''

"Guilty? How come?'' His eyes twinkled as he went on. "Somehow I have a little trouble buying you as the wicked stepmother.''

"Oh, I wasn't mean to her. And I didn't break up their marriage or anything like that. They'd been divorced for a couple of years before I even met Philip. But I wasn't as good with her as I could have been. I was young, and I didn't know anything about chil-

dren, let alone teenagers. I didn't know how to handle
her. Of course, I had no authority with her. I wasn't
her mother, and I was only twelve years older than
she was. I tried to be kind of like an older sister, but
I wasn't even sure how they acted. I was an only
child. She resented me. And there were times when I
resented her. I'd feel like she was messing up my
marriage. When she wasn't there, everything was so
much easier, so much nicer. I know she must have
sensed that lots of times I was happy to see her go
back to her mother's house.''

Cassie stopped, surprised at how much she had just
told a stranger. She was not one to reveal painful
emotions, much less to people she didn't know well.
She guessed the stress of dealing with a crying baby
had taken down her defenses.

''I'm sorry,'' she said quickly. ''I shouldn't burden
you with all that.''

''It's no burden. I was glad to listen.''

''You've been awfully kind,'' Cassie said. ''I
mean, all this…'' She made an encompassing gesture
that included the baby he was holding. ''…is really
above and beyond the call of duty.''

''What are neighbors for?'' he responded lightly.

''No, I'm serous. It was very nice of you, especially considering the fact that I was rude to you yesterday. I'm sorry.''

''Don't worry about it. You weren't that rude. Besides, I have been known to be kind of pushy. I apologize, too. There's no reason for you to sell me your

land just because I want you to. Sometimes I get a little carried away.''

He smiled and stood up. ''Well, I better get to work. I have crews going on two new houses.'' He looked down at the baby, whose hand had latched on to a fistful of his shirt. ''Will you be okay here?''

''Yeah. I'm sure I will be. It was just kind of a rough start to the day,'' Cassie said more confidently than she felt. ''I'll get some books on babies. And hopefully Michelle will call me before too long.''

''Okay.'' He held out the baby, and Cassie took her, settling her into the crook of her arm.

She walked with him to the front door. He reached down to scoop up the rolled-up plan he had dropped there and turned back to her.

''Well...'' He hesitated, then said, ''Look, call me if you need something.'' He reached into his pocket and took a card from his wallet. ''There's my number.''

Cassie took the card. ''Thank you. That's very kind of you. But I'm sure I'll manage.''

He nodded and left. Cassie closed the door after him. The house suddenly seemed very quiet and empty. She looked down at Sydney, who gazed solemnly back at her.

''Looks like it's just you and me, kid,'' Cassie said.

Sydney gazed back at her. Pursing her mouth, she made a noise, one of her eyes closing in a way that made it look as though she had winked. Cassie had to laugh. At that, the baby gave a big toothless grin.

Cassie bent and kissed her forehead. Sydney's skin was the smoothest, softest thing she had ever felt.

"Okay," Cassie said. "What do you suppose we ought to do next?"

She decided to take stock of what she had for the baby. She walked up the stairs and carefully laid Sydney down in the middle of the bed, then opened the small suitcase and looked through it. She found a number of baby clothes and several light cotton blankets, as well as a couple of small stuffed animals, a plastic rattle and a doughnut-shaped ring filled with some sort of gel. Picking up one of the animals, she sat down on the bed and held it over Sydney. Sydney's arms came up, and her fingers curled into the stuffed bunny's fur.

Cassie watched as she brought the small, soft bunny to her mouth. Her mind was filled with questions. It was amazing, really, how little she knew about babies. *What was going on inside Sydney's head? What toys should she have? What did she do all day long?*

Cassie stroked the back of her hand across the baby's cheek. *This was Philip's granddaughter, linked to him by blood.* She tried to imagine how he would have reacted to Sydney, what he would have said and thought. And Cassie knew then that there was nothing she could do except take care of her. It didn't matter whether it turned out to be for a week or months or years. It didn't matter that a baby intruded on her life or that Sydney would disturb her tranquility, or even that she was not actually related to Cassie by blood. This child was a part of Philip, and now she would be a part of Cassie's life.

She bent over the baby, and Sydney's hand fisted in Cassie's curls. Cassie chuckled. "Hello, sweetheart. I guess we're in this together now."

Suddenly tears welled up in her eyes and spilled over. Cassie picked up Sydney and cradled her against her heart. Her little body was warm and soft and indescribably sweet. Softly, quietly, she patted Sydney's back and cried.

She was working in the dark, Cassie knew. She was also certain she was missing a lot of the equipment she should have. A car seat and a crib, for instance—and, first off, a book so she could figure out what she was supposed to be doing.

There was a bookstore in the village of Crescent Lake, she knew. She had been in it only once or twice, since she usually purchased her books online, a method she had found infinitely easier than facing people since Philip's death. But today she could not wait for a book to arrive in the mail; she needed it immediately. And after that…well, where did one go for baby things? In L.A., she knew, there were stores catering solely to baby furniture, clothes and toys, but she did not think that any place as small as Crescent Lake would have such a specialty store.

There was a big discount store on the edge of the town, she remembered, an ugly sprawl of a place. She supposed that was the best place to go. It surprised her a little to think she hadn't been in a store like that

in years; she hadn't realized how sheltered her life
had become, buffered by Philip's wealth.

But even as she thought about going into town to
get a book and the things she would need, she realized
that she couldn't because she didn't have a car seat.
She couldn't take the baby with her without a car seat,
and obviously she couldn't leave her in the house
alone.

Cassie went out to the side porch to see if, by
chance, Michelle had thought about the car seat and
taken it out of the car before she left. But there was
nothing on the porch, nor on the driveway where Michelle's car had been sitting. Cassie sighed. It was
typical of Michelle that she would have driven off,
forgetting to leave such an important item.

Cassie went back inside and contemplated her di-
lemma. In Los Angeles, she would have called a
friend and asked for a favor. Of course, in Los Angeles, she could simply have called a delivery service
to pick up a car seat and bring it to her, or probably
one of the tonier baby stores would even have deliv-
ered a car seat and crib and whatever else she wanted.
But she didn't think the local discount store was
likely to do that.

And she had no friends here.

The realization was a little shocking. *Was she really so isolated? So removed from the people where
she lived?* It didn't take much thought to know that
the answer was yes.

Philip had bought the house here as a vacation spot,
and they had come on the weekends sometimes, but

their real life had been back in L.A. Then, when they had moved to the lake permanently after Philip got sick, the focus of their life had been his illness. With the several-acre lots of the houses on this cove, they weren't even close enough to see their neighbors. They hadn't tried to make friends, had really had little to do with anyone in Crescent Lake except for the most basic dealings with repairmen or clerks in stores. She supposed that the person she had spoken with the most in Crescent Lake was the pharmacist at the drugstore where they had filled Philip's prescriptions. What little social life they'd had was with friends who drove up from Los Angeles to visit them.

It was a lifestyle she had continued after Philip's death. She hadn't wanted to see anyone, hadn't wanted to talk or do anything else. The last thing on her mind had been making friends. Often, even the concern of her family and friends had seemed a burden. Wrapped in the cocoon of her sorrow, she had shut herself off from everyone. It was startling, even a little frightening, to realize just how cut off from the rest of the world she had become.

Not sure exactly what to do, she spent the next few hours settling in with the baby. She started to put the baby's clothes away in Michelle's room, but after a few moments' thought, she realized she would feel easier in her mind if Sydney were in the room next to hers instead of farther down the hall. So she carried the baby's things to that room and put away her clothes, and afterward, she carried Sydney downstairs and put her on the floor in the family room on a little blanket, as Michelle had done last night.

She lay down on the floor beside her and watched with some fascination as Sydney raised her head up off the floor and looked around, head wobbling a little, finally sinking back to the floor each time, then doing it all over again.

Watching her, Cassie could not imagine how Michelle's mother could have seen nothing in the sweet creature but a reminder of her own aging. *But, then, that was Trish.* Cassie had never understood the self-centered woman. Still, she felt a little guilty about not telling her about Michelle's disappearance and her leaving Sydney with Cassie. Little as she liked her, Cassie felt that Trish had a right to know.

Finally, with a sigh, Cassie called the woman, aware of a little flicker of fear in her stomach that Michelle had somehow been wrong and that Trish might want Cassie to turn Sydney over to her. She felt amazingly relieved when Trish responded in her usual way to Cassie's story, saying with the most heartfelt emotion Cassie had ever heard in her voice, "What are you saying? Surely you don't expect me to come get the baby!"

"No, Trish. I don't expect you to want the baby," Cassie responded flatly.

"Good. Because I just couldn't. My life is far too busy to have a *child* in it," she explained, her voice investing the word *child* with untold horror.

"I'm sure it is. I just thought you might want to know."

"Oh." There was a slightly baffled tone in Trish's voice. "Well, yeah. Sure. Thanks."

"Okay. Well, goodbye." Cassie hung up, shaking her head, and returned to the baby, her heart lighter.

Just as she was about to sit back down beside Sydney, the doorbell rang. Cassie turned and went to answer the door, aware of a twist of disappointment in her chest. *Michelle must have thought better of leaving the baby behind and had come back.* But when she looked through the peephole, she saw that it was Sam Buchanan who had returned.

The faint disappointment fled, and she opened the door, smiling. Then she saw that in one hand he held an infant car seat, and she let out a gasp of surprise and pleasure.

"I thought you might need one of these," he said genially, holding up the car seat.

"Yes! How did you know? Michelle didn't leave hers behind."

"I didn't see one sitting around, and I figured you wouldn't have one in your car already."

"No. I've been wondering how I was going to get into town to get all the stuff I need. You're a lifesaver."

"Good. I had a job out this way, so I grabbed one at the store and thought I'd drop it off. You want me to put it in your car?"

"Sure. Just let me check on the baby. I put her down for a nap a while ago."

"Hey, sounds like you're getting good at this stuff."

"I just checked her diaper or fed her when she cried, and then I was sitting there rocking her after I burped her, and she just fell asleep, so I decided it must be time for her nap. I'm completely flying by the seat of my pants."

"And such a way to fly," he said in a Groucho Marx way, wiggling his eyebrows.

His joke startled a laugh out of Cassie. Was he flirting with her? she wondered. It had been so long, she wasn't sure if she would recognize flirting.

She led him out to the car, and they struggled, laughing, with the seat belts and the directions, before they finally got the seat installed correctly.

After Sam left, Cassie went back inside and waited for the baby to wake up. When Sydney awakened, Cassie went through the routine of diaper-changing, pleased that it was becoming easier with each repetition. She fed her and, after packing the diaper bag, set off for Crescent Lake Village. It was a small, quaint shopping area, the sort of place designed for tourism. In the winter, skiing brought in the business; in the summer, a smaller crowd came for the beauty of the lake and hiking in the San Bernardino Mountains. As a result, souvenir shops and sports equipment stores dominated the "downtown" area, but there were plenty of coffee shops, restaurants and bars, as well.

The bookstore was attached to a coffee and tea shop. Cassie parked her car down the street and, carrying the baby, walked into the bookstore. The woman behind the counter, a brunette about Cassie's age, looked up and smiled at her as she entered.

"Oh, my goodness," she said, leaning forward onto the counter. "What a pretty one you've got there!" She smiled at Sydney. "How old is she? Four months?"

"Three."

"Well, close. What can I help you with?"

"Actually, I'm looking for baby books."

"Sure. Right back here." The woman left her perch on the stool behind the counter and started toward the back of the store. She stopped before a group of shelves. "Anything in particular?"

"The basics, I guess," Cassie said. "I'm pretty much clueless." The woman looked a little surprised, and Cassie explained, "She's not mine. I'm, uh, taking care of her for someone else. And I think I need help."

"Well, there are plenty of them here. Want me to hold her for you while you look?" She held out her arms, and Cassie handed the baby over to her a little uncertainly. "My babies are all in middle school now, so I love the chance to hold one."

"Which book would you recommend?"

"Mmm. I'm not sure. This one has a lot of information on physical development. This one, probably less so, but it's very practical in its approach."

"I need that." Cassie pulled out both the books and began to look through them.

"I'm Margaret Jamison, by the way. I own the store."

"Cassie Weeks."

"That's why you looked familiar!" the woman exclaimed. "I'm sorry. I've just been trying to remember where I'd seen you before. I have your books over there. I remember your picture from the jacket."

"Oh. Yeah." Cassie smiled, a little embarrassed.

"I'm sorry. Am I too enthusiastic? My husband tells me I scare people off."

"No, it's quite all right. I just never know what to say when people bring up my books."

"Well, you should be proud of them. I'm a big fan of your work. I have both your books at home, too. I had heard that you lived around here somewhere."

Cassie stayed, chatting with the woman for a few more minutes, and then wound up purchasing three of the baby books because she couldn't decide among them.

She left the store, humming. It occurred to her that she had talked longer with Margaret Jamison and Sam Buchanan today than she had with anyone in Crescent Lake in the entire four-plus years she had lived here.

Her next stop was the discount store, where she found there were so many things that were absolutely essential that she was almost embarrassed to get them all, and the total made the salesgirl's eyes pop. As it turned out, the clerk who helped her out to the car could not get the wide box containing the crib into her car and had to lash it onto the top with the help of a middle-aged man in a pickup, who came to their rescue with a roll of twine. She was discovering that everyone wanted to help someone with a baby. Or maybe people were always like this in Crescent Lake Village, and she had just never noticed before.

She spent most of the evening hauling in all the items she had bought—the boxed crib was the worst, requiring the use of a dolly she dug out of the depths of the garage—and taking care of the various things that needed to be done for Sydney. Babies, she realized, required a great deal of time and effort. She finished the evening by giving Sydney a bath in the new plastic tub she had bought her, which was scarier than she would have imagined, and wound up getting almost as wet as the baby.

Sydney once again slept on folded comforters, for Cassie was too tired tonight to set up the crib. Cassie tried to sit up and read one of the baby books for a while, but she was too tired and quickly fell asleep.

The next morning the routine with the baby went much more smoothly—although she could clearly see that she was going to have to begin waiting to get down her eye-opening cup of coffee until after the baby was dry and had a full stomach.

Then, with Sydney on a soft blanket on the floor, the brightly colored play gem set across her so she could pat, ring and squeak to her heart's content, Cassie settled down on the sofa with her books. Later, she opened the large flat cardboard box containing the crib parts and lugged them up the stairs and set up the baby bed. That procedure cost her a pinched finger and several hours of frustration, but at last the thing was up and offered a more comfortable bed for Sydney. She put it to use immediately by laying Sydney down for her nap.

That evening, before supper, she wrapped a light blanket around the baby and walked down to the lake's edge. She sat down on the bench for a time and looked at the water, the sinking sun glinting on its surface. Then she took the path that led east, edging the lake, until she reached the path that led up to Sam Buchanan's house. She stood for a moment, gazing up into the trees, where she could see glimpses of the house he had remodeled.

After a moment, she began to climb the path. As she grew nearer to the house, she could see Sam moving about on his back deck. He turned from what he was doing and saw her, and a smile creased his face.

"Hey! How are you?" He bounded off the deck and down the steps. "I was thinking about walking over to see how you were faring after I finished supper. Would you like some? I have more steaks. I could put on another one for you."

"Oh, no, that's all right."

"No trouble. Come on. At least come up and have a drink with me. I like to grill out on the deck and look down at the lake."

"You have a nice view," Cassie commented, turning to look at the lake.

He nodded. "Yeah. That's one of the main reasons why I bought the property."

"I don't want to bother you," Cassie went on, then drew a breath and said, "I just came over to tell you that I've changed my mind. I'll sell you that piece of property you want."

Chapter 4

Sam looked at her in some surprise. "Are you serious?"

Cassie nodded. "Yes. I've decided I'll sell it."

He started to smile, then stopped and frowned. "Look, I didn't help you out yesterday because I was trying to get you to sell me the land. I don't want you to feel as though you have to sell me the property now."

"No. I don't feel like I have to," she assured him. "And I know you didn't do it so I would have to pay you back. You did it because you're nice. And a good neighbor. And I realized I wasn't being much of either one of those things."

He shrugged. "It's your property. There's nothing saying you have to sell it just to be nice."

"No, but it won't hurt me to be nice." She smiled.

"Let's just say I realized that I was being a little stiff-necked about the whole thing."

"Come on in. Let me get you a drink and show you my plans for the boathouse. I think you'll see that it won't intrude much."

Cassie laid out the baby's light blanket on the floor and put her down on it, then sat down at the table with Sam to peruse his plans for his boathouse.

"It looks very nice," Cassie told him. "And you're right, between the rocks and the trees, I'll scarcely notice it."

"You really won't," he assured her. "The view from your house shouldn't be changed at all."

She nodded. "I'm sure it will be fine. You've obviously done a very nice job with this house."

"You like it?"

"Yes. Very much. The big windows, the deck—it's lovely. I would scarcely have known it was the same place." She paused, then went on. "You know, I realized that I was holding on to that piece of land because...well, not for any practical reason. Just because I couldn't bear to give up any part of it. Somehow, it was as if I was holding on to Philip by holding on to that land."

He looked at her. "What changed your mind?"

She shrugged. "I don't know exactly. You're a good neighbor, and I thought, how stupid to antagonize a good neighbor. But, more than that, I thought about the fact that Philip isn't in that land. He's in Sydney much more than he is in the land. And he's in my memories. They won't change, whether you own that little piece of land or I do.'' She gave him a small smile.

"Thank you. I understand what it means to you. I really do, and you're being very generous.''

They stood for a moment, smiling at each other, then he said, ''Come on, let me put on that other steak for you. Sydney's happy. It won't take long. And I cook a mean steak.''

Cassie's smile broadened, and she capitulated. ''All right. Thanks.''

They talked as he grilled the meat and then as they ate, and Cassie found herself telling him not only about her recent adventures in the world of babydom, but also stories about her photography and her life in L.A.

By the time they finished eating and talking, it was dark, and Sydney had begun to fuss. ''I better go,'' Cassie said, scooping up the baby and wrapping the light blanket around her. ''I think she's getting hungry.''

"I'll walk you home.'' Sam rose to his feet, as well.

"That's all right. You needn't.''

"Nonsense. It's dark, and the path isn't always even. I can't send a woman with a baby out by herself.''

So he walked her home and even up the incline to the back deck of her house. At the door, Cassie stopped and turned to him. ''Thank you. For walking me home and the meal and everything. Just let me know about the papers I need to sign.''

"Sure. I'll call you." He hesitated for a moment, then leaned down and brushed his lips against hers.

A shiver ran through Cassie, and for a moment she could do nothing but stare at him. Sam smiled faintly and leaned in to kiss her again, this time much more thoroughly. Cassie felt suddenly weak all over, and the blood seemed to hum in her veins. She sagged against him, and Sydney let out a squawk of protest.

Cassie jumped back, and her hand flew to her mouth. She stared at him for a moment, then turned and fled inside.

Nerves jangling, she went into the family room to put Sydney down in her playpen while she returned to the kitchen to prepare her formula. Now accustomed to the task, she did it mechanically, her mind flying around erratically. *How could she have kissed him?*

She hadn't kissed a man since Philip died. If anyone had asked her, she would have said she never would again. Romance was over in her life. She couldn't imagine loving anyone as she had loved Philip, and she wouldn't settle for anything less. Nothing could have been farther from her mind than men and dating.

Especially now that the baby was here, she reminded herself. There was no room in her life for a man; Sydney took up all her time. She wasn't sure exactly how this evening had happened. When she had walked over to Sam's house, she had intended nothing except to tell him that she would sell him the property. She had not meant to stay and talk, much less share a good-night kiss. Had he thought that her going over there meant she was interested in starting a relationship?

The thought embarrassed her. She would have to make it clear to him that she did not want any relationship beyond that of neighbor. She would tell him—no, she thought, it would probably be better to say nothing at all. She should simply make it a point not to see him again. That would make it clear that she wasn't interested.

Yet, as she stood waiting for the bottle to heat, her mind went back to the moment when he had kissed her, to the tingle that had spread through her, the way her knees had gone weak and she had wanted to cling to him, the funny feeling in the pit of her stomach, as if she were falling over the edge of some precipice....

Irritated, she shook her head, as if to displace the thoughts that nagged her. She knew, with an inward squirm of guilt, that his kiss had been exciting, that something inside her had burst into quivering life at the touch of his lips on hers. But that was silly. It was ridiculous. She loved Philip.

Pushing the memory out of her mind, she picked up the bottle and tested it. Annoyingly, it was too hot. With a sigh, she ran cool water over the bottle and tested it again. That time it was right. Gripping the bottle, she went back to the family room to feed Sydney.

She managed to keep her mind off the kiss while she fed the baby and even most of the time while she was bathing her and dressing her for bed, tasks that were becoming a little easier, she noticed. But later, after she put Sydney down in her new crib and went to her own room, she had difficulty keeping her thoughts at bay.

It was a relief when the telephone rang, and she picked it up almost eagerly. "Hello?"

"Cassie?" It was Michelle's voice, small and tentative.

"Michelle! Where are you?" Cassie gripped the phone tightly, willing herself to sound calm and unthreatening. If she started in with a barrage of questions, she was afraid Michelle might very well hang up.

"I came back to L.A. Are you mad at me?"

"No, of course I'm not mad at you. But, Michelle, sweetheart, I'm a little confused."

"Kyle is such a wonderful guy. I know you'd like him if you met him."

Cassie had serious doubts about that, but she wisely kept them to herself. "I'm sure I would."

Michelle giggled and said something that Cassie could only partially hear, as if she were speaking to someone else in the room.

"Michelle, I understand that you need a break from the baby for a while."

"Yeah. I really do. And I need to work on our relationship, Kyle and me, I mean, without...without...distractions."

Cassie realized that Michelle was slurring her words, and that fact, combined with the giggle, sent her suspicion into overdrive. Was Michelle drinking again? Or maybe it was some other drug, like the pills that she had taken in the past. Feeling sick, she realized that given Michelle's history, it could be almost anything.

"Michelle, do you want to give me your telephone number there in L.A.? You know, so I could get in touch with you about the baby if I needed to?"

"I don't know. I'm not at home right now."

"Okay. But you could give me your home number anyway." Cassie could feel the beginnings of a headache clutching at the base of her brain.

"It's new. I don't remember it. I'll call you some other time. Anyway, I know you'll take care of Syndney—Sydney, I mean." Michelle giggled again.

"Are you drinking, Michelle?"

"Oh, please, don't start," Michelle said disgustedly.

"I'm not starting anything," Cassie replied with as much calm and lack of inflection as she could muster.

"I just wanted to see how Sydney is. I didn't call for a lecture."

"I know. And I'm not lecturing." Cassie held on to her anger. She knew from past experience that it was pointless to tell Michelle she was being immature and irresponsible. It was true, of course, but saying so just aroused her ire and nothing more. Of course the problem was that she had never been able to find anything to say that really worked with Michelle, especially when she was drinking or getting high.

"I'm going to get off now," Michelle said.

"Okay. But it'd be nice if you'd call me again soon. I can tell you how Sydney's doing."

"Yeah. Okay." Michelle sounded distracted.

The phone clicked in Cassie's ear. She sat for another moment, holding the receiver, then, with a sigh, put it back on its cradle. She was certain that Michelle had been drinking or using drugs, and she didn't do such things just once. She was off the wagon again, and there was no knowing when or how it would end. The worry that had always hung in the back of her mind was that someday it would end with a phone call from the police, saying that Michelle had overdosed or run off the highway in her car.

Cassie had no idea what to do. She didn't know where Michelle was in Los Angeles, and her phone number was probably unlisted or in someone else's name. Like Kyle's. Nor did she any longer know who her friends were—not that Michelle hung out with the sort of person Cassie could call to ask for help, anyway. There was her mother, of course, but Trish usually knew less about Michelle than Cassie did—and would have been of no use, anyway, since her typical response was to have hysterics. Michelle was a grown woman; the police would have no interest in looking for her unless Cassie told them that Michelle had abandoned her child. But that was a can of worms she definitely did not want to open. Besides, she knew from long experience that no one could force Michelle to stop drinking and taking drugs; she had to reach the decision herself.

She had a feeling of helplessness that she had

grown used to long ago where Michelle was concerned. She had no control over anything...except taking care of Sydney. All she could do was take care of the baby and wait for Michelle to call again. And pray that Philip's daughter would eventually come to her senses.

At least the phone call from Michelle had had the effect of driving away any further thoughts of Sam Buchanan and his kiss. But that problem landed on her doorstep the following afternoon in the form of the man himself. Looking out the peephole, Michelle was tempted not to answer the doorbell, but she knew it would be better to nip this situation in the bud, so she steeled her nerves and opened the door.

"Hello, Sam."

"Cassie." He grinned, his long-lashed brown eyes crinkling up in a way that made her chest feel funny. "Sorry to keep dropping in on you this way, but I couldn't find your number in the phone book."

"It's unlisted." Cassie realized that she sounded rude, and she offered an explanation. "Philip was the head of a recording company. You can't imagine how many calls he would have gotten from aspiring singers if his name had been listed."

He nodded, then said, "Well, um, do you want me to just come over when the papers are ready to be signed? I talked to my lawyer today, and he said it'd take him about a week. In lawyer-speak, that means two weeks."

"No, of course not. Come in, and I'll write down my number for you."

"I promise I'll keep it a secret."

"It doesn't really matter anymore, I guess."

Sam shrugged. "Still, probably safer."

She pulled a piece of paper from the notepad by the phone and jotted down her telephone number. Sam took the paper and folded it and dropped it into his shirt pocket.

"Actually, I came here to tell you something besides the thing about the sale. Well, ask you, actually."

Cassie's stomach tightened, and she felt slightly breathless. She wasn't sure whether her nerves came from dread of dealing with whatever he had in mind or simply from the fact that he was standing so close to her that she could feel the heat of his body.

"I'd like to take you out to dinner sometime," he said. "We could even get wild and take in a movie."

"I—that's very nice of you, but I don't think so. I, um…"

He waited, brows raised questioningly.

"Well, there's Sydney. I don't think I'm ready to take a baby to a restaurant just yet."

"My daughter would love to baby-sit her, I'm sure. She's good at it, has her Red Cross certificate and all that."

"I, um, I'll keep that in mind, but…" She straightened, irritated with herself. "Well, frankly, I don't date."

"It's against your principles?"

"No. But I'm a widow, and I'm simply not interested in dating."

"I see." He studied her face. "So, do you plan on never dating again?"

"I hadn't really thought that far. But, no, not at the moment. I'm just...not interested."

He nodded. "In me or in any guy?"

"In anyone," Cassie replied firmly.

"Okay. My mistake. I thought last night, you seemed...a little interested." There was a light in his dark eyes that made Cassie's pulse start to jump.

"No. No. That was...an aberration."

"Oh." He smiled, a dimple popping into his cheek in a way that Cassie had to admit was devastatingly charming. "Okay. But you realize, don't you, that I'm a very persistent man?"

Cassie didn't want to smile back, but she found herself doing it anyway. "I know. And I'm a pretty stubborn woman."

"I know." He grinned and started for the door, turning back to say, "I'll call you when the papers are ready."

He didn't have to add that he hadn't given up. The words hung in the air.

In fact, Cassie did not hear from Sam Buchanan for a week and a half, and she was a bit surprised. She had thought he would be much more persistent, but beyond a glimpse of him and a wave as their vehicles passed on the road, she didn't even see him.

It was what she wanted, of course. She had plenty

to do with taking care of the baby, and that was all she wanted to focus on. Her mind turned to him only because she had expected him to pursue her, and she was surprised that he hadn't. It wasn't at all that she was miffed that he seemed to have given up on her so easily.

And even if she had wanted to date him, she reminded herself, she really did not have enough time. Sydney took up every minute of her day. From the moment she got up until she went to bed, she was doing something for Sydney or thinking about her or reading about babies so she would know what to do for her. A baby, she discovered, was a full-time job.

However, she was also finding that she woke up in the morning with a lighter heart than she had in years. She was always eager to get into Sydney's room and see her. She found herself looking forward to each new milestone in the baby's life. She drove to San Bernardino and spent a most enjoyable afternoon prowling the aisles of a store devoted to baby goods, pushing Sydney along in her stroller.

For the first time in a long time, the aching loneliness eased. It was impossible to feel sad when she looked at the baby's sunny smile. And when she rocked her to sleep, feeling the little body warm on her chest, gradually turning limper and limper, she was filled with a kind of happy contentment she had never known.

One day, as she lay on the floor beside Sydney, watching her bat at the toys above her on her activity gym, Cassie was suddenly seized with the desire to photograph Sydney. It was the first time she had felt an urge to get out one of her cameras and use it in so long that it startled her.

She got up and went down to her darkroom, and dug out one of her cameras. It was odd and yet at the same time a little exciting to hold it in her hands once again. It needed new batteries, of course, and she had to dig out some and put them in before she could use it. The film, she knew, was too old, but she could not resist the urge to shoot a roll anyway. It felt so familiar, so good and right to use the camera once again. She developed the pictures while Sydney was down for her nap, and later, after the baby awoke, she drove into the village to buy some new film. Her mind was already humming with ideas for shots.

She had just stepped back into the house and was carrying Sydney to the family room to put her in her playpen when the phone rang. It was Sam on the other end of the line, and something quivered inside her at the sound of his voice.

"Hey, Cassie, how are you?"

"Fine. And you?"

"Doing all right. The lawyer's got the papers done, so we can sign any time you're ready."

"Oh. Okay." Cassie refused to admit that she felt a little disappointed to learn that her property was the only reason why he had called her. "Whenever you want. I'm pretty free, as long as I can bring Sydney with me."

"Sure. No problem. How about tomorrow afternoon, then? Say around four or so?"

"That's fine. Sydney will be up from her nap by then."

"Good. See you then."

Cassie turned away from the phone, smiling.

The next afternoon Cassie showered and got ready while the baby was napping. Looking through her closet for something to wear, it struck her that there was nothing either new or attractive in her wardrobe. It was probably time, she thought, to do some serious shopping. And she also thought, looking at herself in the mirror, she could use an afternoon in the hair salon. Perhaps she ought to drive into Los Angeles for a weekend. Sandy Bradshaw had been after her for ages to come visit and would be more than happy to join her on a beautifying mission.

She finally settled on a green silk pants and jacket set on the basis that at least it was less than four years old. Cassie had bought it on a trip to L.A. a year and a half ago when her friend Amanda had more or less forced Cassie to accompany her shopping. Gold earrings and a couple of long, delicate gold chains gave it a little more spark, and she decided she looked acceptable.

Sam was waiting at the title company when Cassie walked in, pushing Sydney in her stroller. A preteen girl with the same dark hair and eyes as Sam sat beside him in the reception area, and she looked on with interest as Sam sprang up and walked over to Cassie.

"Cassie. Great. You made it." He bent over to look at the baby, who was clutching a stuffed frog and staring back at him. "Hey there, Sydney. I think you've grown since the last time I saw you."

He straightened and smiled at Cassie. She smiled back, aware that her heart had skipped a little as he walked toward her—and somewhat annoyed by that fact. "Hello, Sam."

"I want you to meet my daughter, Jana." He turned toward the girl, who was now standing, watching them, her hands stuck in the front pockets of her jeans. "Jana, come here and say hello to Ms. Weeks."

Cassie turned toward the girl as she came up beside Sam. "Hello, Jana, it's nice to meet you."

"Pleased to meet you," the girl returned politely, but her eyes were drawn as if by a magnet to Sydney in her stroller. She bent down to look into the baby's face. "Hi there. What's your name?" Jana raised her face to Cassie. "Is this your daughter?"

"She's my stepdaughter's child. But she's living with me right now."

"That's cool. Would it be okay if I held her?"

"Sure." Cassie started to bend down to take Sydney out of the stroller, but Jana was already expertly scooping her up into her arms. "Well, I can see that you're an old hand at that."

Jana grinned. "I baby-sit a lot. I like babies." She turned her attention back to Sydney, cooing and talking to her until Sydney broke into a grin.

"You're very good with her," Cassie said. "Perhaps sometime you'd like to baby-sit her."

"Sure! Any time."

"She's great with kids," Sam assured Cassie and gestured down the hall toward a glass-enclosed conference room. "I think they're ready for us, if you want to get it over with."

They walked down the hall to the conference room, Jana following them with the baby. Jana sat in one of the plush chairs and played with Sydney, while Sam and Cassie went through the formalities of signing the papers.

Afterward, as they strolled back down the hall to the reception area, Sam said casually, "Well, I think a celebration is in order, don't you? What about dinner?"

"Dinner?" Cassie turned to him.

"Yeah. We'll all go. Pizza, say. Jana, you up for that?"

"Sure. Pizza sounds great."

"But I—" Cassie began, then stopped, not sure what to say.

"You, me, the kids," he said to her. "Pizza. A family thing, you know. Definitely not a date."

Cassie raised one eyebrow at him, her voice tinged with suspicion. "You set this up, didn't you?"

"Who, me?" Sam assumed an expression of great innocence. "Would I do something like that?"

Cassie tried to look severe, but she found herself chuckling instead. There was something rather pleasant about realizing that he hadn't given up at all, but had merely been biding his time, planning a way to get her to accept.

"Your father," she said to Jana, "is a tricky one."

"Yeah," the girl agreed, grinning up at her. "You should see what he gets up to on my birthday."

"Well, what do you say?" Sam asked. "Shall we get a pizza?"

Cassie smiled, realizing that for the first time in years, anticipation was bubbling up inside her. "Sure, pizza sounds great."

Chapter 5

The pizza place, it turned out, had karaoke that night, a fact that Jana was delighted to share with Cassie. Giving the baby back for the first time since she met her, Jana ran over to the karaoke books to look up the songs she wanted to sing.

Cassie turned to Sam. "You planned this whole thing. Signing the papers so late in the afternoon. Having your daughter along so it wouldn't be a 'date.'"

He grinned, turning his palms up in an exculpatory gesture. "What are you talking about? Jana and I always have pizza together on Thursdays. That's karaoke night here."

"Yeah, well, you arranged the signing for Thursday, then."

"That I will admit." He smiled, pulling out her

chair for her. "Told you I was persistent. I just didn't tell you I was crafty, too."

Cassie nodded toward the other end of the room, where the karaoke machine was set up and several teenage girls were studying the songbooks. "So, do you sing, too? Or just Jana?"

"I have been known to get up there a few times. Eagles, Bob Seger, some old Springsteen."

"I sincerely hope you're not going to try to make me try it. I have a tin ear and a voice like a frog."

He laughed. "I doubt that. But I promise I won't make you sing." He paused, then said, "So how have you been getting along? It looks like instant motherhood suits you."

"Maybe it does," Cassie had to admit, a little to her surprise. "I've been doing fine, actually. Hopefully Sydney hasn't suffered. I'm getting to where I'm pretty good at the old diapering bit—haven't had one fall off in days."

"That's always good."

"Yeah. And I've established a routine. They say that's important. I've read at least five books on the subject so far and visited a bunch of Web sites."

"Have you heard from your stepdaughter yet?"

"Yes." Cassie sighed, remembering. "Right after I saw you last week. She didn't say much besides what she said in the letter. She wouldn't even give me her number or tell me where she lived. I think she's afraid I'll track her down and lecture her—or, more likely, try to put her into rehab again."

"She's on drugs?"

"I'm not sure. But she sounded drunk or high or something when I talked to her. She was vague and giggling. I don't know what to do."

"I don't know that there's much you *can* do. She's a grown woman."

"Yes. Philip and I learned a long time ago how powerless we are in this situation. Nothing can really be done for her until she's ready to do it herself. But now there's a child involved. What if she *is* on drugs? What if she takes it into her head to come back and get Sydney? I couldn't turn Sydney over to her if I knew she was doing drugs again. But I know I have no rights where the baby is concerned. How could I go to court and try to take Michelle's baby from her?"

"It would be a mess," Sam agreed soberly. "All you can do, I guess, is take things as they come. Hopefully, it will never come to that point."

"Hopefully." She did not mention to him the other fear that was beginning to plague her. She was coming to love Sydney so that she didn't know how she would be able to give her up even if Michelle returned sober and responsible.

Jana came bounding back to them at that point, and Cassie turned to her, smiling, glad to leave the subject. "So what have you decided to sing?"

"I'm not sure. I've sung Britney so many times." Jana launched into a discussion of her favorite songs.

Cassie listened to her enthusiastic chatter, a smile on her lips. Jana was an entirely different teenager from the sort she was accustomed to. Excited and merry, she displayed none of the angst and antagonism that had been the hallmark of Michelle and most of her friends. She was, in fact, incredibly easy to like...another way in which she resembled her father.

They ate pizza, and Jana sang, and later Sam got up to sing, as well. He had a surprisingly good voice, with a gravelly edge to it that, Cassie had to admit, sent a little shiver up her spine. And in the silent spaces between songs, the three of them talked, hitting on all sorts of topics, ranging from Jana's schoolwork to music to world politics. It was a fun, relaxed evening, and Cassie felt a twinge of regret when Sydney began to fuss and wriggle, her hands coming up to scrub at her eyes.

"I have to leave," she said. "I think Sydney's getting sleepy."

Sam stood up. "I'll walk you to your car." He turned to his daughter. "And one more song for you, and then we have to leave, too."

"I know, I know," Jana singsonged. "Tomorrow is a school day."

"You got it."

Sam walked out with Cassie to the car, where she buckled Sydney into her car seat, then stowed the stroller away in the trunk. She was, she reflected, getting rather good at both things. Sam opened her door for her, and she walked up to him and stopped.

"Thank you for the evening. I had a good time."

He smiled. "Me, too. You made a hit with Jana."

"Did I?"

"Oh, yeah. Well, I mean, the baby was probably

enough to put you in her good graces, but then when you liked those crazy platform tennis shoes she had on..."

"They're cool," Cassie defended her opinion.

"So are you." He leaned forward and kissed her forehead. "I'm glad you came." He rested his forehead against hers. "You think there's any chance of us doing this again sometime? Maybe even going out just the two of us?"

"Sam..." Cassie's chest tightened. "I—I loved my husband very much."

"You think he'd want you to spend the rest of your life shut away like a hermit?"

"No. But I—I don't know if I'm ready to—"

"Life just happens. Doesn't matter if you're ready or not. Look, Cassie, I'm not asking for a big commitment here. I like you. I'd like to see you again. That's all I'm talking about. We could go to a movie. Or dancing. Have a few drinks. Whatever you want. What do you say?"

Cassie hesitated, aware of the strong knot of guilt lodged in her chest. She knew what others would say. She had heard them many times. *Philip's been dead over two years. You can't bury yourself with him. It's time to move on. He wouldn't want you to remain unhappy like this.*

In the past, it had been easy to ignore those words. She hadn't wanted to go out or meet anyone else. Her heart had felt as cold and still as Philip's grave. But now, suddenly, everything had changed. For the first time, there was a desire in her to move on. It was only guilt that held her back—guilt and fear.

She raised her head, and in a voice that trembled just a little, she said, "All right. Let's go out."

A slow smile spread across Sam's face, and he bent and kissed her. His lips were soft and warm, moving slowly against hers. Cassie trembled a little, tendrils of pleasure creeping through her. Her hands went up to his chest, but whether to hold on or push him away, she wasn't sure—until her fingers curled into his shirt and she held on, giving herself up to the delightful sensations moving through her.

He raised his head and gazed down at her for a moment. Then he bent and kissed her lightly on the lips again. "I wish like hell that we weren't standing in the parking lot outside the pizzeria."

Cassie smiled and let out a shaky little laugh. "Perhaps it's better that we are."

"I'll call you tomorrow," he said, running his hand caressingly down her arm and taking her hand. He raised it to his mouth and pressed a kiss against it. He rubbed his thumb over the back for a moment, all the while looking down into her face. Finally he squeezed her hand and let go, stepping back from her.

Cassie ducked into the car and closed the door. She put the keys in the ignition and attached her seat belt, all the while trying to calm her shaking nerves. Sam was still standing there, watching her, so she could not just sit for a moment and lean her forehead against the steering wheel until she recovered her breath, as she would have liked to do.

Giving him a smile, she backed out carefully and started home. "Oh, Sydney," she said, and the baby answered her with a coo. "What do you think? Am I crazy? Three weeks ago I scarcely knew him." She let out a little laugh. "Of course, three weeks ago I didn't know you."

Whatever had happened to her quiet life?

But she knew the answer to that question—the baby had happened to her life. And, she suspected, her life would never be the same again. She glanced back at Sydney in her car seat. Her eyelids were already drifting closed, her chubby cheeks relaxing, her head lolling against the cushioned edge of the seat. Cassie smiled, her heart swelling with love. And she knew that, if given the chance, she would not choose to return to a life without Sydney.

The following Saturday, Cassie left the baby with Jana, after long and careful instructions and with some admitted foot-dragging, and she and Sam drove to San Bernardino for dinner and a movie.

"Do you think she'll be all right?" she asked. "I mean, she is only thirteen, and—"

"And she's been baby-sitting for a year now," Sam reminded her. "She's a really competent kid. And if she has any questions or she gets scared, she'll call her mom. Jeanette will be there in no time if she needs her."

"It's just—it's such a lot of responsibility. Sydney's so little...."

Sam glanced over at her and smiled. "You want to

go back? We can all go out for a burger. Or I could take them back over to Jeanette's house, where Jana will have her mom right there to help her."

Cassie chuckled. "I'm being silly, right?"

"No. Not at all. You're anxious. That's only natural. Hell, I remember how with Jana, it took Jeanette two months before she would even leave her with her own mother for the evening." He shrugged. "Mothers worry, that's all. But Jana is very responsible. And she does have plenty of backup. Not to mention those phone numbers you left her."

"You're right." Cassie folded her hands in her lap.

"You can always call her, you know. Before supper. After supper. Whenever you want, just to make sure everything's running smoothly."

"I don't want her to think I don't trust her," Cassie demurred, her fingers itching to take out her cell phone.

"She's used to it. New mothers always call her at least once or twice in an evening."

Cassie dived into her handbag and took out her phone. Predictably, Jana assured her that she and Sydney were fine, and that everything was going along without incident. Cassie smiled at Sam as she hung up the phone. "Well, now I feel better."

"You know," he told her, "in a lot of ways, they're really easier to look after when they're this little. Feeding and diapering and holding them. It's when they start crawling that they really start getting into everything."

"I know. I have to childproof the house pretty

soon—child gate on the stairs, childproof locks on the lower cabinets, all fragile and harmful objects up high or behind doors. I've been reading up on it. I did a walk-through of the house the other day, checking out everything I'd have to move or change." She shook her head. "I never realized how dangerous my house is."

"Yeah. I better tell the folks at Discount City to stock up on their childproof locks."

Cassie glanced at him. "The people in town think I'm crazy, don't they? Buying all that baby stuff."

He chuckled. "No. They think you're saner than a lot of the folks from L.A."

"I'm not sure how much of a compliment that is."

"Good point."

Cassie kept her anxiety at bay with a phone call home after dinner and again after the movie, so she was able to enjoy the evening. The dinner was good, the movie mediocre, but the whole evening was colored with a kind of free-floating happiness that she could only assume came from being with Sam. It was so easy to talk to him, to sit in silence or laugh, yet at the same time, there was a low buzz of excitement and anticipation in her. She could not help but think what it would be like to kiss him again. Nor could she deny that she wanted it to occur.

She didn't know how it had happened, how Sam had managed to sneak past her defenses, to penetrate the gloom that had cushioned and sealed her off from the rest of the world for so long. Perhaps it was the presence of the baby, or maybe it was just the charm and persistence of Sam's personality. But something had changed inside her. Cassie found herself smiling or humming for no reason. She realized, with a start of surprise, that she was actually enjoying herself, not just managing to get through the day without misery. For the first time in a long, long while, she found that she *wanted* to be happy.

And that evening, when they pulled up to her house and Sam turned to her, she found herself going into his arms as naturally as if she'd done it a hundred times. They kissed and clung to each other, his hands roaming eagerly over her, until finally they pulled apart with a little laugh, frustrated by the awkwardness of maneuvering around the console between the front seats.

"I feel like a teenager," Cassie said ruefully.

"I know. Except now it's our kids we're hiding from instead of our parents."

Cassie smiled at him. "I guess we'd better go inside."

"Yeah." Sam kissed her lightly on the mouth. "Another time."

"Another time," she agreed.

They had many other times. They continued to date through the next few months. And every time she was with him, the desire in her grew and it was harder to send him home at the end of the evening. Only the memories of Philip that permeated the house kept her from asking him to stay.

It was easy to be with Sam, and it seemed only natural to spend more and more time with him. Sometimes they went out by themselves, letting Jana or one of the other sitters Cassie had acquired take care of Sydney. Other times they went as a family, the four of them, becoming a regular fixture at the pizzeria on karaoke nights.

Cassie liked Jana. She was, in many ways, the opposite of Michelle. She had an easygoing, loving relationship with her father, which she extended, seemingly without effort, to a relationship with Cassie. Though beset with the usual sort of problems teenage girls faced, she was more likely to ask Cassie for advice than to close herself off behind a wall of sullen defiance. She appeared to be fine with Cassie dating her father, beyond an occasional rolling of her eyes when Sam kissed Cassie in public. She wanted to be friends with Cassie, rather than viewing her as an enemy invading her territory. It was a new experience for Cassie, and one she liked.

Jana was also crazy about Sydney, which made Cassie like her even more. For Sydney was the center of this new life, the life into which happiness had spread like wildfire.

The baby grew by leaps and bounds, and Cassie marveled continually at the miracle that she was. It was an event the first time Sydney, pushing her shoulders up off the floor and craning her head around curiously, managed to roll over onto her back. It startled Sydney so much that her face began to cloud up, but Cassie hurried over, cooing over her with such happy pride that the threatened waterworks turned into a laugh instead.

Less than two weeks later, when Sydney had apparently mastered the art of turning from her stomach onto her back, she managed to roll back the other way. Cassie loved to stretch out beside her on the floor, talking to her as Sydney cooed and gurgled in answer, flailing her arms and legs excitedly. As the weeks passed, and Sydney grew bigger and stronger, Cassie knew that it would not be long before she started crawling. She had already begun to raise herself on her hands, legs tucked under her, and rock. Sam laughed and called her motion "revving up her engines."

Sydney was also approaching her first teeth coming in, and she sometimes fussed, chewing madly away at her teething rings and just about anything else she could get into her mouth. It was clear that she recognized Cassie and Jana and Sam, and she also always seemed to delight in seeing a particular cashier at the grocery store.

Strangely enough, Cassie thought, somehow Sydney's entrance into her life had seemed to open her up to everyone else, as well. She became friends with Margaret Jamison, who owned the bookstore, and they frequently sat down for a cup of coffee at the coffeeshop next door. Margaret was determined to put on an autographing for Cassie, and finally Cassie gave in. She found, to her amazement, that she enjoyed herself, and she spent much of that afternoon happily talking to photography enthusiasts and several of Margaret's friends.

She now knew the names of all the cashiers at the

grocery store and drugstore, not to mention the nurse and receptionist at the pediatrician's office. She was now, she saw, a townsperson, no longer just a pale living ghost who moved among them, unknowing and unknown.

The pictures she took of Sydney seemed to reawaken her love of photography. She continued to take and develop pictures of the baby, but she also began to have ideas about other pictures she wanted to take, even of a theme for a showing.

She began taking photos at every opportunity, often bundling Sydney into a soft carrier she could wear on her back or stomach while she set up and shot the photos or even, if she was in one place long enough, taking along Sydney's playpen for her.

One morning she called her agent excitedly. "I have an idea for a book."

"What? Cassie! Darling, this is wonderful!"

"I was thinking a contrast of old and young. I'd have photos of old people, and photos of children and babies. Black and white. Maybe some of them together. I haven't completely thought it through yet. But I wanted to see what you thought of it."

"What I think is that your editor will be turning cartwheels," Meredith said. "Cassie, this is great. I'm going to call Elizabeth as soon as I hang up. What happened to you? Oh, wait, don't tell me. I think I can guess. Is there a man in the picture somewhere?"

Cassie chuckled. "Yes, there's a man in the picture."

"I knew it! A new love. That awakens a person's creativity every time."

"Yes, there is a new love," Cassie responded, looking across the room to where Sydney was rocking on all fours, babbling. "But it's not the man."

"Not the man? Cassandra, what are you talking about?" Cassie explained about Michelle leaving Sydney with her.

"Oh, dear, that sounds like Michelle. But, Cassie, what are you going to do?"

"I don't know." Cassie pushed aside the familiar fear that rose in her every time she thought about the possibility of Michelle reappearing and taking back her baby. "I'm kind of taking it a day at a time."

"That's a bad situation," Meredith said. "But what about this guy? What does he have to do with it? Do you love him, too?"

"I—I don't know." Cassie said, frowning. "I really like him. But I'm not sure—I mean, Philip—" She stopped, not sure how to go on.

"I see. So you're confused."

"In a nutshell, yes." She paused, then said, "Sometimes I feel as though I'm betraying Philip."

There was a moment of silence on the other end of the line. Then Meredith began, "Philip wouldn't have wanted—"

"I know. I know. Philip wouldn't have wanted me to be unhappy. And I believe that."

"I've read that if a person is happily married and their spouse dies, they're much more likely to remarry than someone who wasn't happily married."

"I'm not talking about marrying him!" Cassie gasped. "I've only been dating him for three months. We haven't even—" Again she stopped.

"I'm not saying you should marry him. I'm just saying you don't need to feel guilty. Being ready and willing and able to love another person is just part of your having loved Philip and his loving you."

"Okay."

"Now I'm going to call your editor. You go think about what I said. Remember, your agent is always right."

Cassie chuckled. "Okay. I'll remember that."

She hung up and moved away from the phone with a sigh, strolling over to where Sydney was still "revving up."

"Easy for her to say," she told the baby. "She's not the one who has to figure out what she's doing."

Sydney's response, characteristically, was to blow spit bubbles. Cassie smiled and lay down beside her on the blanket.

She wished her feelings about Sam Buchanan were as clear and easy as what she felt for Sydney. She liked him. She more than liked him, she knew, but she balked at putting the name love on what she felt for him. She had loved Philip. And when he died, she had felt that she would never love another man.

Surely she could not already have fallen in love with someone else. Surely her love was stronger, more lasting than that. No matter what Meredith said, it seemed a betrayal of what they'd had for her to fall in love with someone else.

Yet she could not deny that the feeling inside her for Sam was growing stronger and stronger all the time. It would have been easy to dismiss what she felt for him as simple lust, for desire was certainly a strong part of what she felt. With every kiss, every caress, she wanted him more. There had been more than one time when she had almost given in to the wild passion that raged through her.

But each time, something had intervened—Sydney had begun to cry. Jana or some other baby-sitter had been waiting for them, or Jana had been up in her room playing video games—and afterward Cassie had been glad they had stopped.

For her, love and making love were inextricably entwined. She did not want a night of passion without love, no matter how much she desired Sam. So the confusion continued to stay in her. And she continued to wait.

"Oh, well, pumpkin, I guess I'm not going to settle it right now," Cassie said, reaching over and picking Sydney up, then lifting her above her head, much to the baby's delight. "And meanwhile, it's time for your bath. Sam's coming over tonight, so we've got to get ourselves prettied up? Isn't that right?"

She jiggled Sydney in the air, and the baby crowed with laughter. She brought her back down and kissed her soundly on the cheek, then stood up and started off for the bathroom.

At six months, Sydney had graduated to the big bathtub and had a number of favorite bath toys, so bathtime was no longer a crying event, at least until it was time to take her out—which meant that it was now a long event.

But there was nothing as sweet-smelling as Sydney when she took her out of the bathtub and dried her off. Cassie always cuddled the baby close to her in her towel for an extra moment, drinking in the sweet baby smell of her.

After she had powdered, diapered and dressed the baby, Cassie put her in bed with her crib gym and a few stuffed toys, and went to shower and get ready herself.

Then she picked up Sydney and went downstairs to feed her and start supper. Sam arrived not long after that, and gave her a hug and a long kiss. He gladly took on the job of giving Sydney her bottle while Cassie finished making spaghetti.

Even though it was Friday evening, they had a quiet evening of dinner and DVD-watching planned, for Sam, as often happened, had crews working on Saturday, so he needed to make an early night of it because he planned to drop by to inspect the two jobs he had going.

It was almost nine o'clock when the telephone rang. They were in the family room with the television on, curled up on the couch while Sydney was lying on her back, chewing on a toy and getting heavy-lidded.

Cassie reached over and picked up the portable receiver. "Hello?"

The only answer was a woman's voice sobbing on the other end of the line.

Chapter 6

"Michelle?" Cassie's hand tightened around the receiver. "Michelle, is that you?"

There was more crying, but finally, on a shaky breath, the caller said, "Yes. It's me."

"Michelle, where are you? What's the matter?"

"Oh, God, Cassie! I've screwed up my life so bad!" She burst into more sobs.

"Honey, it'll be okay. Where are you?"

"At home. He's gone. He left me yesterday." Michelle continued to cry and sniffle, choking out her words between the sounds.

"Kyle?"

"Yes. That bastard!" Cassie heard the sound of a crash, and she assumed that Michelle had thrown something at the wall in her anger.

"What have you been doing since he left?" Cassie

asked carefully. Any direct question about drugs was likely to make Michelle defensive, even hang up, but Cassie knew that was likely what the girl had been doing to ease the pain. She had to find out if Michelle was in danger of an overdose.

"I don't know. Crying, I guess. Being stupid, as always."

"You're not stupid, Michelle. Maybe Kyle was a mistake, but we all make mistakes sometimes."

"Not all the time, like I do." She began to weep again. "You must hate me. I'm a terrible, terrible mother."

"You did the best thing for your baby," Cassie said firmly. "You have to believe that. A terrible mother would not have made sure her baby would be taken care of. A terrible mother would have kept her baby with her even though she was not able to take care of her well at the time. Sydney is fine. She's healthy and happy, and you helped her to be that way."

"Daddy must have been so disappointed in me. He must have been so ashamed of me."

"He loved you, Michelle. He knew how hard things were for you, and he was proud because you always tried to work your way out of it."

"Why am I so weak? Oh, God, Cassie. I've ruined my life. Wrecked it."

She wasn't incoherent. That was a plus, Cassie thought. Cassie had heard Michelle before when she was slurring her words so badly that no one could even understand what she was trying to say—not to mention the times when the words she strung together simply made no sense.

"Help me, Cassie. Please help me."

"Of course I'll help you. What do you want me to do?"

"Help me," Michelle repeated, crying.

"I will. Tell me where you are, Michelle. Give me your address. I'll come there and help you. Okay?"

"Okay." There was a moment of silence, and Cassie thought, sinkingly, that Michelle was not going to tell her where she was. But then Michelle sniffled and gave her an address in the Hollywood Hills.

"Good. I'll drive over there and help you," Cassie told her, jotting down the address. "You know it will take me a couple of hours to get there, right?"

"Yeah."

"Will you be all right? Will you stay there until I get there?"

"Yeah."

"Okay. Have you been drinking? Do you know how many drinks you've had?"

"No. Not that much. I don't have any pills. I'm trying to stop. And I can't!"

"Yes, you can. You just need help. Listen, I'm going to call Mike Goldman. You know, your dad's friend."

"Yeah. Uncle Mike."

"I want to make sure that you're okay till I get there. So open the door when he comes, okay?"

"Okay."

Cassie hung up the phone and turned to see Sam

standing there, watching her, concern on his face. "Are you all right?"

Cassie nodded. "I've got to go to L.A. It's Michelle."

"I gathered."

"Will you stay here with Sydney? It'll be easier without her. I imagine I'm going to have to check Michelle into rehab. And I don't know—it could be even more of a mess."

"I'll do better than that. I'll drive you. You get ready and call this Mike guy you were talking about, and I'll take the baby over to Jeanette's, so Jana can take care of her. Jeanette will be okay with that. Then I'll come back and get you, and we'll go to Los Angeles."

Cassie nodded. She already felt calmer, just knowing that Sam would be with her, that he would be there to support her. He left the room to get Sydney and her things and take her to Jeanette's, and Cassie went into the kitchen to pull out her address book. Mike Goldman had been Philip's friend and attorney long before Cassie met Philip, and she knew he could be counted on to help out Philip's daughter. She didn't think Michelle was in any immediate danger from whatever she had ingested; she hadn't sounded far enough gone. But there was no telling what she might do or take, left on her own for two hours, and Cassie also knew there was a possibility that Michelle might have taken something right before she called that would kick in, perhaps even to a fatal extent, later. Cassie would feel better if someone was there with her.

Fortunately, Mike was home when she called, and despite the late hour, he readily agreed to drive over to the address Cassie gave him and stay with Michelle until Cassie arrived. After she hung up the phone, Cassie put on her shoes and grabbed her cell phone and purse.

She was waiting by the door when Sam returned, and they set out immediately. They were quiet for most of the drive, but Sam's silent presence was a comfort to Cassie. He reached over and took her hand, and she smiled at him.

"Thanks for coming with me."

"Sure." He squeezed her hand. He didn't have to say he was always there for her. She knew he was. It was one of the many things about him that made her love him.

Cassie looked over at him in the dim light of the car's interior. She had been fighting the knowledge for weeks, maybe even months. She had tried to deny it, to think of it as anything but love. But, she knew, she had just been trying to fool herself. It was love.

She glanced away from him quickly, staring out into the dark night. *What was she going to do now?* The thought of being in love again was frightening. It was like standing on the edge of a cliff, with a world of hurt and pain lurking below.

She couldn't think about that now, Cassie decided, turning away. Right now all she could deal with was the crisis of Michelle. Later, she would think about herself. About Sam and the future.

They made the trip in record time. Cassie was sure Sam had broken all the speed limits on the way. They found the address Michelle had given them, a small apartment complex off Vine in the hills above Hollywood.

Mike Goldman was waiting for them when they reached the door of the apartment. A balding, middle-aged man with a kind face and drooping, sad eyes, he looked relieved to see Cassie.

"Cassie. Sweetheart. How are you?"

"Okay. Thank you for doing this, Mike."

"Sure. Anything for you and Michelle. You know that." He looked curiously at Sam, standing behind Cassie.

"Oh, I'm sorry. Mike, this is Sam Buchanan. He's, uh…" She felt strange introducing the man she was dating to Philip's best friend.

"I'm Cassie's neighbor," Sam explained, stepping forward to shake Mike's hand. "My daughter is baby-sitting Sydney, and I offered to drive Cassie."

"Oh. Well, thank you. That's very nice of you."

"He's also my good friend," Cassie said firmly. "He's—I—we're dating."

"Really? Oh. Well, good." Mike gave Cassie a smile in which happiness and sorrow mingled. "I'm glad. I really am." He stepped forward and gave her a peck on her cheek. "You deserve some happiness, Cass."

"Thank you."

He nodded toward the apartment behind him. "Michelle's in there. I think she's okay physically. Kind of a wreck emotionally, though." He sighed. "I'm sorry, but I have an early tee time tomorrow. I need to get home."

"Sure. We'll take care of her. Thanks, Mike. You're a friend in a million."

He hugged Cassie again, nodded toward Sam, and left. Cassie squared her shoulders and walked into the apartment, saying, "Michelle? It's me. Cassie."

Michelle was sitting on the floor of her apartment, back against the couch. She looked, as Mike had said, a wreck. Her hair was dirty and mussed, as if she had been plunging her hands into it. She had obviously been wearing heavy black eyeliner, for it and mascara were smeared around her eyes and down over her cheeks.

She looked up at Cassie, her eyes a trifle vague. "Hi. Here to rescue me again, huh?"

"I'm here to help you," Cassie corrected, walking over and sitting down on the couch beside Michelle. She bent down to talk to her. "I can take you over to Beginnings," she said, suggesting the rehab center where Michelle had gone most recently. "They seemed good."

Michelle nodded faintly. "I guess. Didn't work, though." She shrugged. "I know. I know. It's me, not the program."

Cassie put her hand gently on Michelle's shoulder. "It's hard, Michelle. It's not as though, if you fail once, you're doomed forever."

"I've failed a million times."

"But you keep trying. That's good. You only have to succeed one time."

"You sound like a self-help guru." Michelle rubbed her hands over her face. "God, I'm such a mess!"

"I'll help you clean up." Cassie hooked a hand under Michelle's arm and pulled.

Sam quickly came over and reached down to take Michelle's other arm and pull her to her feet. Michelle looked up at him and frowned. "Who are you?"

"He's my friend," Cassie told her. Michelle looked from Sam to Cassie.

"You're dating him," Michelle said flatly.

Cassie nodded, and an odd, almost frightened look flashed across her stepdaughter's face.

"But what about—what about Dad?" Cassie had the distinct impression Michelle had been about to say something else and changed it at the last moment. "Are you going to marry him?"

"No. I mean, we're just dating. It doesn't change how I feel about Philip." It dawned on Cassie then what the fear in Michelle's eyes had meant. Cassie put her hand on Michelle's arm. "It doesn't change how I feel about you, either. I'll always be here for you. I promise."

She could feel Michelle's arm relax a little under her hand, but Michelle only shrugged and said in an indifferent voice, "It doesn't matter."

Cassie linked her arm with Michelle's and walked her into her bathroom, where she wet a cloth and gave it to Michelle to wash her face while Cassie combed through her hair.

Then Michelle sat listlessly on her bed while Cassie filled up a couple of suitcases with her things. She had called the rehab center on the way to Los Angeles and arranged to bring Michelle in tonight. Michelle would stay in the small hospital-like detox center for a few days to a week; then she would move over into the rehab portion for the remainder of her stay.

"It's good that it's in Palm Springs," Cassie said as she stowed clothes away in the suitcases. "It's closer to Crescent Lake than L.A. is. I'll come down and see you as soon as they let you have visitors. I can bring Sydney with me, if you want."

"Okay." Michelle nodded. She looked at Cassie and gave her a wry grin. "It's weird, but, you know, I kind of like it there. I mean, it's not fun, but it's all so—everything's laid out. They keep you from doing anything wrong. It's like—it's boring, and I feel bad, but I don't have to worry about screwing up."

"It gives you a structure."

Michelle nodded. "Yeah. I guess. That's another thing that means I'm weak, right?"

"Don't worry about it. We all need help."

"You really think I can do it? That I can change this time?"

"Of course I do."

"St. Cassandra." Michelle's faint smile took some of the sting out of her words.

"That's me," Cassie agreed cheerfully, picking up one of Michelle's suitcases and heading for the door.

They drove to Palm Springs and pulled up in front of the modernistic rehabilitation complex. Palms and eucalyptus trees and a number of flowering shrubs added calm, soothing green to the desert landscape, and a discreet metal sign by the door proclaimed its name. Cassie walked with Michelle into the foyer, Sam following with the suitcases.

Michelle gripped her arm tightly during the whole process of checking her in, and it was with reluctance that she let Cassie go and allowed the attendant to lead her off. She cast one backward glance at Cassie, and Cassie gave her a stiff-upper-lip smile. She sagged a little when Michelle and her attendant turned the corner.

"I'm sure she'll be okay," Sam told her, curling his arm around her shoulders.

"I know. It's not even as if Michelle and I are really close. Most of the time, I think she wishes I didn't exist in her life. But it's weird. Despite it all, somehow I really care about her. I feel responsible."

"You're doing the best thing for her."

Cassie nodded and turned away. "Let's go home."

It was a quiet drive back to the lake, with Cassie sunk deep in her own thoughts. When they reached her house, Sam walked her inside.

Cassie turned to him. It was late, but she wasn't sleepy. She still felt too charged up from the rush and worry of the evening.

"Are you hungry? I could probably find something in the kitchen. Or would you like something to drink?"

He shook his head. "No, I'm fine. I better get home. Unless you want the company?"

"No. That's all right. I just feel a little odd being here without Sydney."

"Yeah."

She smiled at him. "I'm sure you need to get to bed. You have to get up early tomorrow."

"That's the good thing about owning your own business. Nobody gripes at you when you come in late."

"Thank you for all you did." Cassie stepped closer, and Sam opened his arms. She moved into them, wrapping her own arms around him. "I really needed you tonight."

Sam kissed the top of her head. "I'm glad to hear it. I want to always be there when you need me."

"Sam..." Emotions welled up in her. She wanted to tell him that she loved him, yet the words would not come out. Cassie tightened her arms around him.

She could feel the hard bone and muscle of his chest beneath her head, the heat of his body. She snuggled closer. His hands stroked down over her back and onto her hips.

"Cassie." His voice turned deeper and rougher. "I don't know if this is the time or the place..." He nuzzled her hair, and she could hear his breath grow uneven.

Cassie slid her hands up his back. "I think maybe it is," she murmured. "I think maybe it's exactly the time and place."

His arms tightened, pulling her up into his body.

She could feel his desire, sudden and urgent, and a hunger just as fierce rose within her. Cassie turned her face up, gazing into his dark eyes, alight now with passion. She was acutely aware of the need humming in her. He bent his head, and for a moment it seemed as if everything stood still, time and place frozen. Then their lips met, and the passion that had been simmering inside her for months exploded.

Cassie clung to Sam, straining up to meet him. His hands were on her hips, pressing her against him even more tightly. They moved slowly, sensuously, every movement fanning the fire between them. They kissed again and again, their hands exploring, teasing, caressing, until the heat was all-consuming.

He tore his mouth from hers and rained kisses over her face and down her neck. His fingers fumbled at the buttons of her blouse, clumsy in his eagerness, until, in frustration, he jerked at the last button, popping it from its moorings and sending it flying. As he shoved her blouse back impatiently, his mouth roamed down over her chest and onto the quivering tops of her breasts. His breath seared her skin. His fingers dug into her buttocks, and he groaned low in his throat.

"I love you," he breathed. "I love you so much."

"Sam. Oh, Sam." Cassie clenched her fingers in his hair, her flesh trembling, aching for his touch.

He pulled her down to the floor with him. The wood was cold and hard beneath them, but neither of them noticed the discomfort. Panting, eager, they stripped their clothes away. His callused fingertips were rough against her smooth skin, setting off shimmering tendrils of delight. Cassie caressed him with an eagerness that surprised them both a little, her hands roaming his chest and back, then sliding down onto his buttocks.

He sucked in his breath sharply at the stab of pleasure and slid down over her, then began to love her breasts with his mouth. With teeth and tongue and lips, he moved over every inch of the soft white orbs, arousing her to an ever higher frenzy of desire. Cassie moaned, her heels digging into the hard floor, her nails scratching lightly down his back.

As he suckled at her breast, each tug of his mouth sending a frisson of pleasure through her, his hand crept downward, sliding between her legs and sending the heat inside her spiralling out of control. He moved between her legs, and then he was inside her, filling and fulfilling her. Cassie gasped, tears coming to her eyes at the fierce pleasure. She dug her fingers into his back, her hips moving with him, urging him on.

Their lovemaking was fast and hot and hard, need driving them onward, until at last passion exploded within them. With a cry, he collapsed against her, his face buried in her hair.

He murmured something she could not understand and rolled over, his arms going around her and pulling her on top of him, off the hard floor. He kissed her shoulder, damp with sweat. For a long moment they simply lay together, too spent to say anything.

"Well," he said at last, his voice drolly self-deprecating. "I had meant to be much more suave about it than that."

Cassie chuckled. "I don't care about suave."

"That's a relief." He stroked his hand down her hair. "In my fantasies, I always swept you up in my arms and carried you up the stairs."

"Ooh. Sorry I missed that."

"You don't have to." He scrambled up, pulling her with him, then bent and lifted her in his arms. Turning, he carried her up the stairs and along the hall to her bedroom.

By the time he reached the bed, he was panting exaggeratedly and pretending to stagger, and they fell onto the bed in a heap, laughing.

"Oh, yes," Cassie agreed, as their laughter subsided. "That was ever so much suaver."

"Perhaps suave is not my strong suit."

"I don't mind."

She turned on her side, rising up on her arm and stretched up to kiss him lightly on the lips. "I like you just as you are."

"Do you?"

"Yes." Cassie lay back down, her head on his chest. He stroked his forefinger lightly up and down her arm.

"I've been thinking," he went on, his voice more sober. "About what Michelle said—about us getting married."

"What?" Cassie went still.

"What do you think about it? Our getting married."

Cassie raised up again to look into his face. "Do you mean how do I feel about it in a general way, or is this a specific question?"

"It's a very specific question," he replied, gazing searchingly into her eyes. "I want to marry you. I love you. And I'm wondering whether you feel the same."

Cassie stared at him, stunned. Thoughts tumbled about inside her head in rapid confusion. "I—I'm not sure what to say."

"It's okay. You don't have to say anything. I'm not trying to pressure you."

"I love you," she said. "I realized that tonight as we were driving to get Michelle. You mean so much to me. But…marriage! I don't know. It's so sudden."

"I know. I'm like that. It doesn't take me long to know my mind. I've known it almost from the moment I met you."

She gave a shaky little laugh. "I'm afraid it takes me a little longer. I'm not…everything is so confused right now. I mean, there's a lot to consider. Your daughter, for one thing."

"Jana thinks you're great. She was asking me the other day if I was going to marry you."

"And there's Sydney. A baby is a big burden to take on."

"A lot of fun, too. In fact, I don't think I'd mind if we had more babies in the future."

The prospect of that filled Cassie with a fizzy burst of happiness and left her a trifle breathless, as well. "Yes, but—everything's so up in the air. What about

Michelle? When she gets out of the clinic, she's probably going to want Sydney back. And then I don't know what I'm going to do. I don't—I don't know how I can bear to give her up. But more than that, I'm scared to death that it would be the wrong thing to do. For Sydney, I mean. What if Michelle falls off the wagon again? She's always been so unstable. I'm afraid I would be hurting Sydney if I gave her back to Michelle. But on the other hand, how could I keep her from her natural mother? I have no legal rights over the baby. I would have to go to court and convince a judge that Michelle is an unfit mother. And how could I do that to Michelle? She needs for me to believe in her. She probably needs the responsibility of having a baby to care for. If the courts rule against her, it would probably send her straight back to drugs and alcohol. I can't risk that.''

"Sweetheart. Wait. Don't borrow trouble." Sam cupped her face in his hands. "You can't make plans for everything. You can't protect everyone from getting hurt. Maybe it isn't even possible to do what's best for both the baby and Michelle. All you can do is wait and see what happens. You can't control it. See how Michelle does at rehab this time. See what she's like when she gets out. You'll do what's right. I know it.''

"But I don't *know* what's right!''

"You just have to go with your instincts. I know they're good.''

"But what about you? I can't ask you to get embroiled in all that mess. And Jana? How can we marry and have that nice warm little family and then have it torn apart? How would Jana feel if Michelle takes Sydney back?''

''She would be sad, the same way you and I would be. But that's what life is. The only way she could keep from being hurt is not to love the baby. But that's no way to live. We all have to do what we can and hope for the best. It's no reason to not marry you, just because there might be some hassle later. I love you. I'll take the hassle along with the rest of it—the joy and the fun. It's all part of the package.''

Cassie looked at him. She wanted to say yes to him, to be ready to risk everything, dare everything. The thought of a life with Sam shimmered before her, beckoning her.

But she could not take that step forward, could not grasp what she wanted. Fear, too, lay in her, cold and foreboding. Happiness was so elusive, so quick to disappear.

''I—'' she began, then could go no farther.

''Don't worry about it,'' Sam said easily, sitting up a little and kissing her on the forehead. ''I don't need an answer now. We've got all the time in the world.''

He wrapped his arm around her and gently tugged her back down on the bed beside him. ''Forget I said anything. Let's just savor the moment.''

When Cassie awoke the next morning, the sun was spilling into the room between the curtains she had not thought to close last night. She sat up slowly and looked around. Sam had already left.

She turned to the clock and saw that it was already nine. She scrambled out of bed. She would have liked to stay there, daydreaming about what had happened a few hours earlier, but she knew she had to get Sydney. She had imposed enough on Jana's mother. Even though it was a Saturday and Jana was out of school and could take care of the baby, there might very well be things her mother wanted to do.

Cassie hurried to the bathroom but stopped at the sight of a note stuck to the door. The torn-off piece of paper was scribbled on in Sam's angular handwriting: *"Cassie: I called Jana, and the baby's fine. You can pick her up whenever you want. I'll come back when I check on my crew. I love you. Sam"*

The note was as simple and direct as Sam himself, and Cassie smiled to herself. She wondered if life with him would be the same.

She showered and dressed and ate a quick breakfast of cereal and milk, then drove over to Jana's house. Jana, predictably, was sorry Cassie had arrived so early to take Sydney away. She helped pack up Sydney's things, chattering a mile a minute, her conversation jumping from the baby to the dance next week at school to her most recent favorite record, all at a pace that left Cassie dizzy.

She drove home and went inside, the diaper bag on one shoulder and Sydney settled on the other hip. Sydney was cooing and blowing bubbles, and energetically patting her hands against Cassie's shoulder. Cassie kissed her on the forehead and stood for a moment, luxuriating in the scent and feel of her pudgy little body. Her heart swelled with warmth and love. *How could she ever stand to give Sydney up?* Just the thought made her eyes fill with tears.

Sydney began to kick her heels and wriggle, wanting her to move.

"Sorry, sweetheart." She carried her into the family room and over to the playpen.

Sydney immediately grabbed one of her small stuffed toys and began to shake and pat it, happily engrossed. Cassie stood looking down at her for a long moment.

Love always seemed tied to unbearable loss.

Cassie turned and walked back out of the living room and down the hall to the door of Philip's room. She stood in front of it for a moment, then reached out, turned the knob and walked inside.

Just the sight of it filled her with bittersweet memories. She looked all around the room, remembering Philip—how he had looked, how his laugh had sounded, how he had smiled at her in that certain way. She strolled over to the hospital bed in which he had been imprisoned the last few months of his life. She remembered the bite of her emotional pain, the agony of watching him being pulled inexorably away from her. She remembered the long hours and days and months of grief after he died.

She realized, with faint surprise, that the memories no longer tore at her like the claws of an animal. She could remember those days, remember Philip, and no longer feel as if she were being torn apart by pain. She could remember, too, the love.

Cassie sat down on the chair in which she had sat so many times before, watching him slip away from her, and she thought about those days…and all the ones before them. And she knew, as she sat there, that if she had been given the opportunity to live her life again, she would do exactly as she had done before. Even knowing that Philip would die, that he would be torn from her and she would suffer the grief and pain of loss, she would still choose to live those years with him, to have the love and happiness they had shared.

The sound of Sydney fussing in the other room brought her back to the present. She got up and walked out of the room, thinking she would have to pack up the things in that room and store them away.

She walked over to the playpen and picked Sydney up. "Hello, sweetheart. Was I gone too long? I'm still here."

She nuzzled the baby's sweet-smelling neck. The doorbell rang, and Cassie settled Sydney on her hip and went to open the door. It was Sam, carrying a bouquet of roses.

"Sam! They're beautiful!"

He stepped inside, handing her the roses and leaning forward to kiss her on the cheek. Sydney happily reached out to him, and he took her, grinning. "Good. I'm glad you like them."

"You're back earlier than I expected," Cassie said, sniffing the flowers.

"Couldn't stay away. I looked in on the crews and decided they were both doing a great job."

They strolled into the kitchen, where Cassie pulled out a large vase and put water in it, then unwrapped the paper from the roses and arranged them.

She turned back to him, smiling, then took a deep breath and began. "I've been thinking about what you said last night—well, I guess really this morning. The thing is—well, is your offer still open?"

His brows rose, but he said only, "Sure. It'll stay open."

"Not anymore," she replied evenly. "I accept."

"You accept?"

"Yes. I *will* marry you."

Sam let out a whoop and came to her, pulling her to him with his free arm. Cassie buried her face in his shirt. She could feel Sydney patting at her hair.

"I love you," she whispered. "I love you."

Epilogue

Cassie glanced over at the clock. It wouldn't be long now. In an hour she would be married to Sam. She smiled to herself. The ceremony made her a little nervous, but she had no qualms about marrying Sam. She was as certain as she had been years ago with Philip. She loved Sam, and there was nothing she wanted so much as to be married to him.

Jana bounced in the door, saying, "How do I look? How do I look?"

"Beautiful," Cassie answered honestly. The girl was wearing a simple pale blue dress, with her hair pulled back at the crown.

She was to be Cassie's only attendant. Cassie wanted a simple wedding with only their closest family and friends. She hadn't even invited anyone from

Los Angeles except her agent, her friend Amanda, and Michelle.

Sydney, sitting on a blanket on the floor, had been occupied with alternately chewing on a plastic doughnut toy and banging it against the post on which it was supposed to sit. But now she looked up and saw Jana, and she grinned and began to bounce on her bottom, holding out her hands and making the "Nn…nn…" noise she usually made when she saw Jana.

"Hi, Sydney," Jana said, going over to squat down beside her. "Sorry. I can't pick you up. I have to be careful of my dress."

Sydney crawled over to her and pulled herself up, using Jana's knees as support, and stood wobbling and grinning.

"Hey, look at you!" Jana laughed, reaching out to take her hands and steady her. She glanced over at Cassie. "What are you going to do with her during the wedding?"

"Margaret is going to take care of her," Cassie said, naming the bookstore owner who had become her close friend over the past few months. "She should be here any minute. You want to help me choose my eyeshadow?"

"Nah. I promised Dad I'd just show you how I looked and then come right back. He doesn't want me in your hair."

"You never are," Cassie said, smiling over at the girl.

"Thanks. But I better get back anyway. Dad's so

nervous he's about to have a hernia. See ya. Bye, bye, Sydney.'' She planted a kiss on the top of the baby's head, then jumped up and ran out of the room.

Sydney set up a screech of disappointment at Jana's departure and started crawling after her.

''Oh, no, you don't,'' Cassie said, hurrying over and scooping her up before she could reach the open doorway. She continued to the door, but as she started to close it, she glanced down the hallway and saw her stepdaughter walking toward her.

''Michelle!'' she exclaimed, a smile breaking across her face. ''You made it! I'm so glad.''

She hurried down the hall toward Michelle and gave her a hug with one arm, then stepped back and looked at her. ''You look great.''

''Thanks.'' Michelle smiled a little shyly and looked over at Sydney. ''Is this—''

Cassie nodded. ''Yes, this is Sydney.''

''She's gotten so big!''

''Eight months old. You want to hold her?''

Michelle nodded, reaching out tentatively toward the baby. Sydney curled one fist into Cassie's blouse and regarded Michelle. She did not move toward her, but she didn't protest when Michelle's hands grasped her waist and she lifted the baby to her.

''My goodness, you must be crawling and everything,'' Michelle said to the baby.

''Yes, she scoots around all over the place. Come on to my room and let's talk while I get ready.''

Michelle followed her and sat down on the bed while Cassie went to her vanity table and sat down to put on her makeup. Sydney immediately left Michelle's arm and crawled across the bed to the edge. Michelle lifted her down to the floor, and the baby took off across the carpet, crawling over to Cassie and pulling herself up on her chair. She patted Cassie on the leg, babbling. Cassie looked down at her and smiled.

"Hi, sweetie." She leaned down and kissed the top of her head.

Michelle, watching her, said, "You love her, don't you?"

"Oh, yes," Cassie answered honestly, looking up at her stepdaughter with a smile. "How could I not? She's a wonderful baby."

"I knew you'd take good care of her," Michelle said.

Cassie didn't know what to say. Her heart sank within her. She was certain Michelle was about to say she was taking the baby back, and she wasn't sure what she would do. She didn't want to have that conversation, not now, right before the wedding.

Fortunately, there was a knock on the door right then, and Margaret stuck her head in. "Hi! I've come for the baby. Sorry I'm running late."

"Oh!" Cassie glanced over at Michelle. "Margaret was going to hold Sydney for me during the wedding. Would you rather—"

Michelle shook her head. "No, that's okay. I wanted to talk to you, anyway."

So she wasn't going to be able to avoid that conversation.

Cassie managed a smile and introduced Margaret and Michelle. Margaret sent Cassie an appraising look, then picked up Sydney and carried her out, closing the door behind her.

"You're looking really good," Cassie said, hoping to stave off the inevitable.

"I'm doing good. I really am. I think I'm going to make it work this time."

"Good. I'm glad to hear that, Michelle."

"I know I always say that kind of thing, but this time I mean it. I mean, before, I always knew deep down that I was lying or trying to kid myself. But this time it's different. I'm really going to work at it."

"I'm so happy," Cassie said sincerely, going over to Michelle and bending down to give her a hug. "I know your dad would have been so proud of you."

"You think so?" Michelle asked, her voice sounding almost like a little girl's.

"Oh, yes. He loved you very much."

"Sometimes I think about all the hard times I gave him. I was a real pain in the butt, I know. There must have been times when he hated me."

"No. Never. He was concerned, but I know he never, ever stopped loving you."

Michelle's smile was a little tremulous. "Thank you. I feel bad about the way I treated him. You, too."

"Don't worry about it. He understood. I understood. It was hard for you. And I know it didn't make it any easier for you when Philip and I got married."

"You were fine. You were good to me. I knew it, even when I acted so crappy to you. Somehow I just couldn't be any other way."

"I know."

"In the center, we have these therapy sessions all the time. And one day we had to talk about a time in our lives when we were really happy. You know what mine was?"

Cassie shook her head, watching Michelle.

"Do you remember that day when I came over, and I was so upset 'cause Katie Inman had been mean to me? I was crying and all."

"I remember."

"And you took me out shopping at the Beverly Center."

Cassie chuckled. "I remember. We bought a ton of stuff."

"Yeah. And had ice cream. And then I put on some of my new clothes, and we went out to eat at Spago." Michelle grinned reminiscently. "And you didn't act embarrassed even though my hair was that fuchsia color and I had the barbell piercing in my eyebrow."

Cassie nodded. "I remember all that. I just—I didn't realize that you had a good time."

"Yeah. I mean, I couldn't let you see that I enjoyed it. That would have been against the rules. You know? But it was the nicest thing anybody had ever done for me. Not spending the money, 'cause Dad or Mom would have given me that. But, you know, you were working on something when I came in, some pictures for your first book. And you just put it all aside and said, 'Well, let's go shopping. That'll raise your spirits.' And you went with me and listened to me gripe about Katie. And, well, it was more than my own mother would have done for me. She would have been embarrassed to even be seen with me in Spago.''

Cassie could feel her own eyes growing moist with emotion. ''Michelle...I—I that means a lot to me. I was always sure I was messing up with you.''

Michelle shook her head. ''I knew you were a better mother than mine was. Or me. That's why I left Sydney with you. I knew you were the best one to take care of her.''

''Thank you.'' Cassie slipped her hand in Michelle's and squeezed it.

Michelle squeezed it back and drew a breath, straightening a little. ''Anyway...what I'm trying to say is, I'll be leaving rehab in a month. I'm staying in the halfway house now. You know how in rehab, the first month they don't let you go anywhere, and the next month, you can leave but you have to get permission and all that? And now I'm starting in the halfway house, where I can leave, but we still have the weekly sessions and all. Then, when I get out, I'm going to move.''

''Move? What do you mean?'' Cassie felt sick to her stomach. Michelle was planning to move far away and take Sydney with her, and Cassie didn't know how she could bear it. Yet how could she refuse to let Michelle have her own daughter? How could she battle her in court when Michelle was at such a crossroads, when there was the possibility she might actually get her life in some order?

"Beginnings has another rehab center in Florida. They want you to continue coming in for weekly sessions for another six months after you leave. You know, to keep you on track. I've never lasted the whole six months before. Anyway, I could move to Florida and still go to the weekly sessions, see."

"But why do you need to move?"

"You're supposed to cut yourself loose from all your toxic relationships—the people that you got high with and all that. But I've never done that. Every time I've gone back and taken up with my old friends, and pretty soon I was back doing the same thing. I think I need to move away, get away from all of them, so I won't be tempted to go back. I need to make different friends, live a different lifestyle. And if I go to Florida, I can do that and still go to the out-patient program."

"That sounds smart."

"Yeah." Michelle flashed a quick grin. "Quite a change, huh?"

She paused, then went on, "The thing is...what I wanted to know is, would you keep Sydney?"

Her words were so far from what Cassie had expected that for a moment she could only stare. "What? But don't you—don't you want her with you?"

"Yeah. In a way." Michelle stood up, walking away and then turning back. "The thing is, I'm not a good mother."

"Oh, Michelle, I'm sure—"

"No, you don't need to deny it. We both know I'm not. I wouldn't have abandoned Sydney here if I was a good mother."

"Honey, that's not true. It was a good decision. It was the best thing you could have done for Sydney, given the circumstances."

"Yeah, it was the best thing for her—giving her to you. And it's still the best thing for her. It's the best thing for me, too. I mean, I love her, I miss her, and sometimes I think, if only I could hug her, I'd be so much happier. But the fact is, I wouldn't be. Right after I had her, I hired this woman to come in and help me take care of her and all. And I managed the first month, but then she quit, and I figured I could take care of her by myself, but it was just so hard. She'd make me so nervous and irritated. Half the time I wanted to run away."

"But you're doing so much better now."

Michelle nodded. "Yes, but it's hard for me. I'm going to be trying to take care of myself. I mean, really take care of myself, without drugs, and that's going to be hard enough. I know I couldn't take care of a baby, too. She would be better off with you. And I'd have a better chance without her, too. Trying to take care of a baby would be one more stress factor, and I need to keep everything as unstressful as possible." She paused and looked at Cassie. "I mean, unless you don't want to have her?"

"Oh, no! Of course I want her. I would love to take care of her. I love her."

"I do, too. I really do. That's why I want you to have her. I mean permanently. Not just while I'm still in rehab or something."

Cassie stared at Michelle, trying to fight down the joy that was rising in her and do the right thing. "Permanently?" she repeated. "Honey, are you sure?"

Michelle nodded. "Yeah. I'm sure. I want to do what's best for her. I know what it's like growing up with a—okay, maybe not crazy, but not stable—mother, and I don't want that for Sydney. Maybe I'll pull my life together and be okay, but I'm afraid I can't do that with a baby. Maybe, someday, I'll be able to handle everything. Maybe I'll be able to have a baby and be a good mother. Hey, maybe I'll even find a nice guy somewhere down the road and not screw it up. But not now. I can't be a good mother to her. But maybe I can be a good aunt or something, you know, who comes to visit and brings cool toys, or that she could come stay with for a visit sometimes when she's older."

"Of course you can."

"Yeah, I hope so. So I already called Uncle Mike."

"Why?"

"I told him I want to set up the papers. You know, so you can adopt Sydney and I can give up my parental rights."

"Michelle!" Cassie stared at her. "That's such a big step."

"Yeah. But it's what I need to do. I've been talking it over with my counselor at the rehab center, and she agrees. It'll make it easier for you, being her legal parent. You know, with school and hospitals and stuff. My counselor told me that. But most of all, it would protect Sydney from me. I mean, if I can't make a go of it and I start taking drugs again, I don't know what I might decide to do. I can be really stupid when I'm not sober, you know? What if I decided I wanted Sydney back? It wouldn't be good for her, to be jerked away from the only mother she's known. And it wouldn't be good for her to be caught in some big court battle over her, either.'' Michelle looked at her levelly. ''I want to be responsible. I want to do the best thing for her. So I'm going to sign the papers. I'm going to give her to you.''

''Oh, sweetheart!'' Cassie went to her stepdaughter and hugged her fiercely. Her heart was filled with love. ''I'm so proud of you. I know you're going to make it this time. You're so strong now. And I promise you, I *will* take care of Sydney. I will love her with all my heart. She will always be doubly my baby, because she's your daughter and you're mine.''

She kissed Michelle on the cheek, then stepped back and gazed at her for a moment, smiling into her eyes.

''Come on,'' Cassie said. ''We've got a wedding to get to.''

''I know. And I hope you are very, very happy. I really do.''

''I will be,'' Cassie told her confidently.

Then, linking her arm through Michelle's, she walked downstairs. Michelle went on into the family room, which had been cleared out and filled with chairs for the wedding guests. Cassie paused at the doorway.

Sam was waiting for her, smiling across the room at her. A lump rose in her throat. She knew she was the luckiest of women, to have known such love not once, but twice.

The music started, and she stepped forward without hesitation, walking to where Sam and her new life awaited her.

* * * * *

THE BABY BOMBSHELL

Victoria Pade

Dear Reader,

When I had my daughter Cori, I had grand illusions of what it would be like to have my very own baby. Babies were beautiful, cherubic, pink and plump and precious. I had no idea what it would actually take to be her mom or how busy she could keep both her father and me. One tiny bundle had two adults hopping nearly around the clock. It was really a form of culture shock. So when I started to think about "The Baby Bombshell" (which was actually what Cori seemed like to me) I wondered what if Mom was a full-throttle career woman dealing with suddenly, shockingly, inheriting a baby? And how nice it would be for her to have a neighbor who might lend a hand. And if that neighbor was a gorgeous, sexy hunk of a guy on top of it… That seemed like a pretty good way to blunt the edges of that culture shock. So that's how "The Baby Bombshell" was born. I won't confess to which parts of Robin Maguire's foibles came from my own experiences, though. You'll just have to guess.

Happy reading,

Victoria Pade

Chapter 1

"*And what this all boils down to is, well, you're a mother.*"

Those words kept echoing in Robin Maguire's mind over and over again.

You're a mother. You're a mother...

But that was the problem—no matter what her late cousin's attorney had said, Robin *wasn't* a mother. What she was—suddenly and without warning—was the guardian of her late cousin's baby daughter, Mazie.

Mazie, who for the past two hours had been right in the middle of the lovely, luxurious living room of Robin's high-rise Denver loft, screaming her little head off.

"Please be quiet. I don't know what you want and

I've already had three complaints from my neighbors," Robin pleaded with her new charge.

But of course the seven-month-old infant went right on wailing.

Then the phone rang to add to the cacophony. Robin considered not answering it, since she was sure it was just complaint number four, but the ringing seemed to agitate Mazie all the more, leaving Robin with no choice but to pick it up.

"Hello, Mr. Simmons. Or is this Mrs. Reed again?" she said with a warning edge in her voice.

It was Mr. Simmons from two doors down.

"Yes, I know you like to go to bed early and you can't sleep with the noise from over here," Robin repeated what the elderly stockbroker said. "I'm doing my best to get things under control. I apologize for the disturbance, but I'm afraid you may just have to bear with me for the time being."

That made it sound as if they were only in for a short duration even though Robin was well aware that she had a full three days of Mazie ahead of her. It was her own fault. Her late cousin's attorney had wanted her to meet with him the day before. But she'd been too busy, and because he'd given her no clue as to what the meeting was about, she'd put him off until six o'clock tonight.

Friday night.

Friday of a three-day holiday weekend when all agencies were closed until after the Fourth of July. Which meant that Robin had no hope of calling either Social Services or a private adoption agency to broach the subject of finding Mazie a more suitable home with more knowledgeable and adept caretakers.

No, for three days Robin was in possession of a child she had absolutely no idea what to do with. But Mr. Simmons didn't need to know the details.

Mr. Simmons ignored her apology anyway and was shouting that if she didn't quiet the baby he was going to call the police and report Robin as a child abuser. Then he slammed the phone down so hard the reverberation hurt Robin's ear.

She made a nasty face at the instrument, hung it up for only a moment and lifted the handset again to leave it off the hook.

At least that was one problem solved.

But the bigger problem of Mazie remained.

Robin returned to the baby, who was in the infant carrier she'd been in since the attorney's secretary had presented her to Robin. The infant carrier that was on Robin's chrome-and-glass coffee table, exactly where Robin had placed it when she'd come into the loft.

"I don't understand why you were so good at the lawyer's office," Robin lamented, recalling that Mazie had been sleeping like an angel with her long dark eyelashes resting against her chubby cheeks and her tiny hands in two fists up near her rosebud mouth.

The secretary had even whispered to Robin, "She's a sweet one," and then kissed the top of Mazie's head where there was barely enough downy honey-colored hair to support a pink bow tied around one wisp of it.

And Robin had thought, *Okay, you're cute, you're*

sweet, babies sleep all the time anyway, I can make it through the next three days...

Then the attorney had carted infant and carrier out to Robin's car for her, showed her how to strap the carrier into the back seat, and closed the door, sending a stunned Robin and a still-sleeping Mazie on their way.

But three blocks from the office Mazie had awakened and begun the screaming that hadn't stopped since.

"Just go back to sleep," Robin begged, her own voice barely audible over the racket she thought surely should be winding down any minute if she could just wait it out.

The loft's air-conditioning didn't seem to be keeping the space as cool as usual and Robin was roasting in the linen suit she'd had on since early that morning. She pulled off the jacket, leaving only the silk tank top she had on underneath it and then disposed of her shoes and slacks, too.

"I'll be right back," she informed Mazie, making a dash into her bedroom for a pair of filmy pajama pants she took from the dresser drawer.

As she did she couldn't help catching sight of herself in the mirror above the bureau.

Haggard. She looked as if she'd been run through the wringer. Her blush and lipstick were long gone, leaving her fair skin pale and her cupid's bow mouth almost indistinguishable.

Her light blue eyes were even wider than usual— as if she were afraid of something—and even a great haircut hadn't been able to keep the sleek, short bob of her auburn hair in place.

"You're probably scaring the poor kid," she told her reflection.

She ran a comb quickly through the reddish-brown locks and jammed a headband on to keep it out of the way. Then she reluctantly returned to the living room and the crying baby.

"Listen," she said as she stood in front of the car seat again, desperate to stop the infant's lament. "You have to help me out here. I'm a business person—the business of hardware. You know—nuts and bolts, lumber, plumbing supplies, wiring—that kind of thing. Everyday Hardware—that's me. My company. My stores. I'm nobody's mother. I've never been around babies, and the one time in my life when I was anywhere near a child a little older than you something bad happened. What I'm saying—in a nutshell—is that I don't have the foggiest idea what to do with you. So if you would just please go back to sleep, I have a plan that will make everything okay when you wake up tomorrow."

Naturally Mazie was uninterested, but Robin was at wit's end and felt driven to expound. "I have this assistant—Amy. Amy is great at everything and she might know how to take care of you. It's just that right now Amy is on her way to Chicago for her grandfather's birthday and the holiday. But her plane lands at O'Hare in about two hours and I'll have her paged. If I can convince her to come back, she'll be able to do whatever needs to be done to make you happy until Tuesday. But the thing is, you can't scream for the next seven or eight hours until I can get her here. So if you would just sleep until then, we'd all be a lot better off.''

By the end of that Robin's voice was as loud as the tiny noisemaker's, and just as upset. So she took a deep breath and blew it out slowly, trying to regain some control.

She hadn't quite accomplished it, though, when a knock on her door penetrated the din.

Robin closed her eyes and shook her head. She was sure this was another of her neighbors there to complain. Or maybe it was the police Mr. Simmons had threatened to call. Police who would probably believe she was abusing the child.

If the apartment had had a back door, Robin thought she might have used it. But as it was she knew she had to answer the only door the loft did have and face whoever was out in the hallway.

So, with her stomach in knots, that was what she did.

Only, on the other side of that door she didn't find Mr. Simmons or the police, or even Mrs. Reed. She discovered her neighbor from directly across the hall instead—an attractive man she'd seen once or twice from a distance since he'd moved in a few weeks ago.

But attractive or not, Robin was convinced he was there to register his lack of appreciation for the decibel level, and she was too frazzled to give him the chance. Before he could open his mouth she launched into her own diatribe.

"Look, I know, I'm disturbing you and everyone else around here. But that's just the way it is and the way it will probably stay for a while because, as unbelievable as it sounds, I have just inherited a baby. *A baby.* I know as much about what to do with a baby as I'd know what to do with a two-hundred-pound kangaroo. I've asked her to be quiet and go to sleep, but that doesn't have any impact at all. So I guess she's just going to have to cry until she wears herself out. And we'll all have to suffer through it."

Meltdown. She'd reached meltdown. Right in front of this guy.

But he was just standing there, staring at her with an impressive amount of patience.

Then he craned his head enough to glance past her into the apartment and, in a rich baritone, said, "May I?"

It took Robin a moment to realize he was offering some kind of aid, and at that point she would have accepted help from Attila the Hun himself. She stepped aside and ushered him in with an elaborate wave of her arm.

"Be my guest," she said, her voice full of frustration.

"Leave the door open," he instructed as he went in.

His door across the hall was open, too, and Robin did as he'd told her, following behind as he went immediately to Mazie.

He unfastened the straps that held her in the car seat and lifted her out of it like a pro.

"Diaper," he ordered.

Robin's expression must have told him she didn't have a clue as to where to get one because he said, "Didn't she come with some equipment? Like a bag?"

"A suitcase," Robin said, just recalling it. "I thought it only had clothes in it. I'll get it."

She felt like an idiot for not having thought of a diaper change and for not even having looked inside the suitcase. She rushed to the spot near her open door where she'd dropped the suitcase when she'd gotten baby and luggage into her apartment.

Bringing it back with her, she set it on the floor and opened it. Sure enough, there was a package of disposable diapers right on top.

Robin handed one to her neighbor.

He laid Mazie on the suede sofa and unsnapped the stretchy suit the baby had on, making quick work of changing her very wet diaper and refastening the snaps.

Then, amidst Mazie's continuing cries, he said, "Is there something in there to feed her, or at least instructions for it?"

Again Robin turned to the suitcase, finding a typewritten paper that informed her that at about the time Mazie had been turned over to her, the baby should have had an evening meal of strained peas, strained carrots and applesauce, followed by a bottle.

"Let's just try the bottle now," her neighbor suggested after she'd read him that portion of the note.

Robin located a Ziploc bag in the suitcase that held several bottles. But they were all empty.

"She's probably on regular milk by now. Do you have any?"

"As a matter of fact, that's one of the few things I do have. I like it in my coffee," she said as if it were a great accomplishment that she stocked the staple.

"Pour eight ounces into one of those bottles, microwave it for about thirty seconds to start and let's get something into this baby's stomach."

Robin again did as she was told, returning with the bottle and handing it over to him without a single thought of feeding Mazie herself.

Instead she watched her neighbor expertly test the temperature of the milk on the inside of a thick, masculine wrist before he judged it acceptable. Then he settled back onto the couch with the infant in his arms, offering the nipple that Mazie latched on to as if she had been starving to death.

And like magic, the moment the bottle was in the baby's mouth, silence reigned.

Robin closed her eyes again, only this time it was blissfully. "Nothing has ever sounded as good as that." Then she opened her eyes and added, "Thank you."

"Sure," the man said amiably enough.

Robin collapsed into the oversize leather chair that sat at a right angle to the sofa and, as relief settled over her, she took her first really good look at her helpful neighbor.

He had dusty-blond hair that was shorter on the sides than on top; a face of rough-cut angles and planes; a slightly long, slightly hawkish nose; very sensuous lips; and striking silver-gray eyes. And it occurred to her that those scant noticings of him in the past that had catalogued him somewhere in her mind as attractive hadn't done him justice. He wasn't merely attractive. He was ruggedly, staggeringly handsome.

"My name is Robin Maguire, by the way," she said then, just realizing they hadn't introduced themselves.

"Dean Machlin," he countered.

"I can't tell you how much I appreciate this. I'm afraid I'm in *way* over my head with this whole baby thing."

He smiled a small smile that put a dimple just off the right corner of his mouth. "That's okay. It seemed like the only way we'd have any peace around here," he joked a bit wryly.

"You're surprisingly good at it, though," Robin said, observing Mazie, who was gazing up at him as she took her bottle.

"I'm an old hand."

Robin's confusion must have again been obvious in her expression because he said, "That little boy I drag around with me is my son, Andy."

If Dean Machlin had had a child with him any of the times Robin had seen him, she hadn't paid enough attention to the child for it to have registered. It was bad enough that she was so inept when it came to

Mazie, but she didn't want to admit that she hadn't even noticed his son.

"Your wife must be happy to have so much help with him," Robin commented, wondering if she'd encountered the woman and overlooked her, too.

"There's only Andy and me."

Robin hadn't been trying to find out if he was single, but for some bizarre reason, hearing that he was pleased her.

Probably it was just that she was glad no other woman had to know she was so lacking in maternal instincts, she told herself. Certainly it wasn't that she was interested in him. There wasn't any more room in her schedule for a relationship than there was for a baby, and no one knew that better than Robin.

Dean Machlin nodded down at Mazie then. "Looks like she's falling asleep and we'll be able to put her down for the night."

Robin breathed a second sigh of relief at that news.

"Is her crib in the other room?" he asked.

"Crib?"

"That's where babies sleep—in cribs."

"I don't have one," Robin answered with a new wave of tension to make her relief short-lived.

Her neighbor's well-shaped eyebrows arched slightly at that information. "No crib?"

"No nothing. Being left as Mazie's guardian came without any warning and I couldn't be more unprepared."

He shook his handsome head. "I think, as my reward for tonight, I want to hear how you came to *inherit* a child. And without any warning. But for now we'd better make sleeping arrangements for her. Can you lay a blanket on the floor at least?''

"I can, but that seems so mean. I don't mind if she sleeps in the guest bed,'' Robin said.

Still patient, her neighbor explained, "Babies roll off regular beds. What I had in mind was you laying out a blanket so I can put her down and go get my portable crib. I'll loan it to you.''

"Honestly? That's very nice of you.''

"No big deal.''

But to Robin, who was realizing she was terrified of Mazie waking up and beginning that inconsolable crying again, everything he was doing was a big deal.

"Blanket,'' she said, to remind herself and to draw her focus off the man she was having trouble not staring at.

"Blanket,'' he confirmed.

Robin headed for the linen closet but spotted a baby blanket in the suitcase before she got there and didn't need to go farther. She took the soft pink-and-white quilt and spread it on the thickly carpeted floor.

When she had smoothed it out, her neighbor set the empty baby bottle on the coffee table, burped Mazie and brought her to lie on the blanket.

Robin held her breath in fear that the infant's big brown eyes would fly open and the wailing would begin all over again. But amazingly, Mazie stayed quietly snoozing.

"You're a miracle worker,'' Robin murmured.

"Not quite. For the most part babies can be made

happy with dry diapers, full stomachs, rest and a little attention.''

Robin repeated those four things, making a genuine effort to commit them to memory.

Something about that seemed to amuse Dean Machlin; he looked as if he were fighting not to laugh. Then he leaned in close enough to her ear for her to feel a warm gust against her skin and said, ''It's not that complicated.''

''Balance sheets are not that complicated. Babies are a whole different world to me.''

Her neighbor straightened up, smiling again now. ''You'll get the hang of it. We all do.''

''Famous last words,'' Robin muttered, trying not to think about the last time that had been said to her and what had happened to disprove it.

But Dean didn't question the comment. He just headed for the open door. ''Let me get the crib.''

Robin watched him go, which she probably shouldn't have. Because not only did watching him make her very aware of how tall he was—probably two inches over six feet—but she also took in what a great body he had. Broad shoulders, narrow waist, long legs. And worse than all that, a great rear end. A rear end to die for. None of which was relevant or should have been distracting her from the major problem of Mazie.

Yet when Dean Machlin reappeared a few minutes later with crib in tow, Robin felt her heart take a fully inappropriate little leap of joy at having him back with her. A leap of joy that wasn't entirely due to the help he was supplying for her current predicament.

"Where do you want it?" he asked, yanking Robin out of her reverie.

"Oh. The guest bedroom, I suppose," she said, leading the way and wishing for the first time that she was dressed better than she was and had fixed her face. Even though she knew she had no business wishing it at all.

Her guest bedroom had only a twin-sized bed in it so there was ample space for the crib. Once Dean had it set up and made with the sheet he'd also brought with him, he pulled the blinds on the curtainless window.

Then he returned to the living room and brought the still-slumbering Mazie—quilt and all—back with him to lie her carefully in the small crib, where the baby curled onto her side, put her thumb in her mouth and went right on sleeping.

And then Robin truly relaxed.

"I owe you big-time for this," she told her neighbor once they'd silently left the bedroom and were safely in the living room again. "You can't even begin to imagine what you've done for me."

"It's okay," he assured her.

"I hate to ask for even more, but do you think you could run the quick course in baby care by me so I'll know what to do if she wakes up in an hour?" Robin asked, thinking that maybe she could learn enough not to have to drag her assistant back from Chicago.

"Sure," Dean said.

He did a brief summary of the things she should do both if Mazie woke up in only a short time and to get the next day underway.

Robin concentrated so hard it must have shown because afterward he said, "You really are in no-man's-land with this baby, aren't you?"

"Oh, you don't have any idea how far into no-man's-land I am," she answered.

"You're going to need a lot of gear for her, too," he observed. He hesitated then, as if weighing his words before he said, "You know, tomorrow Andy and I have to go to Kid Mart—Andy's outgrowing his high chair and needs a booster seat instead. They have everything you need for about any age kid. You and Mazie are welcome to come along. I could point out what you should have for her and do a little more of the how-to-take-care-of-a-baby lecture. If you want."

It was on the tip of Robin's tongue to tell him she didn't require too much equipment as Mazie would only be here for the next three days.

But then she realized that—like the portable crib—there were definitely other things she needed, and that in the process of acquiring them, she could also gain more information to help Mazie through those three days a little better, a little more safely.

And the fact that accepting Dean's help also meant she would get to see him again certainly wasn't a negative.

So she said, "If that wouldn't ruin plans for you, it would be great for me."

"Andy and I didn't have any plans other than the trip to Kid Mart."

"Great. Then it's a date." Bad choice of words. Robin knew it the moment they came out of her mouth.

"Well," she amended in a hurry, "not a date. But you know, a plan. It's a great plan."

Dean Machlin smiled that small smile again, but he didn't address her blunder. Instead he said, "I know you said your baby's name, but now I can't remember it."

"Really, she isn't my baby," Robin heard herself say as if merely referring to Mazie that way threw her into a panic.

When Dean frowned, though, she pretended she hadn't made the frantic qualification and went on to answer his question.

"Mazie. The baby's name is Mazie."

He still looked confused but let the other comment slide and continued. "Do you think you can make it with Mazie on your own until afternoon?"

"The best I can say is that I'll try," she concluded.

He chuckled at that. "If you get stuck, just pound on my door and I'll see if I can help."

For a moment Robin studied him, taking in the expressive eyes that focused only on her and his oh-so-handsome face. She had to marvel that, in that gorgeous package, there was a man willing to lend her aid at the drop of a hat.

"Are you always this nice a guy?" she asked out of the blue.

"No, usually I'm a big creep," he said facetiously. "I'm just trying to turn over a new leaf."

"Honestly, why are you doing all this?" Robin felt the need to persist.

Dean Machlin stared down at her and smiled again, this time a secret sort of smile. "Maybe I'm just a sucker for ladies in distress."

"I hope you're referring to Mazie because I don't know that I like being put in that category myself."

"Mazie. Definitely Mazie," he assured, his smile gaining a twist of mischief that Robin liked much too much.

Something seemed to hang in the air between them then. Something oddly like that moment at the end of a first date when neither person can be sure whether or not to let a good-night kiss happen.

But that couldn't be what was going on, Robin thought, even as she suddenly found herself curious about what it would be like to kiss this man.

Then he took the high road and stepped out into the hall. "Good luck."

"Thanks. I'll probably need it," Robin answered a little too brightly in order to cover up what had just run through her mind. "And thanks again for the use of the crib and everything you did with Mazie."

"Sure."

His gaze lingered on her briefly and then he raised one big hand in a wave and disappeared into his own apartment, closing the door behind him.

It took Robin a few minutes before she could do the same.

She just kept standing there, thinking that she really had been working too hard if she'd been living this close to a man as incredible as Dean Machlin seemed to be and she'd barely known he was alive.

Chapter 2

By seven-thirty the next morning Dean was out of bed, showered, shaved, dressed and ready. Ready to see to the needs of his son and prepared to dash across the hall to help Robin with Mazie if the need arose.

He was fairly sure the need would arise even though he hadn't heard anything from that quarter since he'd left there the night before. But any minute Mazie was going to wake up, and he doubted that Robin Maguire would be able to take care of the infant on her own, despite his instructions.

Not that it was his responsibility to step in if she couldn't meet Mazie's needs, he reminded himself for about the fiftieth time as he gave Andy breakfast.

Although he could hardly sit idly by and let the infant suffer for a lack of knowledgeable care. And he certainly didn't want to spend his holiday weekend enduring the unrelenting sound of a baby's cries.

"Can you say 'bull,' Andy?" he asked his son as he handed the toddler his sippy cup of milk.

"Bu-ww," Andy complied.

"Clear enough. That's what your dad is full of."

Because although the other infant's well-being mattered to him, and so did having peace and quiet, Dean knew those weren't the only reasons behind his offer to help his neighbor. No, Robin Maguire herself had had a little something to do with it, even though Dean didn't want to admit it.

He'd only seen her twice in the three weeks since he'd moved in, both times in the elevator on the way out in the morning. She'd been talking on the cell phone on each occasion, juggling a briefcase and a number of files, folders and papers.

And despite the fact that he hadn't been able to ignore her beauty, he'd known by her absorption in those phone conversations, by her intensity, and by her total lack of awareness of Andy at his side, that she was a woman he should avoid.

Sure, she had incredible long legs for a relatively short stature of what he'd guess to be five foot four or so. Sure, she had a perfectly proportioned body with breasts just big enough to make him curious. Sure, she had alabaster skin and glistening burnished-brown hair. Sure, she had a perky little nose and eyes as clear blue as a flawless summer sky. And sure, she even had great lips—lips he'd actually thought about kissing last night in a crazy moment he still couldn't explain.

But the way she looked wasn't the point.

The point was, he was a year out of a divorce from a woman whose priority—whose whole life—was her career, and he could spot one like her a mile away. Or one sharing an elevator with him. And Robin Maguire was just that kind of woman.

Which meant that he should be running as fast as he could in the opposite direction.

"But what am I doing?" he said out loud.

"Feedin' me," Andy answered reasonably.

Dean laughed. "Uh-huh. Feeding you and getting sucked in by a pretty face."

The pretty face of a woman who had a child under circumstances he didn't understand. A child she didn't know what to do with and didn't seem to want.

Again, just like Joyce.

But there he was, listening for even the first peep of a baby's cry from the other apartment to give him an excuse to run over there again. There he was, so eager to see Robin once more that it had him all churned up.

And even though he had no doubt he could teach her what she needed to know to meet Mazie's needs, he had to wonder when he was going to learn himself.

When he was going to learn to steer clear of women who were on a different track than he was.

So stay away from her. He thought to remind himself that he had that option.

It would be easy to do. He could slip a note under

her door saying something had come up and he had to leave the city. Then he could pack his and Andy's things and stay at his folks' place for the whole weekend. By the time he got back the work week would be upon them and he could just go about his business like before, with nothing more than a courteous hello to Robin Maguire if they happened to meet up.

But was that what he was going to do?

No, it wasn't.

Because it wasn't what he *wanted* to do.

What he wanted to do was sit tight and see Robin again.

"I'm just asking for trouble, you know," he muttered.

"Twubble," Andy repeated.

"On the other hand," he said, as if arguing with his son, "it isn't as if I'm getting involved with the woman because I'm helping her out. I'm not putting anything at risk."

"Wisk," Andy parroted as if he agreed completely.

"I'm just being neighborly. No harm in that. Not as long as it doesn't go any further."

And he would make sure it *didn't* go further, Dean vowed to himself.

So why worry about it?

He didn't see any reason to.

Except maybe that he actually *had* thought about kissing her last night...

"Are you sure it wouldn't be better if *you* gave her the bottle?" Robin inquired.

"Come on, you can do it," Dean cajoled. "You changed her diaper and fed her cereal and fruit. You even gave her a bath."

"You did more of that than I did," Robin pointed out.

"Still, a bottle is a cinch. And only one of us can hold her and give it to her, so I think that should be you," Dean reasoned.

Mazie had been awake for about two hours. At the first stirring Robin had heated a bottle and tried standing at the side of the crib to give it to her before the baby could start crying. But Mazie had not accepted the bottle and instead had begun to scream, throwing Robin into another panic until Dean had come to the rescue once more.

He'd talked Robin through a diaper change, showed her how to feed the baby the more substantial stomach-filler of cereal and strained fruit, and demonstrated how to give the infant a bath before decreeing that the bottle should be offered again now.

"Sit on the couch so you can use the armrest to support your elbow," he instructed, standing with Mazie and the reheated bottle at the ready.

Robin did as she was told. But she did it tentatively, afraid she was going to foul up the equilibrium Dean had established.

Then Dean placed the baby in her arms and Robin's fears were met as Mazie stiffened on contact and let out a wail.

"Baby cryin' again," Andy said from his perch on the leather chair where he'd been content to watch cartoons since Dean had set him there and turned on the television for him.

"That's because she hates me," Robin informed the toddler.

"She probably senses how nervous you are," Dean said. "Relax and she will, too."

Robin tried. But it didn't help that, when Dean handed her the bottle and she offered it to Mazie, Mazie turned her head away and went on crying.

"Let me see that," Dean said, referring to the bottle.

Robin would rather have handed over the baby, but she refrained and merely passed the bottle back to her neighbor.

Once he had it, he coaxed Mazie into accepting it and then made Robin take over.

"See, there's nothing to it," he said as he stepped away, relinquishing the duty completely to her as he went to his son.

He picked up Andy, sat in the leather chair himself, and positioned the little boy on his own lap as he settled into a purely observational posture.

For his part, Andy nestled against his father comfortably and aimed a stubby index finger at the TV. "Toons," he said with glee.

"I know, you like cartoons, don't you?" Dean responded.

Robin couldn't deny that it was a nice sight—the miniature boy cradled against the big man who cared for him so gently, so calmly, so lovingly.

The two-year-old resembled Dean although his

eyes were more gray than silver and his short, spiky hair was a brighter blond. But when Andy smiled he had the same dimple over the corner of his mouth and Robin thought the toddler would probably grow up to be as great looking as his father.

And Dean was great looking. Robin's opinion hadn't changed on that front since the previous evening. Even dressed in a pair of age-worn blue jeans and a navy-blue mock-neck T-shirt he was a sight to see. His broad shoulders and substantial biceps filled out the knit shirt to perfection, and the jeans seemed designed especially to hug his narrow hips and thick thighs. Plus he was clean shaven and he smelled of a citrusy scent that went right to Robin's head.

"Okay, pay up," he said to her then.

For a split second Robin wondered if she'd missed something while she'd been studying father and son.

"Pay up?" she echoed.

"Tell me how you *inherited* a baby. Remember I said last night that that was the price for my services?"

"Ah," she said as the light dawned. Then she shrugged a shoulder. "What can I say? I just inherited her."

"From?"

"A cousin. My father's brother's son. Apparently he and his wife were killed in a car accident."

"I'm sorry."

"Thanks. Although it seems kind of strange for me to accept condolences. Jon and I had drifted so far apart. We spent summers together as kids, but I haven't seen him since he got married eight years ago and moved to Arizona. We've exchanged Christmas cards but that's it. In last year's he wrote a note saying he and his wife had had a baby, but there was no mention of me being appointed the baby's guardian in the event of Jon's and Melena's death."

"It was a *surprise* inheritance?" Dean said with an arch of both well-shaped eyebrows.

"A complete surprise. I didn't even know anything had happened to them when their lawyer called. And he didn't tell me until I got to his hotel room late yesterday what exactly it was he was delivering."

"Wow."

"To say the least."

"I can't imagine wanting someone to be Andy's guardian and not checking with them first, let alone choosing someone who isn't even a part of his and my life," Dean said, amazement filling his voice.

"The asking-first part is definitely something that should have been done," Robin agreed. "But it seems that neither Jon nor his wife had any friends close enough to take Mazie and, according to the lawyer, I'm the only living relative either of them had."

"So you were the *only* choice," Dean concluded.

"That's what I've been led to believe."

"And as a result, overnight and without warning, you became a mother."

Robin flinched at the words that were so similar to those of the attorney.

"No, not really," she insisted. "I mean, of course I can't keep her."

Dean's handsome face showed his confusion. "You can't keep her?"

"Well, no," Robin said as if she were stating the obvious. "I don't know anything about babies or kids. And I tend to be disastrous for them."

"I wouldn't go as far as that. There haven't been any *disasters*."

"Not yet. But it's been known to happen," Robin said ominously but without any explanation of just how disastrous she could be as the caretaker of a small child.

"I'm just not the parenting kind," she continued. "And even if I was, I work eighteen hours a day, sometimes seven days a week. I don't have time to raise kids."

"You make time," Dean said practically.

Robin shook her head. "It's just not me. I know power drills, not pacifiers."

That made him smile just enough for his dimples to come out.

"What are you going to do with her then?" he said, calling her bluff. He must have thought she wasn't quite serious about not raising her.

"On Tuesday, when the world is open for business again, I'll contact Social Services or someone who does private adoptions to set the wheels in motion to find a home for her where she'll be better off than she'll be with me."

"You're giving her up?"

Dean's shock was evident. And it made what she was planning seem so bad.

"It isn't as if I'll stand on a street corner and turn her over to the first person who'll take her," Robin said defensively. "I'll make sure I can handpick a home for her and keep in contact with the family to guarantee she's always taken care of and has everything she needs."

"But you'd be giving her to strangers."

"*I'm* a stranger to her," Robin said emphatically.

"But at least you're a blood relative. The blood relative her parents chose for her," Dean persisted.

"The blood relative they chose without even asking if I was willing to take her. I'll do it more responsibly than that."

"Before you've given raising her yourself a try?"

"Don't make me feel more guilty than I already do." Or more inadequate. "Mazie deserves to be raised by people who know what they're doing, who can keep her safe and healthy and happy."

"And you don't think you can do that?"

She already knew she couldn't. "Let's just say I'm not the best woman for the job."

"You might be," Dean persisted. "How will you know if you don't try?"

She knew. She just didn't want to tell him how. "Take my word for it."

"You have three days to give it a shot," he pointed out.

"You know, not all women have a maternal instinct," she said.

"I'm well aware of that, believe me. But you might have and you just don't know it yet."

"Right. Because I'm doing such a bang-up job with Mazie so far," Robin said facetiously.

Dean smiled again, this time more softly, and nodded at Mazie. "You're doing fine."

Robin glanced down at the baby she held. The baby who had snuggled up against her, who suddenly seemed to trust her enough to be falling asleep in her arms.

"Sure, but it took you to get us here," Robin said, unwilling to take credit that wasn't her due.

Dean paused a moment, much as he had the night before when he'd ended up offering to take her shopping for baby things this afternoon.

But the moment was brief and then he said, "What if I spend the whole weekend showing you the ropes? Proving that parenting is worth all the time and all the compromises and all the sacrifices?"

"I'd still probably be lousy at it."

"Okay, if you're lousy at it and you hate doing it, then call Social Services on Tuesday. But at least keep an open mind until then."

The man was tenacious, she'd give him that.

Unfortunately, Robin doubted that even tenacity was enough to turn her into anyone's mother.

But all he was asking was that she keep an open mind in return for his help the whole time she had Mazie. And while she didn't know how open she could keep her mind, she did know that she could use his help.

Not to mention that his company wasn't exactly unbearable…

"The free three-day in-home trial of parenthood, complete with an ever-available salesman?" Robin joked.

Dean laughed again. "Yes, all of that."

"And you're willing to give up your whole weekend?" Robin asked with a note of disbelief in her voice.

"I won't be giving up anything. Today we're shopping and I'm picking up things I needed to go out for anyway. Tomorrow Andy and I are going to Ocean Journey, and you and Mazie can come, too. Monday you can go with us to my folks' barbecue and see what it's like to be on the family plan."

"That's your whole weekend," Robin repeated.

"But I'm not giving anything up. I'm just playing teacher and advocate-for-parenthood along the way."

Robin thought that over, paying particular attention to the fact that she was very attracted to this man and wondering if it was wise to indulge in concentrated time with him. Especially when she already knew just enough about him to know she shouldn't. Because, like Cam, he was a man with a child. A man who was determined that she discover maternal instincts she honestly didn't believe she had.

But she was facing three days looking after a baby she was woefully incapable of caring for, and here was an incredibly handsome, personable guy, offering to help out just so he could put in a good word for parenthood. How could she turn that down?

"Okay," Robin finally agreed. "If you're willing

to have me tag along on your weekend, I can certainly use the help with Mazie."

"And you'll keep an open mind about raising her," Dean reminded.

"As open a mind as I can keep. But don't say I didn't warn you when Monday night comes and I still can't change a diaper without you telling me I'm putting it on backward."

"I'll bet you don't approach your job with this much self-doubt, lack of confidence and defeatism."

"That's because I *know* I can do my job and I also know that I'm a failure as a parent," she responded with the conviction born of experience. Bad experience.

"That's the second time you've made a reference that makes me think you've had something to do with kids before," Dean said.

"Not one of my own. Let's just say that I was once entrusted with someone else's, though, and it made the evening news." And her tone this time made it clear she didn't want to expound on that.

"Well, as far as I can see, you have one of your own now—at least for three days—and having one of your own is a whole different world."

"Mmm, I just hope you don't come out of this weekend feeling that you've wasted your time if I don't end up being Mother of the Year."

"I don't consider it a waste of time to try convincing you that you and Mazie might actually have a chance at becoming a family. If I'm wrong, well, at least I tried. And it only cost me three days of doing what I was going to do anyway, but now I'll be doing it with company. Pleasant company,'' he added with a slightly different tone. A tone that was much more intimate than conversational.

A tone that stirred something inside her that felt like a tiny whirlwind.

"Okay, I guess if you're game, so am I,'' Robin said, reminding herself that she needed to keep things like that little whirlwind of delight under control.

Because this weekend was likely to end with Dean as disappointed in her, as disgusted with her, as Cam had been.

And if that happened and she'd let down her guard, she could end up hurt again.

Both Mazie and Andy had naps before Robin and Dean took them shopping that afternoon.

With Mazie in a stroller Dean loaned her, Robin followed him up and down aisles of baby equipment while Andy enjoyed himself in the supervised play area of the store.

Robin resisted purchasing anything that couldn't be sent along with Mazie to a new home. She did buy a portable crib so she could return Dean's, and a stroller, but those were the only large items. Beyond that she invested in disposable diapers, a few baby spoons, more bottles, some towels and washcloths that were softer than what she had for herself, sheets for the new crib, and a pacifier and teething ring Dean said she might try when Mazie was fussy.

She also bought some toys and several new outfits—complete with tiny baby shoes—because they were just too cute to resist. Although in doing so and letting Dean know that's why she was doing it, she opened herself up for a commentary on that being one of the fun things about having kids.

Tearing Andy away from the play area was not an easy task when they were finished. But the promise of pizza for dinner and buying him the magnetic drawing board he'd become attached to helped.

After the pizza supper Robin shared with father and son, Dean set up the new portable crib and removed his, and did some minor assembling of the stroller, all with Andy's inexpert assistance.

But watching Dean's patience with the tiny tot was interesting to Robin. She was amazed that Dean never lost his temper regardless of how many times Andy misplaced his tools or got in his way. She marveled at Dean's ability to pause over and over again to show his son how to do something to help or to distract the little boy so Dean could actually accomplish something.

For Andy's part, it was evident that he adored his dad. He wanted to be just like him, to do anything he was doing. He mimicked his mannerisms, almost his every movement, in a sweet pantomime.

It was slightly demoralizing to Robin to see it all. She doubted she would ever have that kind of rapport with any child. But it was an impressive thing to watch. Dean really was a wonderful father and although that had never been one of Robin's requisites in a man, she found Dean's gentleness, his calm strength, his leashed power, increasingly sexy for no reason she understood.

That evening, when it was time for Mazie to be put to bed, Dean didn't step in to do it. Robin was still clumsy and inept at diaper changes and bottle feedings, but he offered more moral support than hands-on aid so she could learn by trial and error. Actually, more by error than trial because she made so many of those.

But finally Mazie was down for the night and it occurred to Robin that that brought her day with Dean to a natural conclusion.

It wasn't a realization that thrilled her. In fact, she discovered in herself a longing for that not to be the case.

But she'd already imposed so much on him that she didn't feel she could ask him to hang around longer just because she was enjoying his company. So she didn't say anything when he picked up a sleepy Andy to take him home. She merely drank in the sight of the drowsy little boy hanging limply on to his dad, resting his head on Dean's shoulder, one of Dean's big hands tenderly pressed to the boy's small back.

"You know," Dean said as he headed for the door, completely unaware of how appealing he was. "I'm the proud owner of a bottle of wine that's supposed to be something special—don't ask *why* it's special but the person who gave it to me last Christmas told me it was. I haven't opened it yet, but I was just thinking…maybe you'd be interested in a little winding-down nightcap after I get this guy tucked in?''

He could have offered her orange juice and she would have jumped at it just to have the evening extended.

And even reminding herself that she was supposed to be keeping things under control, and that she was going out on a very weak limb not to, didn't keep her from saying, "That sounds nice."

"Great. Give me half an hour to get Andy to bed and I'll be back."

"Okay," Robin agreed, sounding as if she were taking it in stride.

But the instant Dean and Andy were out the door, she spun on her heels and ran for her bedroom.

Off went the jeans and shirt that Mazie had spewed strained spinach on, as Robin charged into her walk-in closet.

On went a pair of lightweight black lounging pants and a filmy white blouse designed to reveal the lacy camisole she wore under it.

Then she made another dash into the bathroom, splashing cold water on her face, blotting it dry and then reapplying mascara and blush, and a deep mauve lipstick that was guaranteed not to wear off.

She'd barely put a comb through her hair and gone into the kitchen to take out wineglasses when Dean knocked on her door again.

Only as she crossed to it did it strike her that the quick change might not have been the best idea, that it might convey a message she shouldn't be sending.

But by then it was too late and she had to open the door.

It helped that Dean had changed, too. Not his clothes, but he had combed his hair, shaved off the shadow of beard that had reappeared as the day wore on, and applied more of that tantalizing aftershave.

Still Robin greeted him with an excuse for why she'd spruced herself up. "I had to get out of the spinach splatter."

Dean smiled, gave her the once-over and said, "Yeah, kids are hard on the wardrobe. But I approve, if it matters."

It did, but she didn't tell him.

Like the night before, they left both his apartment door and Robin's open even though Dean had his baby monitor with him so he could hear any sound Andy might make.

Once Dean had set the monitor on the end table, he took the wine into Robin's kitchen and opened it, pouring it into the two glasses she'd left on the counter and handing one of them to her.

Then he clinked his glass against hers and said, "To the hours *after* parenthood."

Robin smiled her amen to that and they both tasted the wine.

It *was* wonderful, and after the first sip they took their glasses and the bottle back to the living room where they sat at either end of the couch.

"You know," she said then, "I just realized that all we've talked about since last night is babies and kids. I don't even know what you do for a living."

"Mmm. True," he agreed. "I'm an architect. What about you? Why do you know more about power drills than pacifiers?"

She liked that he'd caught the reference and remembered it.

"I own the Everyday Hardware stores," she informed him.

"Really?" he said, sounding surprised and impressed.

"Really. My father started with a corner hardware store and I branched us out. We have over thirty stores now, nationwide."

"You and your dad?"

"No, actually the *we* is me and my stockholders, since I've just taken the stock public. Dad passed away a few years ago."

"But he lived long enough to see what a success you'd made of his company?"

"He did."

"How about your mother? Is she still living?" Dean asked then.

"No. She died in childbirth."

"Having you?"

"Yes. I'm an only child. Which is probably why I ended up so work-oriented—I was raised at the store. We even lived right above it. Hardware was the main focus of life for Dad and for me."

"Was that okay with you? I mean, didn't you miss having brothers and sisters? Or other things going on?"

"Sure, when I was young. I even tried a few times

to fix up my dad with teachers I liked and once with a woman who had opened a bakery next to the store. But after Mom, he wasn't interested in anyone else and eventually I got so involved in plans to expand the store that I stopped caring.''

"No wonder you know more about power drills than pacifiers then."

"Exactly."

Dean leaned forward to take the wine bottle from the coffee table and refill both their glasses.

When he sat back again he was angled more toward her than he had been, creating a stronger sense of intimacy that Robin tried not to like so much.

"What about you?" she asked. "I assume your parents are still alive if we're going to their barbecue Monday. But do you have brothers or sisters?"

He smiled with only one side of his mouth, showing that single dimple, but it was enough to set off a little twitter in the pit of her stomach.

"Yes, my folks are still alive. They live in Evergreen. My dad is retired, but he was a prominent neurosurgeon. And as for brothers and sisters—hold on to your hat," he warned. "I have five of each."

Robin knew her shock was reflected in her expression. "Ten? You have ten siblings? Eleven kids in the family?"

Dean raised one hand to scratch his jaw.

"Yep, eleven kids," he confirmed. "They were going for an even dozen but number twelve never happened."

"Where were you in the birth order?"

"Fifth. There are two brothers and two sisters older, and three of each younger."

"No wonder you know so much about taking care of kids," she said, rephrasing his comment about her and power drills. "You must have done a lot of baby-sitting."

"You could say that," he said wryly.

"Did you like that—growing up in such a big family?"

"For the most part. There were times when I wanted to be an only child, but on the whole I didn't mind. As you may have guessed by now I'm a pretty family-oriented guy."

"Does that mean you want eleven kids of your own?"

Dean laughed. "No. I think three or four will do. But to me that will be a small group in comparison."

The entire idea of being from a family that large was hard for Robin to grasp. "Are you close to each other?"

"Why do you say that as if you can't imagine that we would be? Everybody lives in Denver, believe it or not, and there's always something that's getting us together. Plus we baby-sit for each other—that's why I keep the portable crib around, I never know when I'm going to have a niece or a nephew for a night."

"Are all your brothers and sisters married with kids?" Robin asked, her curiosity still at the forefront.

"Seven of eleven are married. I'm divorced and so is one of my sisters. Two of my brothers haven't taken the plunge at all yet."

"And how many nieces and nephews do you have?"

Robin watched him calculate, wondering as he did if all of his siblings were as attractive as he was. If they had his magnetism. Or his charm. If they were as interesting...

"Thirteen," he finally said. "Andy makes fourteen grandchildren so far. But my youngest brother's wife is due any day with their first."

It was Robin's turn to say "Wow," as she thought that this explained why he'd been so shocked by the notion of her giving up Mazie. He came from a group of people for whom parenthood seemed to be a calling.

They'd both finished their second glasses of wine and when Dean offered a third Robin declined. She wasn't much of a drinker and her head was already a little light.

Dean didn't refill his glass, either, but he did check his watch.

"I should let you get some rest," he said then.

Did she look tired?

She hoped not. But she thought she might sound desperate if she tried to get him to stay longer by insisting that she wasn't. So she didn't say anything one way or another.

And as a result, Dean stood to go.

"Think you can handle tomorrow morning on your own?" he asked.

"I make no promises," she said, her continuing uncertainty when it came to Mazie echoing in her voice. "Do you have suggestions on how to improve over this morning?"

"Well, for one thing," Dean said as he moved toward the door with Robin following behind, "When babies wake up, they want out of their cribs. You can't just hope to jam a bottle into their mouths without touching them. And they need a diaper change first thing, even before food, and even if they cry during it."

She was grateful that he'd pointed out the mistakes she'd made in a tone that sounded more like teasing than criticism.

"I'll try to keep that in mind."

"You're not doing so bad at holding her, do you think?"

She was still not great at it, or confident that she wouldn't drop the child if Mazie wiggled or arched her back, so the most Robin would concede was, "I guess not."

"And you survived lunch and dinner with the spoon, and two bottles on your own today. You're getting to be an old hand at the feedings."

Again, not things she was comfortable with even if she had managed to get through them with Dean's support.

"We'll probably be okay," she said without any conviction whatsoever, but because that seemed to be what he wanted to hear.

"You'll do fine," he assured, clearly more to boost her flagging confidence than out of any real belief in her.

But with that assurance came a hand to her arm, one big, strong hand that squeezed just enough to send tiny sparkles all through her.

Only once the gesture was complete, he didn't take the hand away again the way he might have.

Not that it seemed by design. If the two lines between his brows were any indication, that simple, innocent physical contact had done something to him, too. Something that surprised him. Or maybe confused him.

But suddenly it was as if sparks were flying all around them and the touch of his hand wasn't as casual as it had begun.

He rubbed her arm with his thumb, making small circles there as he studied her with those striking silver-gray eyes of his.

It seemed to Robin that what had brought them together initially didn't matter anymore. They were just two people who had had an extremely pleasant day and evening together. Who had shared wine and conversation, which had let them get to know each other and only brought to the surface the attraction that had been simmering below it since they'd met.

And once again Robin discovered herself thinking about him kissing her...

Then Dean came closer. Slowly. As if he wasn't sure he should.

Robin tipped her chin upward, knowing she shouldn't.

That was when he kissed her, softly, just a bare brushing of his lips against hers for a brief, testing time before he raised away from her and searched her face with a heated gaze.

But if he was waiting for her to tell him no, he needn't have. Because all that was going through Robin's mind was that she wanted him to kiss her again.

Then he did. More deeply the second time, wrapping his arms around her and cupping the back of her head to brace her against that kiss that grew deeper still.

His lips were warm as they settled over hers, and Robin parted her lips in answer to a kiss more incredible than any she'd ever had in her life. A kiss that chased away all thoughts. That sent more of those sparks glittering through every inch of her.

She raised her hands to his back, filling her palms with the hard hills and valleys of honed muscle and broad shoulders, letting him pull her even closer. Close enough for her breasts to press into the steely wall of his chest, for the tight knots of her nipples to let themselves be known.

Her nerve endings seemed to rise to the surface of her skin. Her head felt light and her knees felt weak—but in the best way.

And just when she was reveling in every bit of it, he ended the kiss.

Slowly. With one interruption and then a return to kissing her.

With a second interruption and another return to kissing her.

But after the third interruption he didn't come back.

Instead he peered down into her face again, studying it intently.

"Can we say that was for a job well-done today or maybe to bolster you for tomorrow?" he joked in a voice huskier than normal despite the teasing tone he was obviously aiming for.

"We could say it was for both," she responded to keep things light.

"It *was* a pretty good kiss," he said as if he were being forced to brag.

"Well, *pretty* good," she countered to give him a hard time.

"Good enough that you don't want to wipe it off with your sleeve and make a face?"

Robin laughed. "Good enough not to want to do that anyway."

He smiled as if he were pleased with her answer and with himself, too. "I'd better get out of here while I'm still ahead then," he said, stepping into the hall. "If you need me in the morning, holler. But I swear I'm not rushing over here like I did this morning if you don't call me."

"I was glad you did," she said.

"I think you'll be okay on your own, though."

Robin wished she were as sure.

"But don't forget tomorrow afternoon the four of us have a date for Ocean Journey. You'll get a taste of a pretty standard Sunday family outing."

Robin nodded, still too stunned by that kiss to be thinking about much of anything else.

He should have gone all the way across the hall

then, but he didn't. He stayed standing there for another few minutes, as if he didn't want to go.

But he finally did, giving her only a little nod to say good-night.

Robin waved much the way he had the previous evening and closed her door as soon as he was inside his own apartment.

But despite the separation of two doors and a hallway, she could feel his presence almost as strongly as she had when he was there.

She could still feel the warm embrace of his arms around her.

She could still feel his lips on hers.

And what she really wanted was to have him back there, holding her, kissing her, doing more than kissing her.

Even if he was a man she shouldn't have been wanting at all...

Chapter 3

"Oh! Oh! Oh! What are you doing?"

Robin had Mazie on her bed for the first diaper change the next morning and the moment she'd removed the baby's wet one, Mazie rolled over onto all fours as if she were going to crawl away.

Robin hadn't known she could do that and, with Mazie rocking back and forth, she also thought the infant might actually be mobile.

But she wasn't. Mazie just went on rocking as if she wanted to move but didn't quite know how to put everything into play to accomplish it.

It was so cute, though. That tiny, perfect little baby butt and those chubby legs and itty-bitty feet, all right there in the open without any inhibitions whatsoever.

Robin couldn't help smiling—something she didn't

think she'd done even once in regards to Mazie since she'd brought her home.

It was kind of nice.

Until she thought about the seven-hundred-fifty-dollar quilt Mazie was on and the possibility of the baby wetting it—or worse. Then she knew that, adorable or not, she couldn't let Mazie go for long.

"Now don't get mad, but you have to have a diaper on," she said in a high, lilting, completely nonthreatening way as she reached for Mazie and turned her over. She hoped to high heaven that that wouldn't be enough to make Mazie cry since Robin had not yet been able to stop it without Dean's help and guidance.

But Mazie surprised her by doing nothing more than giggling, as if the whole thing had been a game. Giggling and waving her arms and legs in wild abandon.

"You liked that, did you?" Robin asked, catching hold of Mazie's feet to aid the wiggle.

Mazie loved that, too, and laughed even more, so Robin did it again. Then, on impulse, she bent over and rubbed the tip of her nose against the tip of Mazie's.

This time the baby's reaction was something that sounded like "Ah-goo," just before Mazie grabbed Robin's ears in two tiny hands and latched on to her nose to suck on it as if it were a bottle's nipple.

Robin laughed at the way it felt. "What are you doing to me?" she asked as she pulled away, but not without another nose-to-nose rubbing to let her know she didn't really mind.

Mazie repeated her silly sounding "Ah-goo," and then they both laughed yet again as Robin slipped a clean diaper under her.

But the question of what Mazie was doing to her seemed to apply to more than merely that moment as Robin began to realize that she was actually having fun with her tiny charge. That she genuinely did think the baby was adorable. And that she was experiencing soft, warm, fuzzy feelings for her.

"Still, I'm not cut out to be a mother," she confided in Mazie, not wanting the baby to ever know just how incompetent she had been in the past.

On the other hand, it was something Robin had to keep in mind for Mazie's sake, so she didn't begin to entertain thoughts of keeping her. She didn't want to forget that giving Mazie up was what was best for Mazie.

It was just that, for the first time, Robin felt a deep pang that didn't come merely from the guilt that she was too inept to raise Mazie herself, the way Jon and Melena had wanted.

No, this pang came from the thought of giving Mazie up. And it surprised Robin to realize that a part of her was sad to think of handing Mazie over to someone else.

Not that it mattered. Her own feelings weren't what was important, she reminded herself. What was important was that she do whatever would give Mazie a good, safe, happy life.

But as she finished her first solo diaper change with a reasonable amount of success and found that Mazie had half a pudgy fist in her rosebud mouth and was still managing to smile at her, something inside Robin began to bloom. Something that felt an awfully lot like a bud of attachment.

"But I'm not what's in your best interest even if I am starting to like you," Robin whispered, hating to admit it. "You need someone who can take good care of you, not haphazard care of you. Someone who can give you what you need that money *can't* buy. Someone who knows what they're doing.

Someone like Dean.

Dean, who was just great all the way around.

And who probably wouldn't have anything to do with her if Robin *did* give up Mazie.

That thought brought on another pang.

"Oh wonderful. Am I getting attached to him, too?"

But even without Mazie's third "Ah-goo" to confirm it, Robin knew she was sprouting a little attachment to him, as well.

How could she not? When he was kind and compassionate and patient? When he was fun and good-natured and had a great sense of humor? And he certainly kissed better than anyone she'd ever kissed in her entire life.

Not something she should be thinking about, she reprimanded herself. Or something she should be doing, either.

Because she knew that even though it was the truth, thinking about it—*doing* it—was only starting her out on another road that was likely to end with her as the casualty.

Just then Mazie took her fist out of her mouth and held out her arms for Robin to pick her up, smiling the sweetest baby smile Robin had ever seen.

And that smile and the memory of the kiss that had ended the previous evening with Dean ganged up on Robin to leave her worried.

Seriously worried.

Worried that no matter how much she wished it wasn't so, she was more than just starting out on that road, she was already halfway down it.

Robin wasn't sure if Mazie had been going through a period of adjustment or had just been out of sorts, but the baby's improved mood continued throughout the morning.

It helped considerably not only in lowering Robin's stress level, but in accomplishing the feeding and bathing chores, too. It made it so that Robin's clumsy care didn't seem quite so problematic, and by the time Dean and Andy showed up for their trip to Ocean Journey that afternoon, Robin was proud of the fact that she and Mazie had made it that far without Dean's help.

"See? I told you you'd get the hang of it," he said when he discovered he wasn't coming in on yet another mess.

What Robin didn't tell him was that she hadn't had the courage to chance putting Mazie in the bathtub the way he had and had only given her a sponge bath in the sink. Or that she'd put the baby's pink overalls on backward at first. Or that at least half a jar of strained peaches had ended up down Mazie's front. Or that one bowl of cereal had gotten overturned onto Robin's lap. Or that she herself had had to change clothes twice—once after the cereal disaster and again after dousing herself with Mazie's bathwater.

Of course she might have given herself away slightly when Dean discovered a spot of peaches in her hair, but he didn't say anything about it.

And since he didn't, Robin merely basked in what she considered an accomplishment.

After all, Mazie had come through it none the worse for wear.

And that was an improvement for Robin's track record.

Ocean Journey had only recently been saved from closing its doors because of financial problems, and the threat of that had brought more people out to view the world-class aquarium.

With Mazie in her stroller and Andy pushing his rather than riding in it, Robin and Dean joined the throng of people passing by the displays of common and uncommon aquatic life.

Andy was particularly enamoured of the "feeshies" as he called them, and Mazie—whose good spirits kept up—seemed particularly enamoured of Andy today. Andy, who took special pains to show off for her.

Robin thought it was just the effect the Machlin

men seemed to have on women, since she was hardly immune to Dean either, even though she was trying hard to be.

"So, once you have kids, are these kinds of outings the only kind of social life parents end up having?" she asked.

Dean had seized every opportunity to point out the positives of parenthood throughout the day and she just wanted to tease him a little as they left Ocean Journey amid a crowd of other people with children at the end of the afternoon.

"Sure, that's it—amusement parks, The Children's Museum, zoos, and places like this—the rest of the world is off-limits to you," he answered facetiously.

Then in a normal tone, he said, "No, that's not the end of your social life. There are baby-sitters, you know."

They'd reached his car by then—a big SUV that easily provided room for two car seats in back. But before Dean began the chore of putting kids in them, he gave Robin a sideways glance and said, "As a matter of fact, since you brought it up, how about I call my usual sitter for tonight? She can handle Mazie and Andy, and you and I can get away by ourselves for a few hours. Just to show you that life can be normal even with kids."

"Ah, so it's purely for demonstration purposes."

"Purely."

"And what would we be doing to demonstrate that there is normal life even after kids?" Robin challenged.

"A grown-up, put-on-your-good-clothes dinner and a drive. I'll show you the buildings I've worked on."

"Oh sure, you'll show me your buildings," Robin repeated with a lascivious note to her voice. "I'll bet that's just a line you use to pick up single mothers."

"Only the pretty ones," he countered with a wickedly charming smile that set off tantalizing tingles all through her.

"What do you say?" he added.

She knew what she *should* say. She should say no. Because if a little time alone with him had led to the kiss that had knocked her socks off and had left her worrying about getting attached to him, she could only imagine what an entire *date* alone with him would do to her.

But that was the problem. She *was* imagining it. She was imagining a few hours free of diapers and bottles. She was imagining herself in the little black cocktail dress she'd bought last week. She was imagining Dean looking terrific in a suit and tie. She was imagining them sharing a fancy, uninterrupted meal over nothing but adult conversation. Sharing a drive afterward, all alone together.

And she couldn't say no.

So, a little belatedly, she said, "Can you get your sitter on such short notice?"

Dean shrugged one brawny shoulder. "It's worth a try."

"Then I guess that's what you should do," Robin heard herself encourage even as a little voice in the back of her head cautioned that this might not be smart.

But then Dean took out his cell phone and began to set the wheels in motion, and smart or not, Robin felt a thrill at the thought of where those wheels might lead them.

Juggling getting Mazie ready for bed and herself ready to go out was a new—and unpleasantly frantic—experience for Robin. But by seven-thirty when Dean's baby-sitter arrived, she'd managed it and was only too happy to bring Mazie and the portable crib across the hall, where the plan was to put Mazie to sleep and then wheel crib and baby back again when Robin and Dean returned.

After Dean had thoroughly instructed the teenage girl, advised her to raid his refrigerator, and told her where to find his cell phone number, Robin and Dean were finally out in the hallway between their apartments. Alone.

That was when Dean turned to study her from top to bottom in a long, slow gaze.

"Well, you look amazing," he said.

"Thank you," she said, pleased herself with the sliplike, slinky fit of her dress, with its bra straps and the slit that went from the above-the-knee hem to mid-right-thigh.

"You might turn a head or two yourself," she added.

Certainly he'd made an impression on her. He had on a light gray suit with a barely gray shirt and matching tie, and none of her imaginings of how good he would look had done him justice. The body that filled out a pair of jeans and a T-shirt as if they were designed especially for him, also wore that suit better than any male fashion model could have. Plus he was clean shaven and smelled wonderful, and Robin had a horribly inappropriate urge to lure him into her loft and spend the rest of the evening there, *un*dressing him...

But of course she resisted the urge and instead let him lead her to the elevator to begin their night out.

They had a phenomenal meal at Sullivan's Steak House, an elegant restaurant on Denver's Wazee Street, while Dean talked about some of the buildings he intended to show her and gave her some insight into his philosophy.

He explained that he liked to research the background of the buildings before he began the actual job, checking old newspapers for pictures and becoming familiar with the history. He also appreciated the existence of the original blueprints, and spent time walking through what was left of the places to get the feel of the spirit of them so he could stay true to it.

Then the conversation switched to talk about the house he was remodeling and the fact that he was only in the loft across from Robin until that was complete.

And all the while they ate and chatted, Robin kept watching him, memorizing every angle and plane of that handsome face, and fighting to concentrate on what he was saying when her mind kept wandering backward to the kiss they'd shared the night before, and forward to the end of this evening and whether or not he would do it again.

Being back in his SUV afterward helped distract her. In the dark, facing the dashboard rather than Dean, she could focus more on other things.

Besides, the buildings he gave her a tour of were some of the most noteworthy in Denver, and knowing they were reflections of Dean's vision began to give her yet another view of the man himself and all his complexities. He most certainly wasn't just another pretty face and it surprised Robin that he could do such incredible work and also be such an expert and attentive dad at the same time.

Then he headed out of the downtown area, passing by Cherry Creek Mall and crossing Colorado Boulevard to bring them into an older, very stately neighborhood to show her the house he and Andy would be going to when he was finished with it.

"I have the keys to this one so we can go in," he announced as he pulled into the driveway of a three-story redbrick Georgian-style house.

The electricity was turned off inside so Dean showed her around by the illumination of a construction worker's flashlight. As he did, his love for the place was evident, and his descriptions of what he was aiming for in the restoration were so vivid that even Robin could picture what each of the fifteen rooms would look like when he was through.

She had no doubt it would be beautiful and she told him so.

"But aren't you and Andy going to rattle around in a place this big?" she asked when they ended up in what would be the formal living room, where a hand-carved fireplace was being restored to its initial splendor.

"It won't be just Andy and me forever," Dean answered.

"Oh, that's right, you're going to fill it with those other two or three kids you want. And a wife, I presume," she said.

"Yep," he confirmed.

The living room had two floor-to-ceiling picture windows, and enough moonlight flooded through them to allow Dean to turn off the flashlight. He set it on the mantel and led Robin to the ledge of one of the windows to sit in the milky glow, angled enough to rest their backs against the sides of the frame to face each other.

"What if you never find the wife or have the kids?" she asked then.

"I'm not worried about that," he said as if he knew something she didn't.

"Confidence is good," she conceded.

Dean merely smiled and watched her so intently it made her aware of the warmth emanating from his eyes.

But that was dangerous and she returned to the subject of the house for safety's sake.

"How long have you been working on this place?" Robin asked.

"I've owned it for almost four years, but the renovation has only been underway a few months."

"Why is that?"

"Buying it seemed to be instrumental in the demise of my marriage."

Robin recalled him saying that he was only one of two in his large family who were divorced, and she was too curious about what had happened to resist pushing on the door that his comment opened.

To spur him on, she said, "Your wife at the time didn't like the house?"

"She said she did or I wouldn't have bought it. But once it was ours and Andy was on the way, things started to fall apart."

"Isn't that stuff supposed to be a step *forward* in life?"

"That was what I thought. But the whole family thing—a house and a baby—was more what I wanted than what Joyce did. I'd had to talk her into them both, but I thought that she went along with it all because she wanted them, too."

"But you were wrong?" Robin surmised.

"Oh, boy, was I wrong. She said she'd agreed because she'd known it would make me happy and she'd thought she could grow to like it. But she just couldn't. By the time Andy was born she wanted out of it all—parenthood, the house, the marriage. She loved her work. She was—she *is*—a criminal attorney, and that's what she wanted to devote herself to. So, two months after Andy was born, she left."

"You and Andy or all of Colorado?"

"Me and Andy *and* Colorado. She moved to Chicago and we haven't seen or heard from her since."

"I'm sorry," Robin said, seeing in his expression how much of a shock that had been for him, and how difficult, too.

But then Dean smiled a small smile. "It's okay. I'm over it and I ended up with Andy, so I can't complain too much."

"Andy and this house," Robin reminded.

"Right. But the renovation couldn't get underway while all the divorce stuff was happening. Andy and I bunked with one of my single brothers until we'd gotten through everything. Then I started the remodel, but the place we were sharing with Todd was out in the suburbs and it was tough to supervise the work here and live there. So I rented the loft to be nearby until the house is finished and we can move in."

"It all sounds very complicated," Robin observed.

"The divorce or the renovation?" he asked with a laugh.

"Both. But particularly the end of the marriage."

"Relationships usually are pretty complicated. Or haven't you had any that have taught you that?"

"Oh, very smooth." Robin laughed, commenting on his probing segue.

Dean grinned. "Hey, if you can wonder about my past, I can wonder about yours."

So he'd seen through her.

But she couldn't take offense to the fact that he wanted to know as much about her as she wanted to know about him. Actually, she liked that he was interested.

"I've really only had one serious relationship," she began. "I was engaged until about a year ago. To Cameron Mitchell—man with child."

Dean laughed at her delivery of that information since she'd said it as if it were the title of a superhero cartoon. "His having a kid was apparently a big deal."

"It ended up being the *biggest* deal. He shared custody with his ex-wife so he had Timmie at least half the time and he wanted a mother for him."

"How old was Timmie?"

"Four."

"No diapers," Dean commented on a positive note.

"No, no diapers. But even after the baby stage I'm a failure as a parent."

"What did you do to come to that conclusion? Forget food and water?"

"I lost him," Robin said bluntly, a tinge of the terror the incident had caused echoing in her voice.

Enough so that Dean's expression sobered, too. "You lost him," he repeated.

"Cam was very intent that I get into the role of mother, so he had me take Timmie on my own one Saturday to play mom. I had the whole day planned out—toy store, park, lunch at McDonald's, a movie in the afternoon—"

"Sounds good."

"We never got past the toy store. That was where I lost him."

"How did you do that?"

"I took a business call. Not a long one. And Timmie was right there by my side, looking at some action figures when the call started. Then it ended and he was nowhere around—he was literally by my side one minute and gone the next. And I couldn't find him."

Dean shook his head sympathetically. "That's a horrible feeling."

"I was in a total panic. I went up and down every aisle calling for him, but he was just not there. I got the store manager involved, and when he couldn't find Timmie either he called the police. I had to get hold of Cam and tell him. The police called Cam's ex-wife. We were all upset and scared and thinking the worst. It was awful…"

And the full impact of it reverberated through Robin just recalling how horrible it had been.

Dean must have seen that because he took her hand to hold between both of his. "That's what you meant when you said you made the evening news?"

"Apparently reporters listen in on police scanners, so they picked up on the story. It aired at five and six o'clock, and Timmie was found about seven that night."

"Was he okay?"

"Scared, but okay. He'd spotted a dog just outside the store and run out to see it while I was on the phone. The dog was loose and Timmie had followed it to catch it. By the time he did, he was blocks away from the store and didn't know how to get back. But he kept trying and got farther and farther away until the police finally found him."

"And you hadn't done so well on the mom test."

"Huge understatement. When we finally got Timmie back, Cam's ex-wife blew up. She called her lawyer on the spot and ordered him to start proceedings to have Cam's joint custody revoked for leaving Timmie with someone incompetent. That put Cam over the edge and he completely turned on me. He called me some pretty ugly things, said I was going to cost him his son, that if he couldn't even trust me to baby-sit, how could he trust me to be his son's mother, and by the time I got home that night we were history and I knew better than to think I could ever be a parent."

Dean looked down at the hand he was holding and rubbing gently, soothingly. "So that's what all your self-doubt stems from."

"It stems from the lesson I learned that I'm a walking disaster when it comes to kids," she insisted.

"You know, a four-year-old wandering away from you can happen to anybody."

"Not if you're watching him like a hawk, which is what I should have been doing."

"So maybe that's the lesson you learned, and because you learned it, taking your eyes off a kid you're responsible for is a mistake you'll never make again. Maybe the lesson doesn't have to be that you're a disaster with kids."

"Have you met Mazie? The baby I'm a total klutz with? The baby you had to come over and feed and change after I'd left her crying for hours because I didn't have the foggiest idea what to do for her?"

"But now you do."

"For how long before her needs won't be the same and I won't know what to do with the next set, either? Or the ones after that?"

"You learn, Robin," he said quietly.

But she only learned from mistakes that could do harm, she thought.

She didn't say it, though. Up to that point the evening had been great, and the last thing Robin wanted to ruin it with was conversation that made her feel bad. So she said, "I thought this was supposed to be a night off?"

Dean smiled again. "For parents, even nights off usually involve some talk about kids."

"Okay, we've done that part, now let's move on."

He laughed. "Yes ma'am." Then he let his gaze take a slow roll from her face all the way down her body and back again before he said, "The more I look at you tonight, the more blown away I am by how beautiful you are—shall we talk about that instead?"

"For hours and hours," Robin joked with mock vanity even as his compliment instantly chased away the bad feelings that had risen from telling him about the worst moment of her life.

"You know, I like you way too much," he confided with a sexy half smile.

"In some states there are laws against that."

"Lucky for me Colorado isn't one of them," he said.

Then he stood suddenly, removed his coat and tie to lay on the window seat, and crossed to where one of the workmen had left a radio.

He turned it on and changed it from a salsa station to a station playing dated, slow love songs.

With the volume just high enough to make it background music, Dean retraced his steps to her and took her hand again, this time to pull her to her feet rather than to comfort her.

"Dance with me," he ordered in a tone that didn't allow her to refuse.

Not that she wanted to. Because while she wasn't much of a dancer, being eased into strong arms that wrapped around her was something she had no complaints about.

And in truth, what they ended up doing was only marginally dancing. Really it was just an excuse for Dean to hold her as they swayed in the moonlight, her breasts pressed close to that big, hard body of his, her palms against the broad expanse of his back while his hands massaged hers.

It was easy for Robin to forget the bad recollections of that other relationship, that other attempt at motherhood. It was easy for her to get swept up in the moment, in the return to the pleasant part of the evening. Easy to relax again.

"This is nice," she confessed in an almost whisper, peering up at Dean.

"Oh yeah," he agreed as if that was a vast understatement, smiling another small smile as moon glow dusted his chiseled features and showed her all over again how handsome he was.

Then he lowered his mouth to hers, capturing it with warm, parted lips.

And every minute of mentally reliving the kiss of the previous evening seemed wasted. Because nowhere in those memories was it as good as the real thing.

Tonight there was no hesitancy, no tentativeness. Right from the start, he kissed her as if that was exactly what he wanted to be doing, as if he had no doubts about it.

Certainly Robin didn't. How could she when, the very moment his mouth found hers, she knew that was what she'd been craving since he'd left the night before.

His tongue came to say hello then, testing the edges of her teeth, courted her tongue with mischief.

Robin was only too willing to play that game, to follow his lead.

His massage of her back grew sensual as firm fingers made sexy circles. It felt good. So good. So good she longed to feel it everywhere. To have his hands everywhere. And just the thought of that turned her nipples into solid pebbles that nudged his chest in an unintentional message.

A message her own hands also conveyed as Robin brought them around to Dean's front, exploring hard pectorals from outside the shirt she wished would disappear so she could see and feel his bare torso, his broad shoulders, his flat stomach.

But if she couldn't see it all, maybe she could at least feel it.

Emboldened by kisses that had become a wide-open plundering of her mouth, Robin pulled his shirt from his waistband and slipped her hands underneath.

Satin over steel—that was what he felt like, and Robin reveled in the sensation, in the splendor of male flesh.

The touch of her hands to his bare skin seemed to unleash something in Dean. He abandoned her mouth to kiss the side of her neck, to flick the tip of his tongue into the hollow of her throat, to kiss her shoulder, her collarbone, and then a path that took him much lower as he slid the straps of her dress off her shoulders and let it fall midway down the upper swell of her breasts so he could kiss her there, too.

Robin's head fell back slightly with the pure pleasure of what he was doing to her as he took one breast into his palm and bared the other to his seeking mouth, taking it into that warm, wet, velvet cove of delight.

He traced the outer portions of her nipple with the tip of his tongue. He flicked the rock-hard crest. He teased it with his teeth as his other hand caressed her, kneaded her, tugged at that nipple and brought things to life within her.

Things that actually made her want to rip his shirt, to expose him and allow herself at least a part of what she was yearning for so desperately.

But rather than tearing his clothes off she made quick work of his buttons, sliding her hands inside his shirt again to find the powerful pectorals and his own taut male nibs.

He moaned a little and she liked that. She liked that something she did could elicit that kind of response from him. She liked that she could please him.

She also liked how deeply he was drawing her breast into his mouth as she bent forward enough to kiss his shoulder, to tantalize it with her own tongue as she thought about doing so much more, about *him* doing so much more to her...

But just then the lights of a car driving by flashed into the room and even the momentary brightness seemed to shine a light on other things in Robin's mind. On the resurfacing of those thoughts about her relationship with Cam. On the fact that like Cam, Dean was a man with a child, a man who wanted more children, a man who would never understand it if she ended up feeling the need to find another home for Mazie. Mazie, who was at that moment in his apartment with a baby-sitter...

And something about all that put a damper on what she had been enjoying so freely before. It put it into a different perspective. A perspective that certainly didn't leave her feeling free anymore.

"Maybe we should think about this," she heard herself say, her voice quiet and ragged.

Dean kissed his way back up to her mouth, taking it for one more brief moment with his before he said, "I wasn't thinking about anything else."

"But maybe we should."

"Okay. What should we think about?" he asked as his lips brushed her earlobe.

"About not rushing into…this."

Dean groaned a deep, guttural complaint. But he hooked both index fingers under the straps of her dress and lifted them to her shoulders again.

"I hate the voice of reason," he said as he kissed first one shoulder and then the other, where her straps were now back in place to hold her dress where it belonged.

"I know," she agreed, fighting a wave of disappointment that he'd complied with her request to stop. "But—"

"But you're probably right. What are we going to do here anyway? Roll around in the sawdust?"

Robin laughed, not telling him that a part of her was willing to do just that.

He kissed her again, lightly, and then let go of her, crossing to the radio once more to turn it off.

Then he returned to her and took her hand, bringing it to his mouth to kiss the back of it softly.

He looked down at her with those breathtaking silver-gray eyes and said, "I suppose I'd better get you home."

"I suppose," she agreed, wondering if she really should have ended what she was still craving so deeply it was an ache inside her.

But Dean didn't give her the chance to rescind her decision. Instead, keeping hold of her hand, he led her out of the house.

The ride home was short and what little either of them said along the way was only small talk.

Upstairs Dean paid the baby-sitter and the teenager went to her parents' apartment two floors down while Dean carefully rolled Mazie's portable crib into Robin's loft without disturbing the slumbering infant.

And then he and Robin were at Robin's door and good-nights were all that was left.

Dean cupped the side of her face in his palm in a soft caress and leaned forward to kiss her, tenderly, sweetly, and with passion still simmering beneath the surface.

"So there you have it," he said then, smiling a knee-weakening smile. "I promised you a night to prove that you could still have a full life even as a parent and I think we covered just about all the bases," he said with insinuation in his tone.

"Are you telling me it was *all* just for demonstrative purposes?" Robin joked, referring to their teasing banter of the afternoon.

His smile stretched into a grin. "Maybe not *all* of it. But you can't have any doubts left that you can be a parent and a woman, too, can you?"

"And if I say I still have doubts?" she countered with some insinuation of her own even though they were both well aware that they weren't going to continue what they'd started at his house.

"Okay, right here, right now, in the hallway, I'm all yours."

Robin laughed. "Sorry, you're just too eager."

''Oh, you'll never know,'' he muttered under his breath.

But then he kissed her again and took a step away, lingering a moment before his supple mouth eased into a wicked grin and he said, ''But there's always tomorrow.''

Robin had to laugh even as a little skitter of excitement ran up her spine at the possibilities of what the new day might bring.

''Tomorrow,'' she confirmed. Then, just to be ornery, she added, ''With your family.''

It was Dean's turn to laugh but he didn't refute it. He took a breath deep enough to push his chest against the front of his rebuttoned shirt, sighed it out as if he were giving in to something he didn't really want to give in to and went to his own apartment.

Once he was there he nodded at her door and said, ''You first tonight.''

Robin knew what he meant and she obliged him, closing her door while he watched.

But the last thing she saw before she did was his masculinely beautiful face and it was a mental picture she took to bed with her so she could savor in her mind what she'd denied herself so shortly before at his house.

It was just that fantasy was a poor substitute when what she wanted right to the very center of her being was the real thing.

Chapter 4

"Pick up, Dean. Please, hurry and pick up."

"'Lo?"

"Dean? I'm sorry to wake you—"

"Robin?"

"Yes. I'm sorry, I know it's three in the morning, but something's wrong with Mazie and I don't know if I should call a doctor or take her to the emergency room or—"

"I'll be right there."

Robin hung up the phone and carried the crying infant with her to the loft's front door, opening it and waiting there for Dean.

With Mazie's loud lament again echoing off the loft's walls, Robin unable to quiet her with the methods Dean had taught her, plus the unreasonable fear that something horrible was wrong with the baby, it seemed as if hours passed before Dean's door finally opened and—leaving it that way and carrying his baby monitor with him—he crossed the hall.

"What's the problem?" he asked, concern in his voice.

"I don't know! She just woke up crying and she's really, really hot!"

Dean took Mazie from Robin, pressing the inside of his wrist to the baby's forehead.

"Maybe I should call 911," Robin suggested, hating that she sounded like such a basket case again.

"Let's not jump the gun," he advised as he did something Robin found completely odd—he took the squalling infant with him into the kitchen, washed his free hand and then stuck his index finger in Mazie's mouth.

Robin wondered if that was some way of taking Mazie's temperature but whatever the purpose was, it made the baby scream louder.

And the louder Mazie cried, the higher Robin's anxiety level reached. She was convinced that something was terribly wrong and that something she'd done—or *hadn't* done—had caused it.

A million things ran through her mind. Maybe the water she'd used for Mazie's sponge bath that morning had been too chilly and given her pneumonia. Or maybe the milk had spoiled and she hadn't noticed it and she'd given Mazie botulism. Or E. coli—wasn't there something about kids being particularly susceptible to that and reports of it in apple juice? She'd given Mazie apple juice just before she'd left for her date with Dean. What if she'd done some real harm to her?

"Where are those acetaminophen drops I had you buy the other day?" Dean asked, his voice barely audible over Mazie's wails, but his attitude more calm than Robin could understand.

"Aspirin? You think all she needs is aspirin?" For pneumonia or botulism or E. coli?

Robin had never doubted Dean's wisdom or expertise before, but now she wasn't sure he knew what he was talking about. After all, Mazie was burning up with fever. Surely that must mean she was far too ill for such a simple remedy. Or for taking it in stride the way he was.

"Not aspirin, no," he corrected patiently. "Acetaminophen. Where is it?"

Robin got the small bottle from the cupboard where she'd stored it, but she still wasn't convinced she shouldn't be doing something more.

Then Dean instructed her to put the recommended dose in the tiny medicine dispenser with the miniature nipple that he'd also had her purchase, and while he gave the acetaminophen to Mazie, he told Robin to warm a bottle.

"Tylenol and milk? That's it?" Robin said as she did.

"Tylenol and milk," Dean confirmed over the din that resumed when Mazie had finished taking the medicine.

Once the bottle was warmed, he situated Robin on the couch with it and handed Mazie to her to feed.

"I don't know if this is a good idea," Robin said. "What's that saying? *Feed a cold, starve a fever?* Or even if it's the other way around, shouldn't we find out what's going on before we give her food? I mean, what if she has appendicitis or something? What if—"

"Appendicitis?"

"I had it. It came with a high fever and I had to have emergency surgery."

Dean remained patient though he seemed to be fighting a smile. "I'm sure it's happened that a baby has had appendicitis, but it's got to be pretty uncommon and that isn't what's wrong with Mazie. Just give her the bottle now and see if that doesn't comfort her enough to make everything all right again."

Robin was more than worried that this was the one time he was wrong. Mazie was just so hot—scorching hot. How could that be caused by anything simple?

But certainly *she* didn't know what to do if she *didn't* follow Dean's guidance, so she offered Mazie the bottle, fully expecting the infant to refuse it. To go on wailing. To need to be taken someplace where a medical expert could ease whatever grief Robin had caused her.

But Mazie did accept the bottle.

And just like that, peace reigned once again.

"She's teething," Dean explained when he could finally talk in a normal tone.

"Teething?" Robin said as if it were a mystery of life she'd never heard of before.

"Teething."

"But she's on fire."

"Little kids can spike pretty high fevers without a lot of provocation. The acetaminophen should bring it down, help the pain and put her back to sleep. Unless I miss my guess, she'll be fine when she wakes up again."

"You expect me to just put her back to bed? What if she goes into convulsions or something?"

"I won't have you put her to bed until I know if the fever *is* down. I'm just saying that in my experience, this is no big deal."

Robin didn't believe it.

Then he went on to say, "If I'm right, she'll fall asleep and tomorrow, when she's happier, you can take a look at her gums on the bottom, right in the middle. I can feel a little tooth beginning to poke through."

He said that as if it were cute, but Robin was too upset to consider anything that had caused a fever and a repeat of that inconsolable crying to be any such thing. She'd honestly thought she should rush Mazie to the hospital.

But as the thought was going through her mind again, Dean pointed his chin in the infant's direction. "See? She's falling asleep already and I'll bet she feels cooler, doesn't she?"

Robin rested her cheek to Mazie's forehead, discovering to her total amazement that the infant's temperature now matched her own.

Dean was so sure of himself he didn't wait for her

to confirm it, he just said, "She probably won't even finish that bottle. She just needed the comfort of it."

And he was right about that, too, because when Robin glanced down at the baby a second time, Mazie was hardly sucking on the nipple at all and her eyelids were on their way to a heavy descent.

"I got you over here in the middle of the night for no reason, didn't I?" Robin asked, her intense alarm turning to embarrassment as it began to sink in that she'd once more gone over the edge without a great deal of cause.

"It's okay," Dean assured.

But that didn't keep Robin from feeling like an idiot again. An idiot who couldn't tell the difference between a life-threatening emergency and teething. An idiot who didn't know what to do about either.

But all she said was, "I'm sorry."

"Don't be," he said as if he genuinely meant it.

He was smiling down at her and, even dressed in nothing more than a plain white undershirt and a pair of gray sweatpants, with his hair sleep tousled and the night's growth of beard shadowing his jaw, he looked good to her, compounding her confusion.

"Think you can handle it from here?" he asked.

Robin tore her eyes from Dean to look at Mazie yet again. "I think she's back asleep. Shouldn't I be able to just put her in her crib?"

"You should."

"Well, that I think I can handle." Clearly not much more than that, but that at least.

"Okay, then I'm going back to bed."

Robin tamped down on the inclination to ask him to take her with him. If for no other reason than to rescue her from this situation, which seemed fraught with incidents to prove her lack of qualifications.

Although of course there *were* other reasons...

"If you need me again," Dean was saying on his way to the door, "just call. Otherwise I'll see you around noon?"

Robin nodded and watched him go, watched him pull her door shut and leave her by herself with Mazie again. By herself with Mazie and wondering what she would have done without him. What Mazie would have been submitted to if it had been up to her alone.

The very idea brought a fresh wave of panic to Robin.

What *would* she have done if she hadn't been able to call Dean on the spot? She'd have dialed 911 or raced to a hospital with Mazie and likely traumatized the baby for no reason at all.

"I'm sorry I'm so bad at this," she apologized again, this time to the sleeping infant in her arms.

But even though it sounded simple enough, even though Dean *had* been there to solve the problem without a lot of trauma, it still weighed on Robin that, left to her own devices, she would have likely taken a minor situation and made it much worse. That, left to her own devices, she didn't have a clue what else to do.

And the feelings that came with that knowledge were all too familiar to her.

She felt every bit as much a failure as she had that fateful day in the toy store when she'd lost Timmie.

The Machlin family home was a large Tudor-style place that looked as if it belonged in the English countryside. That seemed appropriate since the area it was in had managed not to be suburbanized despite being close to the city and, instead, had retained a rural feel. A very upscale rural feel, though, since all the houses sat on extensive plots of ground and each one was more estatelike than the next.

But the Machlins themselves were very down-to-earth people who warmly welcomed Robin and Mazie to the July Fourth festivities.

The party was in the backyard, where manicured lawn and a number of ancient trees formed a border around a bricked patio laden with wrought-iron lawn furniture. There was a matching brick barbecue and a pool that separated the main house from a small guest cottage, an even smaller pool house and a tennis court.

Luckily for Robin, she was good with names. It came in handy meeting Dean's parents and all ten of his siblings—complete with spouses or dates and thirteen kids of their own.

Mazie, who had awakened at nine o'clock in fine spirits just as Dean had predicted, reveled in all the attention she received. Particularly from the oldest of the Machlins' grandchildren, Ashley, who took an instant liking to the infant and appropriated her.

It freed Robin of most of the baby care, but still

the afternoon and evening were very different from how she would have spent the day had she gone through with her original plans and attended the party of a friend. And she couldn't help making comparisons.

She would have been poolside just the same, but the guests would have been wearing string bikinis rather than running shorts, boxer trunks and damp T-shirts. There would have been martinis aplenty rather than kids with Popsicles and water pistols. And she would have been eating sushi and sashimi, not hot dogs and hamburgers.

Yet she had a wonderful time just the same. The Machlins were a lot of fun and it was interesting to experience what it was like to be a part of a family that size. To be a part of a family of any size, really. It was interesting to see the affection and closeness they all shared.

But in witnessing it, it also became clear to Robin that the kind of support Dean had been showing her was readily available to him from his parents and siblings, and it occurred to her that it was no wonder he was so in favor of single parenting. She just didn't think he realized that she didn't have that wealth of resources available to her.

Neither Mazie nor Andy could stay awake long enough to see the fireworks display. They, along with several of the other smaller children, were fast asleep by then in the well-equipped nursery where twelve-year-old Ashley had insisted she wanted to baby-sit.

After the city's elaborate show, traffic in the area

around the houses was impassable. Apparently this was a yearly consequence and the Machlins had made provisions for it. When the fireworks ended they adjourned to the house to watch a movie until leaving wasn't a problem anymore.

As much as she'd enjoyed the day and the people, by then Robin was feeling slightly deprived of Dean's company. He'd been attentive and conscientious about making sure she wasn't left on her own with his family too much, but the fact of the matter was that, in such a big crowd, they hadn't had any time alone together.

She couldn't be sure whether he felt the same way or just sensed that she did, but as the rest of the party moved inside, Dean leaned in close to her ear and said, "How about if we sneak away instead?"

"All right," she agreed, keeping the eagerness out of her voice so she didn't give herself away.

"Dad!" Dean hollered to his father, who was holding the back door open for everyone. "Start without us. We're going to take a walk."

The older man waved his acceptance of that and went in the house himself.

Once they were alone, Dean took Robin's hand as if it were something he did every day and led her in the opposite direction.

Robin's only clue that they weren't taking a walk the way he'd told his father came when Dean made a stop at the guest cottage for a blanket before bringing her with him out the cottage's back door and continuing on.

The moon was full but in the shadow of the oak and spruce trees that secluded the property from its neighbors it was very dark. It was like being lost in the woods except that Dean seemed to know exactly where he was going and surefootedly took her through the forest into a clearing on the other side where moonlight beamed into a spot near a natural spring that rolled down a small waterfall of rocks into a small lake.

"This is beautiful," Robin commented. "Why is it hidden back here?"

"My folks thought of cutting down all the trees to incorporate it into the yard, but that would have cost them all the trees. So it stayed a little secret. I used to skinny-dip back here. But don't tell my folks."

Robin had heard a number of stories through the day and evening about his antics growing up, so it came as no surprise to her.

"You were kind of a bad boy. I doubt it would shock them," she observed, not intending to put a sensual inflection on the *bad boy* part of it but hearing it in her voice anyway.

"I raised a little hell," he conceded as he released her hand to spread the blanket on the ground near the lake.

Then he took off his tennis shoes and socks, motioning Robin onto the blanket as he did and joining her once he was barefoot, to sit facing her with one leg folded Indian fashion and the other bent at the knee to brace his elbow.

"Your mother said that of all eleven kids, you were

the worst," Robin pointed out as she kicked off her own sandals and curled her legs to the side.

Both Robin and Dean had on shorts and T-shirts, and Robin had been trying not to pay too much attention to Dean's bare legs all day. Like the rest of him, they were great looking. Long and muscular and athletic.

But for some reason, now that his feet were naked, too—and now that they were alone in that private, secluded spot—it all seemed so much more intimate than it had around the pool before.

"I wasn't the worst on purpose," he defended himself. But the smile that was tempting his features made her doubt that. "I just always seemed to be the one getting into mischief."

"I've never known anyone who actually *did* run away to join the circus."

"It was in town and it sounded like fun."

"You were nine."

"So of course they wouldn't hire me, or right now you'd be here with a lion tamer."

That made Robin laugh, but she didn't tell him that if her response to him was any indication, he was better off as an architect because he did a whole lot more arousing than taming.

Which he was doing right at that moment simply by looking at her the way he was looking at her— with eyes that seemed to know how tenuous was her resistance to him.

He smoothed her cheek with the back of one index finger. "So, have you been thinking?" he asked.

The question baffled her. "Thinking?"

"That's what you said last night—that we should think about what we were doing."

She remembered and amended. "What I said was that we should think about not rushing into anything."

"Oh. Because I haven't been able to think about anything but what we were doing last night."

That simple caress of her cheek was causing the sparks of that encounter twenty-four hours earlier to reignite, but she tried not to let it fog her brain.

"Is that why you brought me out here?" she asked.

Dean just grinned. "Yep."

His bluntness made her laugh again. "To have your way with me?"

"Oh, yeah," he said as if just the possibility was turning him on.

"You really are bad," she said as his thumb began to trace the line of her jaw, following a path to the hollow of her throat and all along the V of her neckline, leaving her skin tingling in its wake.

"Or," he proposed, "we could just go skinny-dipping."

"You wouldn't," Robin said with a note of scandal in her voice.

"I would," Dean answered simply enough, crossing his arms over his middle to grab the hem of his shirt so he could pull it off over his head. "But it'd be more fun if you would, too," he added once he had. "And who knows what might happen from there."

Robin feasted on the sight she'd been avoiding looking at too closely all day. Broad, straight shoulders. Bulging biceps that belied a desk job. Hard pectorals. Flat stomach. And just a faint line of hair that went from his navel to disappear below the waistline of his shorts. And she tried to recall why she was supposed to resist him.

Dean stood and went to the edge of the lake, his hands in his front pockets as if he were only taking a stroll. But the moment the stroll ended, he disposed of his shorts and gave her a brief glimpse of his fabulous rear end before wading into the water until it was up to the middle of his back. Then, with his arms cutting through the water, he turned to face her, an inviting grin on his staggeringly handsome face.

"Feels good," he enticed.

Robin imagined it would. Especially since she suddenly felt in need of some cooling off.

"You know, I've just had one baby bombshell dropped on me. I don't need another one in the form of unplanned pregnancy," she said in a weak excuse when everything inside her seemed to be itching to follow his lead.

"Already taken care of," he said, "on the way into the water."

"Oh really?"

Something about the grin that was still on his supple mouth confirmed the wild streak his family had told her about today. "Let's just say I had hopes," he said.

"Ah, just hopes."

"*High* hopes," he added with a devilish insinuation in his voice. "High hopes that you'd think about last night as much as I have and want to let it take a more natural conclusion tonight."

Robin studied him, trying not to appreciate how great looking he was, how charming, how tempting. Knowing that she really shouldn't let herself be seduced.

But he *was* great looking as moonlight kissed his superb body. And he *did* have a face handsome enough to take her breath away. And as for charming? She'd never met anyone who could get under her skin the way he could with just a smile or a glance from his amazing eyes. She'd never met anyone who always seemed to know just the right thing to say to make her feel better, who could make her laugh through the worst of times. She'd never met anyone as plain sexy.

So how could she *not* let him seduce her? Especially when, truthfully, she didn't think there was ever anything she'd wanted more than to throw caution to the wind and join him. To give herself this one time to do something crazy...

He flung a little water at her and, as silly as it seemed, the few droplets that hit her were enough to make her decision for her. To allow her to let go of her own inhibitions so she could indulge in this simple, playful abandon.

"Turn around," she ordered.

He grinned even wider. And turned around.

Robin got to her feet and discarded her own clothes

with a single thought in her mind—she wanted this man and for this one moment that was all that mattered.

The water was cool and a chill ran up her spine as she took that first step into the lake.

Or maybe the chill came, too, from being naked out in the open, from knowing she was about to do something completely unlike herself.

"Can I turn around yet?" Dean asked.

Robin went to within a foot of him, bending her knees just enough to keep her breasts under the cover of the lake's rippling surface. "Okay."

"If you've come in here with your clothes on I'm going to laugh, but I'll be so disappointed," he said as he spun to face her.

His eyes went from her face to her bare shoulders, and then he grinned all over again. "Glad to see there's a little bit of the bad girl in you," he said in a voice that was suddenly richer, huskier.

He didn't reach for her the way she expected him to, though. Instead he surprised her yet again by wading around to stand behind her. Close enough behind her that she could feel the heat of his body.

He kissed her shoulder as his hands cupped her arms to ease her to stand up straight, raising her breasts above the water.

He looked at her, she knew, from over that shoulder, but doing it the way he did, it didn't make her feel self-conscious.

"Beautiful," he whispered, kissing her neck.

His hands were on either side of her waist and he

moved them upward to cup her breasts and press her back against him.

The combination of the water chilling on her skin and the warmth of his big, adept hands made Robin go weak. She rested her head on his chest, arching her neck to kisses he leaned forward to bestow there. And she couldn't stop the quiet moan that sounded in response to the slow, knowing kneading of her breasts, the tender pinching of her nipples, the feel of Dean's body running the length of hers.

Then, without warning, he released her breasts to pull her around to face him so he could kiss her mouth, tilting his head first one way and then the other in short, sensuous kisses that held on to her lips only a moment and then released them just when she least expected it. Again. And again. Teasing her once or twice by dipping in as if he intended to kiss her and then not. Waiting to see if she would come to kiss him a time or two.

Which she did. How could she resist when she was starved for those lips? For the warmth and the sweetness of that mouth? For the sharp point of his tongue jutting out here and there to torment her a little with promises of things to come?

Their kisses started to linger, to find a new intimacy, a new depth, as his hands reclaimed her breasts. Hot, wet hands that made her want to send her own to do some traveling, some kneading, some teasing, some exploring.

So she did. She let them glide along taut muscles made silken with the moisture, reveling in the power held in check, in the pure, raw masculine grandeur of every inch of him.

His mouth plundered hers, his tongue bold and in command. Sparring, tantalizing, increasing her need for more with each minute that passed as her entire body shimmered to life, as nipples turned to knots and that most secret spot between her legs awoke with a whole new need of its own.

He wanted her as much as she wanted him. She could feel the long, hard staff that relayed that message below the water. And she began to wonder if he would take her back to the shore, to the blanket. *When* he would take her back to the blanket. If she should suggest it before she burst with wanting him...

But no sooner had she considered that than Dean's hands deserted her breasts to grasp her arms again. Only this time they went all the way to her wrists, bringing them up to lock behind his neck before he dropped his hands to her hips.

He lifted her then, raising her as if she weighed nothing at all, and bringing her legs to wrap around him.

This will never work...

But Dean managed it anyway, slipping inside her so smoothly, so easily it was as if he were meant to be there.

It felt incredible enough to force a small gasp from Robin, breaking the seal of their mouths. And once that seal was broken, Dean captured one breast in his mouth, taking her a step closer to the brink with a tongue that circled her nipple, flicked it tip to tip, tugged with tender teeth, all the while he pulsed within her. Slow, steady flexes that still allowed him to work magic at her breast, magic that set sparks raining all through her and made her want—made her *need* more. More than those slow, steady flexes of his body into hers.

Dean seemed to know. Or needed more, too. Because just then those flexes grew faster, stronger. In and out as his hands on her hips moved her up and down in perfect rhythm, in ever-increasing speed. Delving deeper and deeper into her, plunging to her core and drawing out again, only to plunge in again.

Somehow along the way he'd abandoned her breasts to the night air, but she didn't care. She didn't care about anything but the mounting need, the desire that was running through her like a wildfire, building in intensity, flames licking ever higher as he moved faster, faster.

And then the flames turned into a blazing inferno. A blindingly bright burst of the most piercingly exquisite bliss held her in a climax that stole her breath and his alike, that locked them together in one shared moment of mind-boggling physical ecstasy more poignant than anything Robin had ever known before.

And then it began to ebb. The flames flickered. Receded. Calmed…

Dean's forehead fell to her shoulder.

Robin's head dropped to the top of his.

And she wondered how he could possibly still have the strength to bear her weight when she was so spent she could hardly keep her legs around him.

"Are you okay?" he asked in a passion-gravelly voice that brushed hot air against her damp skin.

"Oh, I'm so okay," she whispered. "Are you?"

He laughed, a barrel-chested rumble. "So much better than okay."

Robin let her head remain resting against him, replete and supremely comfortable with his arms wrapped around her, their bodies molded into one.

But she knew that couldn't last forever and she finally uncurled her legs from around him and drifted back onto her own two feet.

But Dean didn't let go of her. He pulled her in close. Close enough for her to have to lay her head against his chest.

Not that she minded. Not when she could hear his heartbeat and savor how wonderful it felt to be there like that with him, to know he didn't want this to end.

Then he drew in a resigned breath, sighed it out into her hair, and said, "We should probably get going before someone comes looking for us."

Robin definitely didn't want to be found by a member of his family—or anyone else. Not like that.

"It must be late," she agreed. "The traffic has probably died down by now."

Dean kissed the top of her head and Robin pressed her lips to his astonishing chest. And then they reluctantly released their hold of each other.

He caught her hand in his as they waded out of the lake. And he kissed her again when they reached the blanket—a kiss so full of passion that Robin thought they might use that blanket yet.

Until he groaned and broke away from her.

"Get dressed and quit tempting me," he ordered, returning to the water's edge to retrieve his shorts. Robin did as she'd been told, replacing the clothes she'd discarded, when what she really wanted was to be lying naked with Dean under the stars.

Neither of them said much as they dressed. Or as they returned to the house, gathered both sleeping children and called a quick good-night to Dean's family where they were still engrossed in the movie.

On the way home Robin told him how much she liked his parents and siblings, how nice it had been to be included.

Then they were back at their respective apartments, each with a child in their arms.

"Let's get these two munchkins to bed and then meet back here to say good-night," Dean suggested.

Robin was only too willing to do anything that didn't conclude her time with him and so she agreed.

She got Mazie into her crib without incident and then padded back through the loft to the door. She was standing with her spine to the frame when Dean rejoined her.

He crossed the hall without any hesitation and, as if they were still in the pond, eased her into his arms to kiss her a long, slow, openmouthed kiss that turned Robin to jelly all over again.

But just when she was sinking into more of the mindless pleasure she'd experienced earlier, he ended the kiss and clasped his hands together at the small of her back so he could gaze down at her with a small smile.

"So, here we are," he said, "at the end of my allotted three days."

"Did the clock strike twelve and your carriage turn into a pumpkin?" she joked.

"I'm just wondering how I did."

"I'd give you an A-plus-plus-plus," she answered with enough innuendo to let him know she was referring to his lovemaking.

Dean squeezed her waist with his forearms. "Thanks, but that's not what I was talking about."

"I can't think of anything I *wouldn't* give you an A-plus-plus-plus on," she admitted a bit dreamily because it was true, and in the afterglow of that lovemaking her guard was down.

"Great," he said. "Then does that mean I succeeded in convincing you you actually can care for Mazie and you'll keep her?"

"Oh." That put a damper on things, and sobered Robin completely.

But before she could say more, Dean continued. "Because I think the past few days have been the best I've ever had and it would be nice if it could go on—you and I, enjoying each other, taking care of our kids together. I think we have something pretty special started here. Something that could have a future."

The idea of a future with him was very appealing and it gave Robin a rush of hope and happiness to hear that he thought so, too.

It was just that the rush was followed up with a little reality when she thought about the *taking care of kids together* part.

"What if I don't keep Mazie?" she had to ask, her voice quiet because she wasn't eager to learn his answer.

Dean's expression turned serious. "You're still considering giving her up?"

"I don't know," Robin said honestly, feeling something clench inside her at the thought. "I know I've gotten a little better at changing diapers and giving her a bottle, but there's so much more to it. And I have to think about what's best for her."

"What's best for her is to be with you," he said unequivocally.

"I'm not so sure. If you hadn't been here in the middle of the night I would have rushed her to the emergency room. Who knows what might have been done to her there before someone figured out what was really wrong? What my ignorance might have submitted her to for no reason at all? And even if I finally got better at the baby stuff, that doesn't mean I'd know what to do with a toddler like Andy. I already know I'm dangerous to four-year-olds. And that's just the start. Kids go through different stages, they all have different needs, and I don't know anything about any of it."

"You get better as you go along," Dean assured.

"Not everyone does," she said ominously.

"They do if they want to. You've warmed to Mazie, Robin, I've seen it. I've also seen that the reason you panic like you did last night isn't because you don't know yet what you're doing, it's because you *care.* And that's something my ex-wife never did. It's the caring that counts. It's the caring that will make you a good mother.''

''It's the caring that makes me want Mazie to have the best possible home and parents and upbringing. A better home and parents and upbringing than I think I can give her myself.''

''*You're* who her parents chose to do that,'' he reminded.

''But they only chose me by default, not because they even knew me or thought I was right for the job.''

''So *be* right for the job.''

He wasn't going to budge on this, she could tell that. She could also tell that he wouldn't accept that this genuinely might be something she *couldn't* do. That he believed it was a matter of choice. The same choice his ex-wife had had.

But Robin was very afraid it *wasn't* a matter of choice. That some people were able to be parents and other people weren't. And that she was one of the ones who wasn't.

Dean must have seen her doubts in her expression because his was a bit sad, a bit forlorn. ''I guess I've done what I can and it's up to you now,'' he said.

''I've appreciated everything you have done, though,'' she told him as if that somehow made things better.

Dean kissed her again, lightly, before he pulled his

arms from around her and stepped into the hall. "I should leave you to figure it out on your own now."

That sounded so fatalistic.

Robin wanted to say something that would reassure him but she couldn't. She couldn't say she was keeping Mazie when she didn't know if that was true. So she didn't say anything. She just watched Dean put distance between them. Watched him step back into his own apartment.

He didn't close his door immediately, though. Instead he took one last look at her and, in a deep, quiet voice, he said, "Don't give that baby away, Robin."

Then he shut his door.

And as she'd done on other nights since she'd met him, Robin was left staring at it.

Staring at it and thinking about him, thinking about the decision she had to make about Mazie, and wondering if she found a different home for Mazie, would Dean ever want to open that door to her again.

She doubted it. Because, after all, he had his own son to think about, and not only had the fiasco with Timmie proved she wasn't mother material, surely Dean would have that confirmed if she gave up Mazie.

And everything would be over between them.

Robin felt a sharp stab at the thought and a part of her wanted to cross the hallway, pound on Dean's door and tell him she *would* keep the baby.

But she didn't do that. She knew she *couldn't* do that.

Because regardless of how awful she felt at the

likelihood of not getting that chance at a future with Dean, regardless of how stunningly handsome he was, how charming, how sexy, how irresistible, regardless of how attracted she was to him, how much she enjoyed his company, how much she was already coming to care for him, he couldn't be what influenced her decision about Mazie. She couldn't keep the baby to keep the man, even if the man was as terrific as Dean.

She had to make her decision based on what was best for Mazie.

And she couldn't seem to shake the feeling that *she* wasn't it.

Chapter 5

"There are instances in which contact is maintained with adopted children but it isn't common. I certainly can't guarantee that you could be allowed visitation privileges, let alone overnights. And frankly I don't recommend it. It would be very confusing for the child and extremely unnerving for the adoptive parents. Not to mention that it would be like giving up Mazie over and over again each time you had her and then had to return her to the adoptive family. A complete severing of ties is what we find works best for everyone involved."

"In other words, if I let you take Mazie right now I'll just never see her again?" Robin asked the caseworker late the next afternoon.

"Yes," the woman from Private Adoptive Services confirmed patiently. "Or, if you'd prefer to turn her over to me another time, we can arrange that, but once that's done she'll be the adoptive family's child and no longer available to you."

It wasn't an answer Robin liked.

"If I lose contact with her, how will I know if she's okay? How will I be sure if she has everything she needs and is being taken care of the way she deserves to be taken care of?" Robin persisted, just as she had with the man from Social Services and the other woman from Families By Choice.

"You have to trust that we will place Mazie in the best possible environment with people who have been rigorously screened." The caseworker paused a moment and then said, "Maybe I'm misinterpreting what you're telling me, Miss Maguire, but I don't have the feeling that you really want to give Mazie up."

"Well, no, but—"

"That no is a very big red flag to me. I'm reluctant to put a couple who have been waiting years for an infant into a situation where I feel the birth mother— or you in this case—isn't serious about actually adopting the child out."

"I just want what's best for Mazie."

"And you don't believe you are?" the caseworker asked.

"I'm just no good at taking care of kids," Robin confessed.

Although there didn't seem to be any ready evidence of her ineptitude. She was sitting on the sofa with Mazie lying in her lap, the baby's feet kicking against her abdomen, her head at Robin's knees, and everything was under control. Unlike the chaos that had ensued before noon, when Robin had been trying to bathe and feed Mazie, make business calls, contact adoption agencies, reschedule appointments and fix a problem with the shelving at the new Everyday Hardware.

But Robin didn't go into details. Instead she said, "I never even baby-sat as a teenager. I had to have a neighbor come over and show me how to change a diaper when I brought Mazie home last Friday."

"Well, you seem to have caught on. Maybe you should keep in mind that none of us starts out an expert. We all learn through experience. And babies are amazingly resilient little beings. The old saying *Where there's a will, there's a way* is true in this case particularly—if you *want* to keep Mazie, I'm sure you would do just fine."

It was what Dean had said the night before. But Robin still wasn't sure she could believe it. Or do it.

The older woman continued. "Parenting is more a matter of doing the best you can than a matter of perfection. If Mazie were to go to an adoptive family those people would make mistakes, too, because they would only be human just as you are. And keep in mind that if you *want* to keep Mazie but simply feel unqualified, there are parenting classes you could attend to strengthen your skills."

That seemed to have brought the caseworker to some sort of a conclusion because, as if she had no more time to waste, she said, "There's nothing that says you can't keep Mazie a while longer and think more about this, which is what I advise since you seem so unsure. Or I can take her with me right now. It's up to you."

Keep Mazie a while longer...

That idea should have sent Robin into another tailspin.

But it didn't. It gave her an enormous sense of relief.

Which also gave her the only answer she could give, even before she thought about what she was saying. "I can't let you take her."

The woman closed her briefcase. "I didn't think you could."

The caseworker stood then and set a business card on the coffee table. "If you change your mind, feel free to call and I'd be happy to come back. But unless I miss my guess, this little girl has wiggled her way into your heart and I'm never going to hear from you."

Robin glanced down at the infant and found Mazie had gotten hold of her chubby little foot and managed to pull it to her mouth so she could gnaw on her big toe. It was funny and cute and endearing all at once and Robin actually did feel something around the area of her heart.

"Don't get up," the older woman said. "I'll let myself out."

"Thank you for your trouble," Robin called to her as she went to the door, leaving Robin alone with Mazie again.

And still Robin felt relieved.

But was it merely a temporary thing? she wondered. The lull before the next storm?

Undoubtedly.

And she wasn't any closer to being sure she could weather the next storm, the next real or imagined crisis if she *didn't* give up Mazie.

So what was she going to do? she asked herself as she watched the baby.

Mazie didn't give her any answers. But she did gaze up at her the way she'd been doing since Sunday morning. She gazed up at her with familiarity. With complete trust. And with something more. Something that made Robin feel as if Mazie liked her.

"But what if I do something awful like take you to a hospital when you don't even need medical care or lose you in a toy store?" she whispered to the infant as if to dispute her right to Mazie's trust, to Mazie's affection.

But as she worried about it, something Dean had said when she'd told him about the incident with Timmie came back to her. He'd pointed out that after that incident with Timmie she knew not to let a four-year-old out of her sight and it was certainly not something she would ever do again. Which was true.

And, in keeping with that, after the middle-of-the-night escapade with Mazie, she would know to try fever-reducing medicine and some comfort before she even considered taking the baby to a hospital.

So she *had* learned a couple of things from her mistakes and they were mistakes she wouldn't make again.

The problem was, she would likely make others.

But the caseworker's words came back to her, too, about all parents making mistakes, about no one being perfect or starting out an expert.

"I'm just not sure you could survive my training period," she confided in Mazie.

Mazie waved her arms and legs enthusiastically in response and for some reason Robin didn't understand, tears came into her own eyes.

She really had come to love this baby.

And if she loved this baby and she didn't want to give this baby away, then there was only one alternative. She had to keep her and learn how to raise her to the best of her ability. To make sure *she* gave Mazie the home Mazie deserved.

"I guess we'll just have to do the best we can and maybe with a little help from parenting classes I can get better at it."

With a little help from parenting classes and Dean...

The thought of him sent another warm rush around Robin's heart. And not only because he was everything she could ask for in a man. It also helped to know that he had faith in her as a parent. That he believed she could do this. That he would be there as her safety net.

And maybe as more than her safety net...

"I know you don't understand how totally weird this is," she said to Mazie then, "but I'm actually picturing you and me and Dean and Andy and even more kids—all of us together as one big happy family. Me, the totally obsessed career woman who just put hardware on the stock exchange and didn't even know how to change a diaper four days ago."

But it was true that she was imagining the future Dean had said he thought they had a chance at. And liking the image.

"But can I do it all?" she asked Mazie.

Not easily, seemed to be the answer.

But when she looked down at Mazie again and basked in the baby's smile, when she thought about Dean, about being with him the way she had been this past weekend, when she thought about Andy and more kids and being a part of a whole family like the Machlin family, she was shocked to find that she felt, no matter what it required of her, it would be worth it.

"So I guess we're going to do this," she told Mazie. "You're going to be my daughter—"

Oh, that sounded so strange.

But so nice, too.

"And I'm going to be your mom."

That sounded just as strange. But it suddenly occurred to Robin that, unlike at the beginning of this, when the lawyer and Dean had referred to her as Mazie's mother and it had freaked her out, now that idea appealed to her so much it actually made tears roll from her eyes down her face.

"It's okay," she reassured her new daughter. "They're happy tears."

And it was true. Now that the decision was made,

she really was happy about it. And so full of feelings for Mazie it seemed like they might spill over, too.

So full of feelings for Mazie and for Dean that she wanted to share it all with him. She wanted to let him know that his efforts hadn't been in vain.

She just hoped that he was as patient and understanding as she thought he was, and that the fact that it had taken her some time—and getting very close to giving Mazie up—before she'd decided to do anything she could to become a good parent hadn't changed the way he thought of her.

Mazie was already asleep for the night when Robin finally heard Dean at his apartment door. She thought she probably should have given him a minute to settle in, but she just couldn't wait. Not to see him and not to tell him what she'd done.

As he was stepping into his loft, Robin opened her door and said, "Hi, remember me—the crazy lady from across the hall?"

Dean smiled at her, a tentative sort of smile that let her know he was still worried about what she might have done with Mazie.

"I was just going to put down my stuff and come over there," he said by way of greeting.

He looked like a man who had put in a long day, and yet he wore it well. He had on tan suit pants with a pale cream-colored dress shirt tucked into them, the collar button unfastened and his brown tie loosened at the knot to hang slightly askew. But still his hair was combed and the shadow of his day's growth of beard only added a sexy scruffy addition to his appearance that Robin liked.

"Where's Andy?" she asked, proud of herself for having noticed immediately that the little boy wasn't with him.

"Some problems came up at work and I couldn't get away so my sister kept him for the night."

His sister provided day care for Andy.

"Think Peggy would take Mazie here and there if I needed backup?" she asked, seizing the segue.

"I don't know," Dean said as if the announcement didn't shock him at all, even though his eyebrows had shot into high arches.

Still he pretended to take it in stride by leaning a nonchalant shoulder against his doorjamb. "So you're in need of day care?" he asked.

"Looks like I will be," Robin answered. Then she gave in and confessed. "I couldn't do it. I couldn't send her off to be raised by someone else and never see her again."

Dean smiled and his entire expression, his entire body, seemed to relax, as if a burden had been lifted from his shoulders. "I didn't think you'd be able to. I *hoped* you wouldn't be able to."

"So is your offer of help getting me up to speed as a parent still good?"

"Absolutely," he said without hesitation.

"How about your other offer?"

"What other offer?"

"The whole maybe-this-thing-between-us-could-have-a-future offer?"

His smile stretched languidly into a devilish grin. "Was that an offer?"

"I don't know—was it?" she asked quietly.

He pushed off the doorjamb with one of those broad shoulders and came across the hall then.

"Is what you're proposing that the *four* of us actually see if we can make some kind of full relationship work out?" he said, teasing.

Robin played along. "I know it's an outrageous idea."

"Coming from the woman who knows power drills not pacifiers? Pretty outrageous, yeah. Think you can handle it?"

"You're the one who keeps telling me I can," she reminded. "Besides, it occurred to me that I was raised in the back of a hardware store and—with the exception of not knowing much about babies or kids—I didn't come out too badly. And since I own the place, if I want to bring Mazie to work with me who can complain?"

"True."

"Plus, as you so artfully illustrated, there are baby-sitters. You leave Andy in day care with your sister. There are ways to work things out."

"No? Not really?" he said with elaborate exaggeration since she was repeating his own message back to him.

Then he leaned forward to confide, "And I'm right here if you get in trouble."

"You're here all right," she reiterated with enough breathiness to her voice to make it a double entendre.

He smiled again and stood up straight so he could pull her into his arms, and Robin went willingly, wrapping hers around his waist as he kissed her so deeply it made her toes curl.

Then he said, "You made the best choice. For you and for Mazie."

"I hope so. I keep worrying that she'll end up looking like an old Raggedy Anne doll I used to have. I loved her, but I dropped her in a mud puddle once, and I accidentally yanked off one of her arms, and when her button eye fell off I tried to glue it and staple it back on."

Dean laughed, a deep, throaty, sexy laugh. "I don't think it'll get that bad. You made it through this whole day on your own with her, didn't you?"

"I did," Robin said, not having thought about that milestone until he pointed it out.

"And did you drop Mazie in a mud puddle or yank off one of her arms or glue and staple her eye?"

"No, but I did give her milk that wasn't warm enough and she spit it at me."

"So she let you know what you did wrong and no harm was done."

"That's what I need, someone who can put a positive spin on my slipups."

"Happily at your service," he said. Then, in a serious tone that let her know he meant it, he added, "Happily at your service from here on."

He kissed her again, his lips parted, his tongue coming to do an arousing dance with hers, and Robin melted into his arms.

But even as he began to stir all the things inside her that he'd awakened the previous night, Robin couldn't help marveling at the change her life had taken in such a short time. At the fact that in only a matter of a few days she was suddenly on a completely different course. With a beautiful baby of her own. And a man more incredible than she'd imagined existed.

And while she was sorry her cousin and his wife were lost to her and to Mazie, and while Jon may have flung her onto this course against her will, she thought she owed him a great big thank-you.

Because she honestly did love Mazie, and she believed that she and Dean really did have a chance for a future together.

A wonderful future full of kids and family and a man who made her pulse race like no one ever had before.

A wonderful future unlike any she'd thought she would ever have.

*   *   *   *   *

LIGHTS, CAMERA...BABY!
Myrna Mackenzie

Dear Reader,

Babies bring such joy into our lives. They're precious beings, but I remember that when my first son was born my joy was tempered by an astounding fear of my own ignorance. He was so tiny, so helpless, and all that stood between him and disaster were two completely clueless parents. How could this have happened to such a sweet little child?

Sure, I'd read the books, I'd taught school, but nothing had prepared me for this new role. Sometimes at night I would slip into his room just to watch him breathe and marvel that he had made it through another day with me.

Of course, I gradually gained confidence and skill, but writing Eve and Nick's story in "Lights, Camera…Baby!" I recalled all the panic as well as the lighter and sometimes embarrassing moments of being a parent-in-training. It was great fun to write. I hope you'll find it fun to read, and for those of you who've lived through the terror of being a novice parent, may you enjoy a trip down memory lane.

This time you won't even have to worry a bit. The baby lives happily ever after. I guarantee it.

Happy reading,

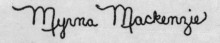

Chapter 1

"**Y**ou want me to do *what?*"

Eve Carpenter tried to keep the squeak and panic out of her voice as she stared up into her boss's blue eyes. There had been many times in the two years since she'd come to work for Burnside Baby Foods that Eve had looked at Nick and felt fight-or-flight panic start to build. Tall with pirate-black hair, a rogue's wicked smile and an easygoing manner, Nick Stevens made even the most sensible woman feel like she was trying to cross a raging river on a shaky six-inch log.

So Eve was ready for almost anything where Nick was concerned. She had known from day one that she needed to stay smart and aloof where her boss was concerned. Looking into those lake-blue eyes, she was always scared that she would do or say something stupid. Be like the other women in the office who came on to Nick and received a patient smile for their efforts. Still, never before had Nick scared her this much.

As his assistant, Eve was expected to be adaptable, but baby-sitting for the company president while he was out of town? It just wasn't possible for a woman like her. And it was such an odd request. Maybe he'd just been kidding.

"You didn't really mean that, did you?" she asked, keeping her fingers crossed.

Nick arched a speculative brow in that way that must have fueled a thousand women's fantasies. "Um, Eve? That was not a 'yes, Nick' that I heard. So...I take it that you have a problem with this assignment? That's not your usual style."

Uh-oh, he really had been serious. Darn it all!

"I know. I know. I'm the original 'yes, boss' type. It's programmed in my genes, but taking care of a baby is not exactly the kind of thing you've ever asked me to do before," she explained, trying to keep her voice calm. She hoped he'd just find someone else to do the job, and she wouldn't have to explain any more.

Staring up at Nick, Eve wished yet again that she were taller. Having to tip your head back to look up at a man, especially a man who had such an unmistakably nice physique, made her feel uncomfortably feminine—not forceful, which is what she really needed right now.

She crossed her arms, trying to achieve the right

effect, and for a minute she thought she detected a trace of amusement in his eyes.

But then he blew out a breath, leaned his palms on his desk and shook his head. "You're absolutely right. This isn't the kind of thing I'd ask you to do under normal circumstances."

"Maybe I'm just confused about the specifics," she ventured. "Maybe you didn't say 'baby.' Maybe you said... 'dog.' You want me to take care of the president's dog."

Nick grinned, and those blue eyes became more dangerous. "Eve, you're reaching, and you even look like you may be hyperventilating. I didn't say 'dog' and you know it."

He was right. She was nearly hyperventilating. She, the cool and calm one who never let anything spook her, was twisting her fingers in a nervous attempt to latch on to something solid.

Nick's grin was fading fast. He was studying her intently. Could he tell just how badly she was shaking inside? Please, no. She'd worked hard to perfect her image at Burnside; she'd been mom, apple pie and completely professional to her colleagues. Never had she allowed anything of her private responses to situations to show through, and she'd done her best to be the consummate assistant to the director of public relations. Now, with this one request, everything was set to come crashing down.

"Eve," Nick said, more solemn now. "I *am* sorry. You understand this is not something *I'm* asking you to do. The request came straight from Larry Burnside.

He specifically asked that you be the one to watch his nine-month-old son, Charley, while he and Sandra are on vacation in Italy. I'm afraid he's pretty much sold on the idea of having the company's 'most perfect mother' watch over his child.''

Eve's heart started pounding even harder. She had an urge to walk around that desk, lean forward and place her hands on Nick's broad chest to brace herself. That phony perfect-mother image had stood her in good stead while working for the company, but now it was backfiring in spades. She kept her gaze on Nick's eyes, even though she knew it was risking fate. After all, he was a man used to looking into women's eyes. He might well see things she didn't want him to see. Things like the truth.

"I don't understand." She almost whispered the words. "I've been working here for two years. You know I'm single and I don't have children. Larry hired me to be your assistant. That's all. And as for taking care of his child, well…Burnside Baby Foods is his company. He and Sandra can afford to hire the best professional baby-sitters in the world. They can hire ten."

"I know that. I mentioned it to him, but he specifically asked for you."

"How long?"

"Two weeks." He might as well have said two centuries. It would be as if that baby were her own. The responsibility would be enormous, the risks too high. Eve's knees felt as if they were melting into uselessness. The thought of watching a helpless baby had her remembering, starting to sway.

Stupid. So stupid. She had to get hold of herself.

"Eve?" Nick came around his desk and stopped in front of her. "Hell, I'm sorry, Eve. I know this intrudes on your personal life. And I probably shouldn't have hit you with something like this when you were standing. Come here, let me help you." Nick's voice was low as he took her hands, his fingers warm and strong. He led her to a big burgundy chair. "Sit. Breathe. I know this must have caught you unawares. Guess you're just too good at what you do, kid."

He smiled, and she couldn't help but smile back, especially considering the fact that she was no kid. She was twenty-seven and he was only four years older.

"Are you trying to shmooze me, Stevens?" she asked, her voice a bit shaky.

Nick pulled up a chair in front of her and leaned toward her. "I'd love to say yes, just to see you get that chin-in-the-air, I'll-show-you look that you wear when you're determined to prove yourself—but in this case, I can't lie. You know that ever since you came to Burnside, you've presented an image that has been a real boon to the company. Frankly, you've become the perfect mother in Larry's eyes. You do the baby kissing and cuddling thing better than anyone I've ever met."

She knew that. It was planned, intentional. After being passed over for good positions because of her small size and small voice, she'd been grateful when

Larry had given her a chance. She'd worked so hard to establish that image of the best mom in the world because it was what her job at Burnside Baby Foods seemed to require, with all its public contact with parents and their children. She'd sworn to try harder and become the ideal mom for the public whenever the company staged events. Thank goodness no one knew that it really was just an image. But now?

"This is different, Nick. Taking complete responsibility for the president's baby? I really *can't*, and I'm not a woman to throw the *C* word around lightly."

Nick gazed directly into her eyes. "I'm aware that you don't say no to much. You're a whirlwind, Eve, the hardest worker I've got."

"Thank you." Her fear eased just a bit.

"You know, I've always wondered what would happen if you ever had to do the baby thing full-time." His tone was gentle, he was studying her carefully. Maybe too carefully.

"You did?" Eve suddenly found her backbone. She sat up ramrod-straight. Nick's gaze zoomed in on her like a peregrine marking its prey. No one knew her secret. She was sure of it.

"Oh, yes, I did. I'm a bachelor, Eve. By choice. I know my own kind when I see it."

"And what is your kind?"

"Independent. A loner. A person who works for a baby food company, but is secretly a bit afraid of babies."

His last few words fell like a heavy rock into the

conversation. Fear roiled within Eve. She wasn't just a bit afraid of babies. Oh, she loved them to pieces, but to take care of one? The thought petrified her.

She clenched her hands on her knees. "But you never said anything. You let me pretend."

He shrugged. "Why not? You do your job well. Heck, you do your job stupendously. Larry was certainly right about that. To the average observer, you are the perfect mother. And who am I to criticize, anyway? Heaven knows, I'm not even close to being father material. It takes a certain steadiness to do that. It's not for a guy like me."

Instantly, indignation filled Eve. "You're a wonderful director, and you're going to be a wonderful vice president when Larry cuts some of his duties and you move into that position next month."

"Thanks. I do all right. After all, a man needs to eat and have enough money to support his bad habits," he said dryly.

She was pretty sure most of Nick's bad habits involved naked women and beds.

"And," he continued, "I believe that if you're going to do a job, you should darn well do it right. But I'd never choose to be domestic material, so don't think I'm criticizing you, Eve. I've never had a better assistant, and I'm hoping Larry chooses you to take over my position when the time comes. So I'm definitely not judging you. I'm simply saying I've always suspected that you could be the perfect mother at work and still take the costume off when you go home at night."

She licked her lips nervously. For a second she thought she saw Nick flinch, and she realized that the lip-licking thing was something she'd seen one of his women do when she'd come to see him in the office. So, it was probably foolish to be doing something that could be misconstrued as flirting. She and Nick worked so well together because she didn't come on to him the way other women did. It was crucial that she remember that.

"What tipped you off?" she asked, desperately trying to think back to what mistake she'd made. If she'd messed up, she sure wasn't going to do it again. For while Nick might be understanding, there was no question that her worth to Larry Burnside lay primarily in the image she'd projected since she'd been hired. He liked the women of his company to be maternal, and she had done her best to comply.

So where had she gone wrong? How did Nick know she was a fraud?

"Did I say something wrong publicly?" she asked.

He grinned that grin that was so deadly to other women. Eve reminded herself that she wasn't "other women."

"Don't worry, no one else would have noticed," he said in a conspiratorial voice, "but when my sister came to visit me one day and remarked that you were so good with kids that she couldn't wait to see you with your own, well…"

Eve remembered. She had been caught off guard. Her distress had probably been noticeable, especially to someone as tuned in to women and their moods as Nick was.

"All right, I do have a few problems with babies. I'm certainly not the right person to watch one twenty-four hours a day," she said.

Nick leaned forward and took her hand. "Eve, I'm sorry I brought this up, and I don't want you to worry. We'll just go see Larry and tell him that you won't be able to take this job."

And just like that, the fear faded. Eve realized that Nick's body was awfully close to her own. Looking into his eyes, it was difficult to remind herself that she was never to think of him as a man. His shoulders were broad, his neck was tanned and strong, and the hand that was holding hers was so large and male and so...

Eve shifted on her chair, trying to ignore her thoughts.

Not that she was ever in any real danger of falling for Nick. He was casual, friendly and a good boss, but he certainly wasn't a man to get serious about. Besides, she had it on good authority from the watercooler crowd that Nick didn't date women from the office. It was too uncomfortable and too disruptive to the office routine when the inevitable happened, as it did with all of Nick's relationships.

Only here he was, just inches from her, his lips close enough to have her thinking that he was probably a master at using those lips.

She glanced into his eyes and realized that he'd

probably noticed her staring. Those blue eyes looked suddenly hot.

Then he rose, unfolding the long length of his legs. "Let's go have that talk with Larry," he said tersely, and Eve got to her feet.

But at that moment, there was a knock on the door. A technicality, since the door immediately flew open and Larry Burnside entered. The small chubby man was rubbing his hands together. He had a look of glee on his face.

"Did Nick tell you, Eve?"

"Yes, I—"

"Isn't it great? Sandra and I are so excited. I wonder that I didn't think of it sooner."

"I'm flattered, Larry, but really I can't—"

"You can't believe your luck, can you? Charley is a charmer. Any baby-sitter who gets to spend this much time with him is one lucky woman."

Eve lost her voice. What could she say? That she didn't want to baby-sit Charley?

"I'm afraid Eve has some other commitments, Larry," Nick said. "It's not going to work."

Larry looked as if someone had just dared to try to steal his skybox seats at a Bears game. "Of course it is. Whatever the problem is, I'll handle it. If it involves money, I'll pay twice as much. If it involves previous appointments, I'll take care of rescheduling. I've been trying to talk Sandra into taking a vacation ever since little Charley was born, and she wouldn't have any of it. No one was good enough, talented enough, caring enough. It was only when I thought of Eve that she relented. In fact, she was overjoyed. So am I. Charley's my boy, my angel, the light of my life, my everything, but Sandra and I need this time away desperately. Our anniversary is next week, you know. You've got to do it, Eve.''

"Larry," Nick began, but Larry held up his hand.

"And you know what? I've thought of something even better. I've just run it by the boys in marketing and they are completely jazzed about it. It's a great idea, ties everything together and promises to be the best advertising campaign we've come up with in forever.''

Eve hoped he wasn't going to say that he had *two* babies he wanted her to baby-sit. She gave Nick a worried glance.

"I think you'd better fill us in, Larry. Will we need to be sitting down for this one?" Nick asked, with a concerned look at Eve.

Larry laughed. "You're such a kidder, Nick. I know my last idea was unusual, but it was soooo good. This one, well, this one's even better. You know how Eve is going to be staying at our mansion, taking care of Charley while we're gone?''

Eve noticed that Larry spoke of the situation as if it were a done deal. And wasn't it? Her job was her world, her success story, her future. She wouldn't dare risk it.

"Tell us your idea, Larry," she said softly. At least she'd heard the worst. What followed could only make her feel a bit better.

"Okay, here it is. While Sandra and I are gone and

you're taking care of Charley, I'm going to send a camera crew to record your every move. You know, like reality TV.''

Nick moved to stand behind Eve. She wondered if he was afraid she was going to pass out.

''Eve is the top mother in the world. We all know that,'' Larry continued. ''Who better to make a training film for parents?''

Eve felt her legs wobbling. Nick's hands suddenly framed her waist. She felt his warmth enfold her as he kept her in the upright position.

''And there's more,'' Larry said, oblivious to the minidrama unfolding right before him. ''I want Nick to be there. You and Nick are my most treasured employees, Eve. You both look good, you do a great job of representing the company, and now Charley will get to be in pictures. This film is going to be a boon for Burnside Baby Foods. Just what every parent wants and needs—a guide for how to do all the tough stuff that's so confusing after your first baby is born. So...what do you think? Isn't it just the best idea in the world?''

It *was* a good idea. If only someone else were playing the starring role.

''Let me clarify this, Larry,'' Nick said, his hands still resting on her waist. Eve could feel each finger pressing against her gently while still maintaining command of her body, keeping her limbs from folding beneath her. ''You want Eve and me to stay at your house alone for two weeks.''

''Yes. No, of course not. You'll have Charley with

you, and a camera crew. Constant company. And I'll be in touch whenever I can.''

"And Charley is to be the baby we use to show people, um…how it's done."

"Yeah, I love that. My kid in a movie. I think I'll call it *The World's Best Mom and Dad: You*. So? Are you excited yet? I figure we'll wrap this up and then we'll go ahead and move Eve into your job once filming is successfully completed. You're due to make the move to vice president soon, anyway. What do you think?''

As if Eve were one of his women, Nick turned her in his arms. He kept his hands on her as he gazed down into her eyes.

"It's your call, Eve." She knew what he meant. He'd been with the company and Larry so long that he could back out of this proposal with no repercussions. He'd already been slated for the promotion and had already started taking on more duties. But the position of director of public relations had still been up in the air until now. There were other people who wanted that job, most with more seniority than Eve had. Obviously, this "project" was pivotal in Larry's decision, and his mind could be changed if things didn't go well.

"Your choice," Nick said. "I'll stand by you all the way."

Yes, she could back out, but Larry would be hurt and maybe he'd be angry. Nick's credibility might be damaged a little. Besides, she had set out to show Larry Burnside that she could do any job she was given and that she could present herself as the perfect mother because it was a boon to the company. She needed to prove that he hadn't made a mistake in hiring her and giving her so many responsibilities. Besides, she wanted that promotion badly. Surely she could do what Larry wanted for just two weeks?

Eve swallowed hard. She reached out and gripped Nick's arms and managed to nod, though for a few seconds her voice refused to function.

Nick looked over her head at his boss. "Well, Larry, looks like it's a go. You've got yourself a temporary mom and dad."

"A perfect mom and dad," Larry said.

Eve wanted to laugh hysterically. For two weeks she would be, for the most part, all alone with this wickedly sexy man and a baby who was only nine months old and incredibly vulnerable.

And she was scared to death.

Chapter 2

Nick arrived at the Burnside mansion in the exclusive suburb north of Chicago, to find Eve huddled in her car, waiting. When she looked up and saw him, she visibly straightened, shoved her long dark brown hair back from her shoulders and put on her all-right-it's-showtime face.

"Good girl," he whispered. "Don't let anyone see your fear." But, for some reason, he felt a little disgruntled, too. She darn well already knew that he was on to her. There was no need to keep pretending with him.

A low chuckle slipped from him. If his sister were here, he knew what she would say. "Can't take it when one of the ladies doesn't turn to melted sugar in front of you, can you, Nick?"

Maybe there was a tiny nugget of truth to that at

times, but not in this case. Eve Carpenter was pretty enough with her dark hair and her green eyes and her cute, squeaky little voice that did odd things to a man, but she was a serious one. Very dedicated, over-the-top intense, and he definitely didn't do the responsibility thing, at least not outside of work. His whole childhood had been preprogrammed to the stern and somber and dutiful mode, no exceptions made, and he'd had more than enough of that, thank you very much.

So, seeing as how his assistant was in need of some good old-fashioned distraction, Nick threw his silver Corvette into Park, climbed from the car and donned the most encouraging grin he owned. If Eve was scared and nervous, he was honor-bound to make her forget her troubles.

"Come on, little mother, it's time to go play with Charley," he said, holding out his hand.

She gave him a calculated look as she exited her spartan white subcompact and carefully checked all the locks on the doors. "Charley is not a toy," she said in that tight little lecturing voice that made her sound stern but was actually kind of adorable. She was wearing a slim blue skirt that was too long and a white, boxy blouse that should have looked plain-Jane, but somehow made him want to find out what her curves looked like beneath her hide-my-femininity clothes.

"We're here to take care of a baby, to make a film, and I'm here to earn a promotion. Remember?" she asked, just as if she knew that he was imagining her naked. She was right, of course. He had no business imagining anything of the sort. He planned to stop the inappropriate stuff pronto, but he still couldn't help thinking that Eve's prim voice hid a world of fear. He just had to take care of that. After all, she was his employee. He was responsible for her.

So Nick pretended to nod sagely. Then he chuckled. "Okay, you've made your point, boss." He winked.

She blushed, widened her eyes and tried to stand taller by rising on her toes, as if that could make her less petite. "I'm on to you, Nick Stevens. You're trying to tease the butterflies out of my stomach by playing games with me."

He almost managed to look crestfallen. "Darn, most of the women I know fall for that routine."

"I'll just bet they do." Her cheeks were rosy and her voice was soft, but she didn't look as if she was kidding.

Well, she had him on this one, and she was right. Her promotion was at stake here, and he shouldn't be teasing her about a situation that obviously had her so rattled. Larry adored her, but he adored the image she projected. Nick had been singing her praises for all of the other work she did, but it was that mom image that Larry was stuck on. Which was a shame. Eve might be a serious little mouse, but she was the best little mouse at her game in the office. Surely she'd get her promotion as long as nothing terrible happened in the next two weeks.

And what were the odds that anything out of the ordinary would happen?

"I think this is going to work out just fine."

When Eve looked up at him, he realized he'd muttered the words out loud.

"You think there's really any chance anyone will believe that you and I know the details of how to take care of a baby for two weeks?" she asked.

Absolutely not. "Hey, totally green parents manage it all the time," he said. "What could be so difficult?"

Amazingly enough, she smiled at that, a full-lipped, wholehearted smile that turned her from merely pretty to dazzling. "You're amazing, you know that? Doesn't anything ever faze you?"

Lots of things. Women with big green soulful eyes and a no-nonsense attitude. Women with issues he was incapable of dealing with. Serious women who were a risk to everything he held dear.

Not that anything was really at risk here. He'd already picked out his next girlfriend. Phyllis Adderby. She was blond, built, she didn't care about anything beyond the next five minutes and she wasn't anything like Eve. Did anything ever faze him? He'd spent all of his adult years making sure he never allowed himself to be fazed or caught up in anything too serious. Didn't the woman know that was the secret to contentment?

"Eve, you wonderful workaholic, this assignment is going to be as easy as breathing."

She smiled again, that reluctant little smile she

saved for special occasions, and he suddenly had trouble breathing. Damn, this wasn't going to be easy at all, and he knew it as well as she did.

"Come on," he said, taking her hand. "Larry and Sandra are waiting."

"And Charley," she offered.

"Oh, yeah, Charley." A kid. What in hell was he going to do, holed up for two weeks with a kid and a woman with eyes that never partied?

The housekeeper let them into the mansion and Eve felt as if she'd been dropped into a fantasy world. Everything in the place looked like it had been dusted with dollars, and Larry and Sandra were both taking turns talking at lightning speed.

"Now, I've made lists of everything you need to do so that Charley's routines aren't disrupted," Sandra said, taking the floor. "Of course, you already know all about that, the importance of routines to a child, don't you?" she asked Eve.

Well, she knew now. "Of course," Eve said soothingly. She had this awful feeling that Nick was grinning, aware that she was lying through her teeth. As casually as she could, she turned and looked at him. He *was* looking at her, but his grin was altogether absent. That couldn't be sympathy she saw in his dark blue eyes, could it?

"Don't worry, Sandra. Eve and I will follow your instructions to the letter," he soothed. "You said you had everything written down? Step by step?"

Sandra chuckled. "Oh, sure, as if Eve needs step-by-step instructions. I've only written down the things that pertain to Charley's personal preferences and schedule. I wouldn't insult Eve by implying that she needed me to fill her in on the basics.''

Nick gave a quick nod. ''Of course. Eve is the best.''

Eve felt tears form in her throat. She felt inordinately grateful to Nick for saying that, now that he knew she was a fraud, and a liar. Not for the first time she wondered if she was doing the right thing. Was she risking too much, risking a child?

''I'll guard Charley with my life,'' she suddenly said, her voice charged with determination and the tears that threatened.

''That's the reason Sandra and I chose you, dear,'' Larry said, stepping forward. ''Well, that and the great publicity it will bring. Nick, I've laid out the schedule for shooting. When you and Eve have a chance, you just go over it. Anything you need, you order it. Don't worry about the cost. I want this thing done right.''

Nick moved to stand behind Eve. He'd been doing that a lot these past couple of days, she thought. There was something about having a tall, strong man at your back that made you stand taller yourself, even if you were only five foot two and no one was ever going to be impressed by your stature.

''We'll get the job done, Larry. Don't we always?'' Nick asked.

''That's the way,'' Larry said with a big grin. ''Well, now, here's my little man.'' He turned to the woman carrying a little boy with blue saucer eyes and hair the color of sunshine. Charley was laughing. He held out his hands to his father, who took him in his arms and kissed him. "Charley, remember Uncle Nick and Aunt Eve? You met them at Daddy's office."

Charley pulled on his father's tie and stuffed it into his mouth.

"Oh, no, he'll choke, Larry," Sandra said, and Eve felt the sour taste of fear in her mouth. She bolted forward, but Larry was just laughing. He pulled the wet mess from Charley's mouth.

"Now, Sandra, you worry too much. He's fine, see."

But Eve was with Sandra. "No ties," she said, turning to Nick.

He smiled lazily at her as if she'd just said "no clothing."

"My pleasure," he told her.

Sandra chuckled. "That man," she told Eve. "I don't know how you put up with his antics at work."

She didn't. "Nick is always a complete gentleman and a total professional with me," she said, speaking the truth. And for the first time she wondered just how he was with other women. Not that she really wanted to know or had half a chance of finding out.

Sandra shrugged. "Well, let's hope Nick stays that way. This house is big, but it has plenty of cozy nooks. We built it that way on purpose, didn't we, my sweetie-kins?" And she kissed Larry right on his chubby cheek. Larry was no physical prize, but he was a good man, and his wife was clearly in love and in lust with him.

Which made Eve want to squirm, especially with Nick watching the show. She cleared her throat. "Oh, you don't have to worry about us. Nick and I will be completely professional," she assured her employers.

"Well, not too professional," Larry said with a laugh. "Remember, you're pretending to be married for the film. Still, we wouldn't want you to get too carried away with the marriage thing. When this is over, you still have to work together. Don't want Nick treating you like his wife at the office, do we?" he asked, laughing at his own joke. "That could be embarrassing."

Nick tilted his head. "I'm always careful with Eve, Larry. This is a job, remember?"

"Except for Charley," Larry said. "He needs lots of love. Now, if you'll excuse us for a few minutes, Sandra and I need some time alone with our boy before we go. Jenny, our housekeeper, has a house on the grounds. She's here during the daytime and will show you to your rooms. They're right next door to each other, so that you have easy access when you need to consult on anything."

For a moment Eve felt panic building inside. How had her life and her career gotten so out of control?

But then Nick cleared his throat. "Afraid that's not a good move, Larry. I tend to walk in my sleep now and then and I don't always know where I'm going. Might prove to be embarrassing or even frightening if I showed up in the wrong place at the wrong time.

Just put me down the hall from Eve. When we need to consult, I'll walk.''

An inordinate sense of gratitude flowed through Eve, and she smiled up at him. Walk in his sleep? Did that gorgeous big lunk really think she believed that? Of course not, but it had been a very nice gesture, and she could have kissed him for it if they'd had that kind of relationship. Which they didn't.

"Or I'll walk down the hall," she volunteered.

Either way, the important thing was that she and Nick wouldn't be sleeping right next door to each other. There would be no opportunities for her to do something stupid. Like getting all warm and fuzzy about her boss.

Thirty minutes later, Nick finally closed the door behind Larry and Sandra and turned to Eve, who had a sleeping Charley crooked in her arms. She kissed the child's blond curls and looked over his head to Nick.

"Well, it begins," he said. "May I say that you're doing fine so far. You look like a complete natural."

She did, too. Swaying from side to side, she cuddled the baby close, humming softly to him. Some off-key lullaby that made him want to try to remember the words. Tiny as she was, with those big eyes and that slender frame, Eve still looked as if she had been made to hold babies.

"This is the easy part," she whispered, her breath gently stirring Charley's thin wisps of hair. "As the front man for Burnside Baby Foods, I'm used to mothers giving me their babies to hold. And then I give them back," she pointed out. "Do you see anyone here to give this baby back to?"

"Not a soul," he admitted. "Jenny made it clear that she was strictly housekeeping, and, anyway, she's already gone home for the day so that we could have some privacy. Guess that means that neither of us knows what comes next with Charley?"

"Well, not exactly. I do have a few books I bought. Stuff for new parents."

"That would be us, all right," he said, smiling at her. "Brand-new. Take two singles, add one baby and stir for a few minutes."

She smiled at that, a very small smile even as she kept swaying. Nick couldn't help thinking that she had to be getting tired. Charley was only nine months old, but Eve was a small woman.

"Maybe we should put him down somewhere," he suggested softly. "We need to review Larry's notes on the filming schedule."

Instantly, fear entered her eyes. "You mean, leave him alone?"

"In a crib, Eve. Even a rookie like me knows you don't put a baby down just anywhere."

"But we wouldn't be in the room."

"We'd be close by."

"I'm not sure that's wise. What if something happened? Things do sometimes."

Something obviously *had* happened, at some time, to make Eve this nervous about leaving Charley to sleep. Nick didn't know what it was, and maybe it wasn't any of his business, but he did know that they were going to have to work around it.

"Eve, you can't hold him for two weeks."

She took a deep breath. "I know that. I just worry."

"What would make you worry less?"

Eve rolled her eyes. "I don't know, a spy camera on him every second."

"Consider it done."

"Excuse me?"

Nick nodded toward the door. A security camera guarded the entrance. "Why not? Every store has them all over the place, many businesses do, Larry's even got one or two already here. All we need is a few more. I'll call right now."

Eve hesitated. "I feel so foolish. It seems so...I don't know. Extreme?"

It most likely was extreme, but it would help make the two weeks more livable if Eve wasn't worrying about letting Charley out of her sight. "Larry won't mind. He'll just be happy you're taking good care of his son," Nick said. "And I'll ask the security company to make sure the cameras are temporary, not the kind you bolt to the ceiling. If Charley so much as wiggles his little baby toes, we'll know."

Eve nodded. "Thank you. It will help to know that."

"Why don't you go put him in bed now. He'll be more comfortable." Although Charley looked plenty comfortable cradled in Eve's embrace.

"Yes, I'll do that." She headed to Charley's room,

and Nick called a security company he trusted. The supplies would be here within a couple of hours.

"Now," Eve whispered, when Charlie was settled in his crib and she and Nick were staked out in the corner of the baby's room. "What did Larry leave us to do tomorrow morning?"

Nick held out a folder. Together they opened it.

"Oh, my," Eve said.

"Oh, yes," Nick answered.

"A whole script and everything." She tilted her head, an intense look of concentration furrowing her brow.

"Do you think this is how Larry and Sandra actually talk when they're changing Charley's diapers?" Nick had dropped his voice low so that Charley wouldn't wake up. Eve leaned closer to hear him, and the scent of lily-of-the-valley drifted over him. It wasn't the first time he had breathed in her unique scent, but those other times had been in the office amidst crowds of other people. Safe territory.

Here it was just the two of them, alone in a cramped and shadowed corner of a room. If he moved just slightly, his lips would brush against her hair. If she looked up into his eyes, her mouth would be close enough for him to swoop in and capture her lips.

She was chewing on her bottom lip, he realized, the flesh full and pink, her small white teeth raking the surface.

And suddenly, she wasn't Eve the earth mother, or Eve the employee, or even Eve the frightened and brand-new baby-sitter. She was a woman, soft and silky and tempting.

Nick drew in a deep breath. Too deep, he guessed.

Eve frowned. "You wouldn't be in this mess, would you, if not for me?"

He knew what she meant. If Larry hadn't been fooled by her perfect-mother act, he wouldn't have asked her to baby-sit, and if he hadn't asked her to baby-sit, he wouldn't have come up with this crazy training film scheme. Which wasn't all that crazy a scheme, when you came right down to it.

"I'm sorry," she said when he still hadn't answered. She was back to chewing on her lip again.

He couldn't help himself. He gently grasped her chin, turned her face up and rubbed his thumb across the flesh that she'd been torturing. "Don't worry," he whispered. "I'm a real expert at dealing with messes. Been making them all of my life, and I'm rather partial to the adventure of trying to figure out how to worm my way out of a situation. If I didn't want to be here, I'd be five hundred miles down the road leaving only a dust trail."

She shook her head. "You're trying to make me feel better."

He shrugged. "Nothing wrong with that. Am I doing a good job?"

A low, musical laugh met his ears. He leaned closer to catch it. "No wonder all those drooling women drop into your life like willing raindrops," she said. "Do you have even one serious bone in your body?"

"I'm a mean one with customer account profiles."

"That's true."

"I know how to do a few other things, too."

"You do. I've seen you handle the customers and the media and distraught employees. And Larry wouldn't be so enamored of you if your only claim to fame was a wild way with women." She shifted slightly, and his thumb moved against her lips.

She breathed deeply, and her chest lifted against his arm. Oh hell, he thought, don't think of her as a woman, Stevens. You can't have your wild way with this one.

But it was beyond too late. At least, it would be if he didn't back off soon. Right now. Somehow Nick managed to ease his thumb away from her, to release her completely. He cleared his throat.

"Speaking of Larry and work, I suppose we'd better study this plan for tomorrow more carefully," he said.

She nodded, but the look that she gave him was speculative.

"What?"

"How *does* a man do as well in business as you do while maintaining a completely no-commitments attitude in the rest of his life?"

"Simple. I work at it."

She raised one brow in question.

"My parents were super serious, dour, people with a mission, and that mission was to eradicate frivolity from the face of the earth. They believed in all work, no fun. Laughter was the devil's tool, and half the time they thought I was the devil. Toys were out, having friends over wasn't allowed, no movies, no television, just study and work and wait to be old enough to get married and do the same with my own family. I couldn't wait to get out and never do another serious thing in my life. The only trouble was that having fun and mere survival cost money. So it was a simple choice. Make use of those sober skills I'd learned in order to make money, then party the rest of the time. See how it works?''

Eve studied him carefully. "I see. So..." She held out the script for tomorrow's filming. "This is the serious stuff, the part you have to get right?"

"Absolutely."

"Well, then, Mr. Stevens, I guess we'd better start reading my baby manual. By tomorrow morning, you and I have to be experts at getting Charley in and out of a diaper. And we have to remember to call each other 'darling' and 'sugarplum.' Um—"

Her voice broke as she looked farther down the page.

"What?"

She took a deep, shuddering breath. Women had done that before when he was touching them. That was usually a good sign. This, however, didn't seem to be a positive sign.

"Eve, tell me," he said, holding out his hand so she could give him the script.

She held on to it and turned those big troubled green eyes on him. "Um, it says here on page four that I have to give you a kiss once you manage to successfully close the tabs on Charley's diaper.'' Her voice was barely a whisper. Her skin was far too pale.

Nick nearly groaned at the thought of kissing Eve, never mind the bit about getting Charley in and out of a diaper. What had Larry been thinking? And what were they going to do about Larry's script? If he spent the whole night thinking about pressing his lips to Eve's, by tomorrow he was going to have a serious case of arousal that wasn't going to film well at all.

''We've never kissed,'' he said slowly.

''No.'' She looked up into his eyes. She lifted her hands from the page and the script slithered to the floor.

''We'll want it to look natural on film,'' he whispered.

''I suppose we will. At least, Larry will.''

''Well, then, I suppose we should try it. Practice it. We'll go through the motions. Dispassionately, of course.''

''Of course. We should.''

''Just once,'' he said. ''Just this one time.'' And he lowered his lips to hers.

Chapter 3

Eve's breath stopped completely. Her mind seemed to stop working, too. All she was conscious of was Nick's lips moving over hers, tasting, sipping, moving away, then hovering before he claimed her again.

Her hands fluttered like helpless butterflies, then came to rest against his chest—warm muscles beneath white cotton.

She clutched at him.

He kissed her again.

She started to lean toward him, to ask him to please do that again.

A loud horn honking outside sent her scurrying backward.

Nick swore beneath his breath. He gave her one fierce look before he swung away from her.

"I think we've probably practiced enough," he said, his voice thick. "You did very well."

"Thank you. You, too."

And then he was gone, answering the distant and insistent ringing of the doorbell.

A groan escaped her. She cast a nervous look Charley's way, but he was still sleeping. What had she been thinking? She was supposed to be taking care of a child, not melting in a man's arms. She wasn't sixteen and just discovering that kissing existed. She was a responsible executive's assistant, and the man she'd been tasting was her boss.

A man who could write a book on the art of the kiss.

Nick certainly didn't need practice kissing, but maybe he thought that she did. He'd said it would be a dispassionate kiss. He probably hadn't even felt a thing, whereas her heartbeat had been accelerating at an alarming rate.

While he'd simply been teaching her, so that she would get it right on film, she'd been feeling overwhelmed, excited, completely involved.

At that moment, Charley stirred and turned in his sleep, stuffing his fist into his mouth and sucking, his lashes fluttering, then settling back into the peaceful sleep of the completely innocent.

"Oh, Charley, what have we gotten into?" Eve whispered.

But the only answer was the sound of Nick's footsteps echoing down the hallway, moving ever closer.

Eve braced herself to see him again. She hoped that

her lipstick wasn't smeared and that her hair and clothes bore no evidence of her recent tumble into desire. She blinked twice to clear her vision and to pull herself together, smoothing nervous hands over her skirt just as Nick's broad shoulders filled the doorway.

"Who?" she asked, and he held up a huge box.

"Delivery person. Toys," he said with a rakish smile. "The security cameras, some alarms and a few other things." He set down the box and pulled out a doll the size of a small baby, her red hair of molded and tinted plastic.

Immediately Eve's nervousness faded. She stepped forward with a frown. "A doll? I'm not sure he's into dolls yet."

Nick chuckled. "She's not for Charley. Heck, she's almost as big as Charley. I'm not sure we should be giving him toys he'd have to wrestle to the ground yet. No, this is—" he turned the doll over and lifted the tag that was dangling from her neck "—this is Sassy Sheila, and she's for us."

"For us." Eve held out her hands in confusion.

"To practice with," Nick said slowly. "Do you really want to go before the cameras and put Charley through the torture of having two neophyte diaper-changers try to get one of those on him without a few practice runs?" He nodded toward a bag of disposable diapers sitting in the corner.

"Um, of course not. Won't we have to change him between now and then?"

Nick suddenly looked as if someone had crept up

and hit him with a ballpeen hammer. "Damn, I suppose we will. I doubt Charley's going to need a diaper change only at convenient times."

At that moment, Charley rolled over and sat up, rubbing his fists over his eyes. He gazed at the two adults standing in the corner of his room and instantly stuck his bottom lip out. Great tears filled his eyes, and he let out a painful wail.

"Oh hell, I was probably talking too loud," Nick said, then winced. "And I suppose I shouldn't be swearing in front of him, either."

Eve immediately went to Charley. "It's all right, sweetie," she cooed. Charley cried harder. She cast a scared glance at Nick, then bent to pick Charley up. Rocking him in her arms, she tried to quiet him, but he sobbed as if his heart had been stepped on, as if he was terrified.

"He probably doesn't remember who we are. I'll bet Sandra is usually here when he wakes up," Eve said.

"No need to cry, Charley," Nick murmured awkwardly. He tried to pat Charley on the back, and the little boy howled even louder.

Nick, who normally wore a knowing grin, looked horrified. "Did I hurt him, do you think?"

Eve cuddled Charley closer. "No, you're just not his daddy."

"If you're sure." Nick looked slightly mollified, though no more comfortable, but Eve was feeling rather desperate.

"Nick, what if I'm wrong about him just being

scared? Something could be really wrong with him. Something he ate. Some disease. Where's the name of the doctor that Sandra left us? I think we'd better call.'' She put Charley in his crib and moved toward the phone.

But Nick had turned away for a minute. When he turned back, he was holding Sassy Sheila. He lifted the doll up in front of his face. ''Char-ley,'' he called softly. ''Oh, Char-ley. Yoo-hoo.'' He lifted his voice to a phony female pitch.

The unfamiliar, high-pitched tone sounded so ridiculous. Eve wondered if Nick had any idea how he looked and sounded.

But Charley stopped crying suddenly. He gave a soft hiccup, his face still streaked with tears.

''Hi, Char-ley, I'm Sassy Sheila,'' Nick said. ''Would you like to play with me?''

Eve was pretty sure Charley had no idea what Nick was talking about, but he was clearly mesmerized, his blue eyes large and moist, his little hands reaching as they clenched and unclenched while he stood by the bars of his crib.

Nick started to hand over the doll.

Eve welcomed Charley's shy smile, but then she had a thought. ''No!'' she cried.

Nick and Charley froze in midexchange. Charley's mouth started to tremble again, but Eve shook her head.

''Look at all those buttons on her clothes. He'll choke, Nick. Remember the tie.''

Nick cocked his head. ''You've got a point there,

angel. Shh, Charley, my lad. We'll hand over your lady friend in no time.'' And Nick immediately started removing Sassy Sheila's clothes. Eve couldn't help noting that he did it with a certain ease.

She raised an imperious brow as he turned over the naked doll to Charley, who gooed and placed a wet slobbery kiss on Sheila's cheek.

"Fast thinking," she said, nodding toward Sheila. "Another talent of yours. Being good with buttons and snaps."

Nick smiled. "We all have our talents. Thank you."

She lifted one shoulder. "I'm sure other women have already commented on your finesse in the clothing removal department."

"I meant, thank you for stopping me from giving him the doll before he choked on the buttons."

Eve felt herself growing warm. "Oh, well, yes, of course. As for catching the button thing, it just slipped out unexpectedly. I tend to worry a lot."

Amusement lit Nick's blue eyes. "I've noticed. No need to explain. It's endearing—and useful. In this case, very useful."

Nick's voice was low and intimate. She wondered if he even knew, or if it was just his habit to talk to women like that all the time when he was out of the office. As if he was intent on seducing them. No doubt it was just a habit. Nick wasn't planning on seducing her, she was sure of it. And she was very uncomfortable with the way her thoughts were headed.

"Looks like Charley's in love," she said, turning to Charley in an effort to distance herself.

Nick leaned one shoulder against the wall. "Ah, and with a fickle woman at that. Look, she won't even look him directly in the eye. That Sassy Sheila. What a tease!"

Eve couldn't help chuckling. "That Nick Stevens. What a ham!"

Nick took a bow. "And proud of it I am, ma'am."

They stood there grinning at each other for several seconds. Until Eve was uncomfortably aware that Nick was standing only a few feet away from her, that they were alone in the house, except for a baby and a doll, and that Nick knew more about women's bodies and buttons than any man she'd ever met.

She shifted slightly and glanced away purposely to where Charley was gnawing on Sheila's arm.

"Ah, a love bite," Nick said. "What do you think the odds are of getting her away from him so that we can practice?"

"Not a chance. He's besotted."

"So what do we practice on?"

They both stood there watching Charley, who suddenly grew very quiet and still. After a moment, he sighed slightly as if he'd just done something wonderful.

Eve and Nick turned toward each other. "I think," Eve said carefully, "that we practice on Charley. Want to go first?"

For a man who exuded confidence day and night, Nick looked suddenly appalled. "You can have this shift. I'll take the next," he promised. "I'll just go see about setting up the security cameras."

Which made her heart beat a little more evenly. At least there would be security cameras. "How do they work?"

"Ah, these are the best. There's a satellite feed into the security firm. If anything looks even mildly out of order, we'll get a call immediately."

"So someone will be watching over him twenty-four hours a day?"

"That's the plan." He turned to go.

"Nick?"

Nick looked back over his shoulder.

Eve took one step toward him. "Thank you. For agreeing to do this," she said, indicating the whole room, "when you really didn't have to. And for understanding about the need for the cameras."

He studied her carefully, suddenly sober, suddenly not Nick. More dangerous than a smiling Nick.

"I don't understand completely," he said. "You can explain it to me when you're ready."

She nodded. And then she managed to dredge up a smile, grateful that he wasn't pressing her for details now. "And I'll call you when it's your turn to practice changing diapers. Tomorrow we hit the silver screen, Mr. Stevens, as Mr. and Mrs. Perfect Mom and Dad."

As he walked away, Nick's groan echoed down the hall.

Eve would have laughed. If she hadn't been so frightened.

* * *

The next morning the house was full of cameras, and not just security cameras, Nick thought, watching as the film crew set up to begin work on Larry's pet project. Someone had swabbed makeup all over his face and Eve's. She had hit the roof when they'd tried to put makeup on Charley.

"He's a baby," she squealed, grabbing him up and holding him to her body as if to shield him from radioactive material.

"But he'll be too pale," the makeup artist said.

Nick stepped between her and Eve. "Aren't babies supposed to be pale? He'll be just fine, ma'am." He had no idea if he was right or not. Maybe Charley would simply look like a little white blob on film, but he could see the worry building in Eve's eyes, and no one was going to worry Eve when she already had enough to contend with.

She hadn't slept well the night before. He'd heard her get up four times to go to Charley's room. He'd considered going to her to comfort her and reassure her that Charley would be all right, but then there had been that thought, that wholly wayward and off-base thought. The one that said Eve might be wearing one of those short sleep shirts…or a thin white cotton gown that was transparent in lamplight…or maybe just a bathrobe to cover her totally nude body. And it had been all he could do to simply clutch the bed and keep himself from going to her.

So he had been no help at all last night, damn him. But he was not going to let anyone else hassle her.

Besides, watching Charley chew on Sheila's leg, he had to admit that Eve might well be right about the makeup, anyway. Who knew what was in this glop they were both wearing on their faces? Surely nothing that could be healthy for a baby. Maybe even something that might be toxic if Charley ate it, and since Charley appeared to lick and smack and chew a lot, no doubt some of the makeup surrounding his mouth would eventually end up in his tummy.

"Leave it, darlin'" he drawled, when the makeup artist opened her mouth to protest again. "If there's a problem, I'll take the heat."

The lady backed off. Nick turned to Eve to get ready for the shoot and found her looking at him. *Darlin'?* she mouthed.

And for the first time Nick felt uncomfortable for having done what he had been doing all of his adult life: flirting.

"We're nearly ready," he told the cameraman.

"The doll's gotta go, Nick," the man said. "It's as big as Charley. No way Larry is going to want his kid being upstaged by a hunk of plastic."

Uh-oh. Nick and Eve exchanged glances.

"What do you think?" he asked her.

"You know what I think. He's going to cry. He loves that doll. Right from the moment you held her up and gave her that silly voice..." Eve's voice trailed off. "What's that man's name over there, the one who doesn't look like he's doing anything important?"

Nick nearly choked. "You mean Pete, the director?"

Eve smiled. "Yes, him," she said, and she turned toward the man. "Pete," she called, but Pete was busy talking to someone suddenly.

"Pete, darlin'," she drawled in a low, sultry voice that whispered across the room.

Pete's head came up. He started walking their way.

"Pete," Eve said, and her voice was a caress. "Would you mind doing us a very big favor here?" Eve opened her eyes wide, and Nick knew that every man in the room was dying to do something, anything for Eve.

"No problem, Ms. Carpenter," Pete said.

She smiled that glowing smile, the one that made her green eyes luminous, her face a beauty to behold.

"You see, Charley is going to cry big-time when we take his doll away from him, but if he could just see her, if you could just hold her up in front of your face and make her...I don't know, make her dance a bit, I think he'll be all right." Eve finished her preposterous request with another smile.

"You want me to make the doll dance."

"Or something like that. It would be such a help. I'd appreciate it so very much." Blanche DuBois couldn't have been more effective. Pete looked grumpy and uncomfortable and unhappy, but he took the doll, prepared to do his part.

Nick came up behind Eve. "Darlin'?" he whispered at her ear. He felt a shiver run through her, the kind of shiver he'd felt from women before, but this was Eve. Eve, his employee, Eve with the oft-troubled eyes who took things way too seriously. Breathing in her ear like a lover was not something he should be doing, but he couldn't seem to step away.

"We needed his help," she finally said, her voice faint and hesitant. "I know it's not my style."

"Oh, I think it's a style that suits you real well," Nick said, starting to see sides of Eve he hadn't seen before, sides that intrigued him too much, maybe sides she didn't even know she had. Interesting, he thought as he let her go. At Pete's direction, he took his position next to Eve with Charley between them on the changing table.

When Pete gave them the signal and held up the doll to keep Charley happy, Eve looked up at Nick, giving him a wifely smile as the cameras started to roll.

"Honey love," she said, repeating the words of Larry's script, "I know that if I were a new parent, I'd want someone to show me how to care for my baby, wouldn't you?"

"Lovey, you couldn't have said it any better. Remember how nervous we were when little Andy here first came along?"

Eve laughed the way the script had directed her to. "We didn't have a clue, did we, and I was so scared we'd do something wrong. So let's show everyone the proper way to care for a baby. The first lesson, my own true heart, is going to be changing a diaper. All right?"

Nick gazed down into her eyes. "Sweetest, I just can't wait." He knew he didn't have the proper inflection. Instead of sounding like he couldn't wait to help Eve show their audience how to change a diaper, it sounded as if he couldn't wait to get her in bed.

And when her eyes went wide and wary…oh, yeah, he wanted her in his bed. He couldn't wait to have her, even though it was never going to happen. He couldn't let it happen. This was all wrong for him, but even more so for Eve.

Nick pulled back. He cleared his throat.

"Yes, let's show our viewers the right way to change a diaper," he said, toning down the heat.

"All right." Eve's voice was a bit raspier and more nervous than usual.

She reached for Charley, who suddenly giggled and rolled away.

Nick caught him and brought him back.

Charley giggled, rolled over and crawled away again. Changing the diaper had become a big game for him.

Five times Charley crawled away. Nick could almost feel the steam rising from Pete's bald head.

Finally Eve grabbed hold of Charley. She held out her hand to Pete and gave him a meaningful look. Without a word, Pete handed over the doll. Eve gave it to Charley, who rolled over onto his back once more.

Together Eve and Nick managed to get the diaper on halfway straight and held Charley up for the viewers to see, doll and all.

"There, angel face," Nick said, looking down into Eve's eyes. "That's how a new parent changes a diaper."

And just as the script ordered, with Charley contentedly settled on one hip, with Eve's hair in disarray and one tortured lock of his own slipping over his forehead, he leaned forward and gave Eve a kiss. It was supposed to be just a husbandly peck, but after the horror of the filming, he could see that Eve was upset. He made the kiss long and slow and sweet. He made it good.

She kissed him back and made it better.

"What do you think?" he whispered against her hair, breathing deeply of her fragrance.

"I think none of this went as planned. I think I feel very strange," Eve said faintly, and without another word Nick handed Charley and Sheila to Pete, scooped up Eve against his chest and carried her away.

The cameras were still rolling.

Chapter 4

"You can put me down now, Nick," Eve said, blushing as Nick carried her from the room. "Honestly, I'm fine, just embarrassed and chagrined." She tried to sit up and nearly threw him off balance. Clutching at his shoulders, she righted herself.

He held on to her. "You sure you're okay?"

She nodded. "Physically, I'm fine, but did you ever see such an awful fiasco as that filming?"

Nick chuckled. "I don't think we'll win any awards for that one."

"Don't laugh," she said, as he lowered her to the ground and she balanced herself, straightening her clothing. "Larry's going to be so upset. He's completely enamored of this idea, and you and I are just the worst choice possible for this job. Maybe we should call him and tell him.'' She looked up at Nick, hoping he would say yes.

"Eve,'' he said, "do you really want to interrupt Larry's romantic interlude with his wife? It seemed like he'd been waiting for this chance for nine months.''

She frowned and fidgeted with the top button of her blouse. "I guess it wouldn't be fair to cut his vacation with Sandra short just because I'm uncomfortable.''

"Maybe the filming will get better,'' he suggested.

"Do you really think so?''

He shook his head. "Not a chance. Some guys are made to be the perfect dad. That's just never going to be me.''

"So you don't ever want children?''

"Can't do it. I know just what a responsibility the happiness of a child can be. It takes a different kind of man to be a good father. I've lived what happens when a man puts his own desires before what's good for his child, and I don't think I'm any more unselfish about certain things than my father was. Some things probably are genetic. At any rate, I don't want to experiment only to find out that I've been right all along. Too big a risk. Look at Charley. Would you ever want to do anything to hurt him?''

Eve's breath came slow and shaky. She shook her head. "I've played that scenario over in my head before. It's much too easy to hurt a child. I know. I've seen it happen, and through simple accident, the mere act of glancing away for a second. Things can happen so quickly, irrevocable things, and a child's life is changed forever.''

Nick gave her the most somber look she'd ever seen him give anyone. He reached out and gently brushed her cheek with his knuckles. ''What happened to you? Obviously something painful. Tell me.'' His eyes grew dark and concerned. She was certain he was going to take her into his arms and offer her the comfort of his warmth.

Quickly she shook her head. ''It wasn't just one thing, and they didn't happen to me—at least, not exactly.''

''All right, not to you. Explain. Please.'' His voice was soft and coaxing. This wasn't something she talked about, ever, but Nick was still stroking her cheek. No doubt he'd used that same technique with success numerous times. For some reason she didn't care right now. She just wanted him to understand.

''All right. About three years ago, I was at my sister's house. She had been mopping the floor when I arrived, and my visit served as a distraction. We had made tea and had sat down and started laughing and talking. All at once, she realized that things were too quiet. Her little girl, who was a year old at the time and had been playing with blocks not five feet away, wasn't there. I ran into the kitchen and found Minnie had fallen into the bucket of water my sister had been using. When I pulled her out, she wasn't breathing. I've never felt so scared and useless in all my life. I've never felt so…so alone.''

Just saying the words, Eve relived the horror of that

moment, seeing the tiny little girl's limp body, feeling cold fear rip through her own soul. That please-let-me-go-back-five-minutes-and-make-things-right feeling.

She realized suddenly that Nick had taken her hands in his own and was holding them too tightly.

"Minnie's all right now," she said hurriedly, realizing what he must be thinking. "My sister Tracy is a nurse and started doing CPR immediately. I guess Minnie hadn't been submerged for more than a few seconds. We were so very lucky. It could have gone wrong so easily."

"You weren't to blame," Nick said, easing his hold and smoothing his thumbs lightly over her fingers.

"Anyone who is responsible for a child is to blame when something like that happens. They can't be left alone that way. It's just too easy for a situation to turn dangerous. A few months later, my best friend's little boy nearly choked to death on some food right before my eyes. I couldn't help him even though I tried emergency procedures. I realized then that motherhood was never going to be for me. By the time the paramedics arrived and dislodged the obstruction, I had already made up my mind. I love kids, but I would never willingly face the fear of being responsible for one every day of my life. I had nightmares for months after that incident, and I wasn't even Ian's mother."

Nick raised her hands to his lips. He kissed each palm.

"You must think I'm a coward," she said.

"I think you're very brave. It takes courage to give up something you want in order to save someone else from harm. Very few people have experienced what you have, Eve, twice in such a short period of time. That kind of thing has a lasting effect. How could it not? I promise you this, though. I'll help you guard Charley. You won't have to go through this alone."

She raised one hand and cupped his jaw. "I think you're a very good man, Nick."

He shook his head. "No, but I do know that a man has to stop and be serious now and then. The fact that I don't choose to do it often doesn't mean that it never, ever happens."

"How did two people so dead set against having children manage to get themselves assigned to make a film about the perfect mom and dad?" She smiled up into his eyes.

"I don't know," he whispered, and he stepped closer into her space. "But I *will* help you, Eve. Can we call it a deal?"

He didn't have to do this. He wasn't the one who had something to prove to Larry.

"Yes, it's a deal." Eve's voice came out choked. She was so grateful, she couldn't help the mist that dampened her eyes as she gazed up at Nick. "How did I ever rate you as a boss?" she asked him.

Those deep blue eyes stared down at her. "I've been asking myself how I rated you ever since you came to work for me," he replied as he dipped his head and touched his lips to hers.

Eve's mind refused to function. All she could manage was to feel and to touch. Right or wrong, she kissed him back.

"Eve?" Nick slid one arm around her waist, the other smoothing up her spine as he brought her more fully against him. Then he kissed her again, more deeply this time. "Tell me to stop. I shouldn't be touching you," he whispered against her lips. "I know darn well I'm breaking all the rules." He tilted his head and touched his lips to the corner of her mouth, then moved on to her chin.

"Yes, this is…insane," she agreed, as he found the sensitive spot just beneath her jaw. She gasped.

"It complicates the situation in the office." He placed his lips against the hollow of her throat. His fingers stroked lower, just flirting with the curve of her breast, and she thought she'd die of pleasure. So much pleasure. Too much pleasure.

And suddenly Eve realized just how complicated things were getting. She was wrapped in Nick's embrace. Nick, who never kept a woman for more than a month or two. Nick, who didn't date women he worked with. Nick, her boss.

She pushed away. "We can't do this. I can't do this. Really. My job is important to me. What must you think?"

He closed his eyes. "I think I've been a jerk. Look, Eve, it's me, not you. I can't imagine what's gotten into me today. But I swear to you, this will never influence anything that takes place in the office. I give you my word of honor, and I do still have some. I never should have touched you. You and I have rules. We've stood by them for two years. I somehow forgot that, but I'll try not to let it happen again."

"It's not just your fault," she said. "It's me, too. I think it's this whole situation. We're probably just not used to this man-and-wife stuff."

A commotion in the next room reached them.

"Charley," they said in unison.

"Pete must be wondering what's happened to us," Eve said.

But Nick didn't answer. When Eve turned to see why, she heard him swear beneath his breath. He was staring directly at a security camera.

"I think we have to worry about more than just what Pete is thinking," he said. "And just be grateful that I didn't do what I was wanting to do next."

She looked down to the buttons she'd been fiddling with on her blouse earlier and saw that two of them had come undone. Immediately, Nick reached out and buttoned her up as quickly as he had divested Sassy Sheila of her clothes the day before.

Then he turned to the camera and winked.

"Nick!"

He reached down and kissed her once, hard, on the lips. "We've already committed the crime, Eve. Might as well brazen it out and act as if we really are married. Only if we look guilty will anyone think anything wrong was going on."

"How many people at the security firm do you think saw what we were doing?"

"I don't know, but I don't think we can go back

and rewrite history. What's done is done. All we can do is make sure it doesn't happen again."

"Absolutely. Never again," she promised Nick and herself. But her lips ached, and she knew that in her heart she had already crossed some invisible line she should never have crossed.

This was not going the way he'd planned, Nick thought a few days later. As if he'd planned it at all. As if he'd have ever voluntarily penned himself up with a woman he wasn't supposed to want to touch and a baby, when babies weren't for men like him.

All of which was utter nonsense. He wanted to touch Eve every time he got near her now. Funny that he hadn't felt that way before. Or maybe it wasn't so funny. Of course, he'd always seen her as a lovely woman, but there had been those business walls. Now the two of them were together in a situation that had no established rules.

"So make some. Fast," he muttered to himself.

He glanced across the breakfast table to where Eve was reading a book called *Baby Steps to Perfect Parenting*. As she looked down at her book, her dark lashes hid her eyes from view. He could study her as much as he wished. Nearby, Charley played contentedly in his playpen with Sheila, who was letting him do all the babbling.

As Nick observed all this, oblivious to the day's script that lay in front of him, Eve's lips turned up in a smile.

"What?" he asked.

She opened her eyes. They were still a mesmerizing green, with all those gold specks that made a man want to lean closer.

He ignored that fact and nodded toward her book. "Are you now approaching the nirvana of perfect parenting?"

"I don't think so. There are lots of case studies in here, examples of those on the verge of parenting sainthood, women who create glorious Halloween costumes for their children using duct tape and other household products. Did you know that there are women who get up at the crack of dawn and bake cookies, so that the house smells nice when their children come downstairs?" Eve looked suddenly uncertain.

Nick chuckled. "Not into cooking and sewing?"

Were those sparks in her eyes? Ah, she didn't like being teased about her lack of domestic skills.

"I cook sometimes. I'm not starving, anyway."

"Eve, you know you have talents that those women don't have. I've seen you talk men three times your size into doing things they didn't want to do. You've calmed mothers and done wonders for this company. You don't have to make miracles out of duct tape to prove yourself."

"I know. It's just...this morning's filming didn't go much better than the last few went, did it?"

"Oh, I don't know. I thought we both looked pretty cute soaked to the skin when Charley splashed his hands in the bathtub."

She looked up at him, and then she giggled. "Poor

Pete. He had soapsuds right on his bald spot. I think all of this is doing a number on his dignity.''

"No need to feel sorry for him. He's a pro and he knows it. He did his job and never stopped filming, even when I wished that he would."

"Yes, and I thought that was very masterful of you to whisk Charley up in a towel and dance him around the room. It almost covered up the fact that we never really did get around to washing him at all. He liked it, anyway.'' Eve's eyes lit up with the memory of that perfectly awful filming, and Nick wished that he could preserve the memory. Women had often smiled at him that way, but usually for reasons other than that he had managed to make a baby laugh.

"Yes, well, who doesn't like a good dance now and then?"

And he would like to have the opportunity to dance with Eve just once. But then, that wouldn't be right. If he danced with her, he'd definitely wind up wanting to do more. Like peel her dress off her shoulders and sweep his palms down her sides.

"What's on for tomorrow?" she asked, which was a good thing since it dragged his thoughts back to where they should be.

Nick had opened his mouth to describe what little he'd read of the script, but just then, Charley let out an anguished cry.

Immediately Eve rose and ran to the baby's side. She started to take him out of the playpen, but Nick placed his hand on her arm.

"Let's find out what's wrong first before we pick

him up. We don't want to hurt him more if he's injured.''

Immediately he could have cut his tongue out. Eve stopped in her tracks, her body went rigid, and she nodded. ''You're right,'' she said, but the eyes she raised to him were filled with pained memories when she turned and dropped to her knees in front of Charley's playpen.

''What's wrong, sweet stuff?'' she asked.

Nick lowered himself to one knee beside her. He kept his eyes on Charley, but he rested one hand on Eve's shoulder. His grip tightened when he heard Charley whimper, and the little boy raised tear-filled eyes to him.

''Ohhh,'' the little boy wailed. ''Ohhh.'' He held up one finger, but Nick didn't see a thing.

''Eve?''

She shook her head. ''I don't know. I can't believe I let him get hurt when I was this close.''

A world of censure was in her voice. Nick would have told her that she had been as careful as any woman could be, even those perfect mothers in the book, but he knew that she would never buy into that. He understood her guilt, too. He had his own personal demons where children were concerned, and he was facing one right now. That little boy, looking up at him so trustingly, when anyone could tell him that he was not a man who could be trusted for the long term. Oh, yeah, he could make a baby laugh to save a moment, but moments passed quickly. Children, and the responsibility for their welfare, were long-term. They were for men willing to go the distance.

"Here, let me see, sweetie," Eve was saying as she took Charley's little hand between her own. She ran gentle fingers over the baby's skin, but Charley was shaking his head and growing more upset.

"Ohhh! Ohhh," he said, more tearfully.

Eve looked up at Nick, distraught. "I don't see anything wrong, Nick. Maybe we'd better call the doctor."

He was all for that. This called for the services of someone who actually knew what he was doing. Nick nodded, but he took one last moment to run his hands over Charley's limbs.

"I really wish you could talk right now, pal," he whispered to the inconsolable little boy. Tears hung on Charley's lashes.

"Ohh," he said again, and this time he held up Sheila.

Nick closed his eyes.

Eve sat down with a whoosh, her hands over her chest. "Oh, my. Oh, thank goodness."

And Nick realized that in this instance, at least, he could still be good old short-term Nick. He could come through again.

"Here, big guy," he said, gently removing the doll from Charley's hand. Carefully, he turned Sheila's head one hundred eighty degrees, just the way it belonged, facing forward.

Charley squealed and smiled. He took the doll that

Nick handed to him, plopped down in the corner and began to chew on his baby once again.

Nick and Eve looked at each other. He took her hands in his own and placed kisses on each one of them.

"Did that scare you as much as it did me?" she asked.

"Probably more. In spite of my job, I stay behind the scenes. I have zero experience with babies."

"Ah, but you know how to make a female's head spin around, Nick," she said.

It was the kind of thing people said to him all the time in the office. It was the kind of kidding he'd always liked, and he liked it now, coming from so-serious Eve.

"I do my best for the ladies, ma'am," he said, playing up his usual role.

But just once, just this time, he realized, he would have liked to do more. He was very glad that Charley wasn't hurt, but he would have liked to be the kind of man who knew how to handle that kind of situation.

He realized that his father hadn't been able to handle those situations, either.

Ouch, Nick thought, maybe he hadn't come so very far from his roots, after all. Maybe there was no changing the past.

Chapter 5

"We're going to do this," Eve insisted three days later. "I've decided." She stood in front of a table that held a mixing bowl, flour, sugar and various other ingredients. "If we do well on this practice run, maybe we can sneak in one other film tomorrow and add it to the rest."

Nick raised one brow. "Eve, um...sweetheart?"

Eve glanced up so quickly, her eyes wide, and Nick realized that he'd used an endearment. He also realized something else. Larry had never used the word *sweetheart* in any of his scripts.

"Yes?" she whispered, and she looked almost as if she were afraid to hear what he would say next.

Quickly Nick tamed his thoughts. "I don't think Charley is capable of baking cookies," he said.

Eve smiled broadly. She dared to reach up and pat

him on the cheek. "Nick, what happened to that genius mind of yours, the one that came up with the campaign to have all the employees bring their babies to work one day and invite the media in?"

"Obviously, it flew out the window. So if you're not planning on putting Charley in an apron, then...?"

"You and I make the cookies, of course," she said. "Mr. and Mrs. Perfect Mom and Dad on a typical day in the kitchen. And then we bring Charley in, give him a cookie and show off that megawatt smile of his. What parents wouldn't want to make their baby smile like that?"

He studied her. "You just want to prove that you can do it, don't you?" he challenged.

"Absolutely. Let's go. Give me that spoon."

"Eve," he growled. "Have I told you that I love it when you order me around?"

She took the spoon from his hand and bent her head over the recipe book. "That's only because most of the women you date don't ever offer an opinion. They just give you those melting, soulful looks and beg you to take them to heaven."

Her tone of voice indicated that she would never in a million years beg him to take her to heaven. The woman clearly was interested in only one thing right now and that was baking cookies. If a man wanted to seduce her, he would have to jump into the flour with her.

"Not that I want to," he said.

"What?"

"I said, 'What do we do next, Eve?'"

She reached out and grabbed another apron. "Here, bend down," she said.

When he did, she slipped the loop of the apron over his head, then stepped behind him and did up the ties. Small as she was, he could feel her like a flame behind him. He wanted to turn, press up against her and feel her heat full force. Instead, he gave her the butter, just as she had asked.

In truth, most of his job consisted of handing her things and watching her intently attempt to follow the directions.

"There," she finally said. He looked down to see wobbly gingerbread men marching across the silver coating of the cookie pan.

"See, you *are* the perfect mother," he said.

"They're not baked yet."

"A mere technicality. You did this part just great."

But fifteen minutes later, staring down at the pan of singed and slightly shrunken little men, Nick was at a loss for words. Eve looked so dejected, almost as heartbroken as Charley with his broken doll.

"I'm sure I left them in just the right amount of time," she said.

"You did," he agreed. "No doubt Larry's oven is just a little off."

"You're being nice."

"No, I'm not. Sometimes it happens. I've had it happen."

That stopped her cold. "You know how to cook?"

"Now and then."

"You could have told me that my cookies were going to burn!"

"I might have mentioned that we should just open the oven and check them out."

She frowned. "Yes, you did say that, and I told you that I wanted to do the whole thing myself."

"And so you did." He reached down and picked up one of the overly brown and misshapen gingerbread men and bit off its leg. The fact that his tongue was burning was irrelevant. He would have choked rather than say so. Quickly he chewed the bite of cookie.

"It tastes wonderful, Eve. No perfect mom could do better."

She looked skeptical, so he ignored the warning bells going off in his head and reached out to tuck one finger beneath her chin. "I'm not lying." It was the truth, although if lying had been required, he would have done so without hesitation.

"Here." He broke off a bit of the gingerbread man's arms. "Open for me. Taste."

Obediently she opened her mouth. He slipped in the bit of cookie, then watched her lips as she chewed it up. "It's good, isn't it?"

She smiled, almost shyly it seemed. "I didn't do so bad, after all, did I?"

"You did just great. Charley's going to love you." And he bent and started to kiss her.

She gasped, and he realized that there was a security camera aimed directly at their faces.

He placed one hand about her waist, turning her

until his back was to the camera. Then he did what he'd wanted to do all day. He kissed her.

"Gingerbread," he said, "never tasted this sweet."

She kissed him back, twining her arms around his neck. He supposed he should stop her. Her hands were going to show up on the security camera again. But he didn't want to stop her. He wanted her to do more. He wanted her arms around him, her legs around his hips and her body, naked and silky, against his.

He wanted to sprinkle gingerbread crumbs over her, then lick them from her skin.

She wanted to be the perfect mother.

He wanted her in a perfectly carnal way.

This wasn't right. She was so good at her job. Her idea today had been a winner, and Larry would recognize that. It wasn't fair of him to risk their professional relationship.

But she was here, she was touching him willingly. And he was lost, so damn lost. He swept his tongue through the heat of her mouth. Seeking her essence, the thing that made her special, made her maddening, made her the one temptation he couldn't resist, he tangled his fingers in her hair, lifted her against him and slanted his mouth over hers until he could get her no closer. He kissed her many times. She touched him with her lips, the tip of her tongue. She moved against him like a lithe cat. And she entranced him the way no other woman had.

When he let her go, she was trembling, her fingers pressed to her lips.

Nick closed his eyes. "I apologize," he said immediately, regret thick in his throat. "Again. I guess…well, I guess I've gotten a whole lot wilder than I thought I was. I told you I'd behave."

She shook her head. "Don't apologize. I may be small, but I'm twenty-seven years old, Nick. I'm an adult, completely responsible for my behavior, and you've never made any secret about what kind of man you are."

No, he hadn't. He'd often been proud that he'd broken out of that rigid mold that had been imposed on him as a child. He'd learned how to enjoy life to the fullest, or so he'd thought. He'd opened the doors to a world of pleasure.

Only now, he was realizing that in opening those doors he might have closed others.

In the distance, over the airwaves of the baby monitor, Charley began to cry. Sweet, innocent baby sobs.

Instantly, the confidence left Eve's eyes, the passion fled. She left the room in a rush, headed for her charge.

And Nick stood there. Though she'd turned from marriage and motherhood, it was clear that in her heart Eve still wanted to be the perfect mother.

But he was simply a man of passion, and that wasn't good enough to win him the title of Dad of the Year.

"Okay, we're on," Eve said, and she handed Charley a newly made unburned gingerbread man. He clutched it in his chubby fingers, gazed at it a while.

He sniffed it, and someone chuckled in the background. Not Nick. Nick had been uncharacteristically quiet since he'd kissed her last night.

She didn't want to think about why. For a second or two, he'd thought of her as a woman. She knew that. She'd wanted it. Then they'd both remembered who and what they were.

She could still taste him if she closed her eyes and remembered. Gingerbread was never going to be the same after this. But she'd worry about that later.

As Charley took another delighted look at the cookie, Nick moved in. He joined hands with her over Charley's head and gave her the look that a loving husband would bestow on his wife when they both are perfectly in tune and in love with their child.

Isn't film amazing? she thought. People will see this and think that we're really man and wife, that we have this beautiful child and that we sleep together every night.

The thought caught Eve unaware. She felt the warmth climbing up her chest and her throat. She wanted to look away from Nick, whose eyes had turned hot and fierce, but the camera was still running.

Nick's fingers clenching hers, he rubbed warm circles on her wrists with his thumbs. The move was meant to soothe, she was sure. Instead, all she could think of was Nick and herself in the big guest bedroom where she was staying, on the king-size bed, with Nick holding her hands above her head, his lips nuzzling her throat as he moved inside her and gave her what he'd given so many other women.

"Cut," Pete called, and Eve gasped. She broke free and turned her back on Nick, fearful of what he might read in her eyes. The man was an expert with women. Who knew what he was capable of discerning?

Quickly, she turned to Charley and picked him up to cuddle him close. It was a cowardly thing to do, she knew, using a baby this way, but holding Charley was so easy, and holding back her attraction for Nick was so difficult.

Charley instantly settled into her arms, nestling there. A sense of fullness enveloped her. She couldn't help sneaking a peek at Nick, who was studying her from beneath lowered lashes.

Her small movement must have caught Charley's attention because he looked up at Nick and held out his arms.

Nick froze, a wary expression in his eyes. If she hadn't known he was a grown man and Charley only a baby, she would have sworn that he wanted to take a step away from the eager reach of the child.

"Nick?"

He blinked, staring directly into her eyes. Then, shaking himself as if to clear his mind, he reached out and took Charley.

Charley crowed. Nick seemed to relax.

"Time for some fun, big guy?" he asked.

Ah, so that was it. Nick was fine if everything was just fun and games, but if real emotion, real need was a part of the package, that was a different story.

Kind of like Nick's attitude toward women, she reminded herself. Play all you want, be as passionate as you please, but don't take things any further than that.

Which wasn't such a bad way to be, she reminded herself. Maybe she should try it.

"I'm sorry, guys, but we've got to at least keep the baby in the shot," Pete said the next day, when Charley kept rolling around on the table as they were trying to dress him.

Nick gave Charley a what-a-guy look. "You're a devil, aren't you?"

Charley babbled, seeming to agree.

"What do you think?" Nick asked Eve. "Is he faking it or what?"

"Nick." She placed her hands on her hips. "He's a baby. How can he fake things?"

But Nick ignored her. "Are you putting us on today, Charley, my lad?"

Charley was waving both feet in the air, and Nick gently tugged on one pudgy appendage. "Just this morning, we got you dressed in no time. Are you rebelling against all these lights and cameras today? You can't be in this glare long anyway. Need a break, some time just for play?"

At the word *play*, Charley perked up right away, just as if he knew what Nick was talking about. "Come on, we're going to take Charley for a ride around the house," Nick told Eve. "We'll be back in ten, Pete," he said, scooping Charley up.

"Yes, well, all right, maybe you're right. And when you come back, could the two of you put more life in your acting? More of that lovey-dovey stuff that Larry wants? You're both a bit...um, wooden, today."

Which was intentional on his part, Nick thought. He'd awakened last night with dreams of Eve stepping from his bathtub and climbing wet and naked into his bed. If she called him "my dearest sweet darling" and batted her eyelashes one more time like it said in the script, he was going to embarrass both of them in public.

Eve nodded her agreement to Pete, but she looked unhappy. As soon as they were outside the door, he turned to her.

"It's tough pretending you're in love when you're not, isn't it?" he asked.

She gazed up at him. "I just feel like a fish out of water. We're not doing much better now than when we started. I thought it would get easier."

Charley babbled and they both looked down at him. The little boy looked tired.

"Horsey ride?" Nick asked.

Charley bucked, and Nick turned to Eve, handed Charley over and dropped to his knees. "Could you help him up?" he asked her.

But he had only gone around the room once when Charley let go and started to slip off. Nick reached to the side and easily caught the sliding little body, cradling Charley against his side like an oversize football. Once Charley was secured, Nick stood and rested him on his hip.

"No horsey today?" he asked, softly brushing the little boy's curls from his face.

Charley smiled, but he didn't hold up his arms.

"Okay, then, big guy. Your call. No horsey," Nick said as he kept his arm looped around the little boy, easily holding him against his side.

"Are you played out, Charley?" Eve asked.

She leaned in and gave Charley a kiss, and the scent of her perfume swirled around Nick. His breath hitched high in his chest.

"I take it Pete's not happy with us," he said, his voice a bit lower than usual. Well, what could a man do when a woman like Eve got this near?

"Not enough lovey-dovey talk," Eve agreed. "It's still hard to imagine Larry talking like that. To anyone."

"Maybe he doesn't. Maybe he just thought it sounded good."

"Maybe we should improve on the script," Eve suggested. "At least make it sound like we're not doing a sitcom, like we're really in love with each other."

That tense feeling got more tense. But she was right. "Okay, I'm with you. We might as well go back. Charley's not interested in playing."

He looked down at Eve and found her staring at him as if she'd just seen something amazing.

"What?" he asked.

"You. Charley." She gestured to where the little boy was cuddling gently against Nick. "You're swaying,'' she pointed out. "You're cuddling him. No fun. No games.''

Immediately Nick glanced down at the baby. He breathed in that scent of baby powder and baby and felt the small but insistent weight against his side. It felt…comfortable.

"Don't worry, it's an aberration," he assured her, and he didn't know if he was teasing Eve or talking to himself. Not that he hadn't just told the truth. "Charley's easy, and he's so obviously temporary. Who wouldn't eventually fall into his trap and settle in?''

She nodded tightly. "Yes, I suppose you're right. It's a bit of a fantasy, isn't it? All of this. The house, the baby, us.''

"Nice one, too," he agreed.

"Uh-oh, I hear Pete," she said. "Well, it was a fantasy he wanted. Let's give him one.''

She placed her hand in Nick's free one and strolled back into the other room. As Pete called out directions, she turned to Nick. "My love," she purred. "Charley needs to be changed for the party we're going to, doesn't he? Let's show the people how it's done.'' And she gave Nick a look that she hoped conveyed her desire to be with her husband and to share this experience with their son.

"He does, sweetheart. Absolutely," Nick agreed, dropping his voice low. "So let's just see if our son will help us give the people what they need to know.''

"Together," Eve whispered, and she felt a shiver zip through her as Nick gazed down into her eyes.

She suddenly wished the world and Pete would go away. "Are you with me?" she added.

"Try to keep me from your side," Nick said, his voice hot and tight. He took a step closer, and then he heard a sound that made him realize that something wasn't right.

"That was much better, with much more feeling," Pete announced, "but it appears we have a problem."

"Oh, yes, we do," Nick agreed. In fact, they had more than one.

He and Eve were getting perilously close to doing what they shouldn't even be thinking of doing and—

"Oh," Eve said, her voice sad and guilt-laden. "Nick, Charley's fallen asleep," she said as the baby's gentle snores fell into the silence. "We've pushed him too hard today, haven't we?"

He looked down at the sleeping child, at the distressed woman.

"Can we have him back up in ten or fifteen?" Pete asked, but Nick shook his head.

"He's done enough. We'll continue tomorrow. We'll do the right thing," he said, and this time his words were for Eve. "We asked too much of Charley, and now he's exhausted. I see that now. It's important to remember that all of our actions have consequences."

Because if he didn't watch himself, he was going to be having some very serious consequences with Eve.

Chapter 6

The next evening brought a new complication into Eve's life. Several new complications, she thought, as she anxiously held Charley.

Charley wasn't his usual self tonight. He was cranky and fretful, not a smile to be had.

Nick had lost his smile, as well, and a wall seemed to have come up between them. He watched her struggle to calm Charley. Finally he picked up the phone.

"I'm calling the doctor," he said, his voice stiff.

"Yes. Please." Eve shifted Charley in her arms as he whimpered.

She listened as Nick tersely explained the problem to the person on the other end of the line. There appeared to be some difficulty.

"Well, get him or give me the name of someone who can help us," Nick said firmly.

Silence ensued. Minutes passed.

Eve looked down at Charley's pathetic little figure, then up at Nick, who seemed to have turned to ice.

Finally he began to speak again. He rattled off what they had determined were Charley's symptoms: crankiness, tears, not his usual cheery disposition, excessive drooling. Yes, he'd been chewing on things, too. He listened a moment, then motioned Eve over. Propping the receiver between his shoulder and neck, he reached out and gently stroked Charley's cheek until his lips opened. Then Nick brushed his finger inside Charley's mouth. Charley promptly bit down on the digit, but Nick didn't make a sound. He reclaimed his very wet finger, stroked his knuckles across Charley's cheek and shifted the receiver back in place.

"Yes," he said in response to whatever the person on the other end was saying.

More silence. More of Nick listening and Nick frowning. Eve wished she had listened in on another line. She tried to get Nick's attention, but he shook his head.

"That's it?" Nick finally said. "So what do we do?"

He didn't appear to be happy with the result. When he finally set the phone down, he turned to Eve.

"What is it?" she asked. "What's the problem? Do we need to take him in?"

"No."

She frowned. "It's not serious?"

Nick reached out for Charley, who went to him.

"Apparently not." He looked down into the little boy's blue eyes. "Charley, my boy, you appear to have crossed a milestone of sorts. You know, like your first kiss or your first date or the first time you see a good-looking woman in a bikini?"

"Nick." Eve tried to scowl, although Charley did seem to be a bit perkier. Nick was cradling him in his arm in that man-type football hold and stroking his finger across Charley's gums. "What are you doing?"

"Probably the wrong thing, though he doesn't seem to mind. It seems that Charley is getting a tooth. That's why he's so upset. Irritating as heck, isn't it, big guy?"

Charley appeared to clamp down harder on Nick's finger.

"So what do we do? That isn't what they told you, is it?" she asked, eyeing his finger.

"Not exactly. They said that he needs something to chew on, so let's find him something, shall we? I washed my hands, by the way," he said, smiling at her as if he knew all her concerns.

For the first time this evening, her heart eased a bit. And, anyway, now she had something constructive to do.

Within minutes Charley's crib held an assortment of rubber toys, and Sheila, of course. Charley chewed away, but the teething pain was apparently not receding.

"Ice wrapped in gauze," Nick said, "or a cold

spoon. I've also sent Pete out for this gel that you can rub on his gums.''

Charley whimpered and Eve picked him up. She turned to Nick, her eyes filled with pain. ''I know it's just teething,'' she said, ''but he's so little and he can't tell us how he's feeling. He's probably afraid, too.'' Kissing the top of Charley's head, she rocked.

''I know, sweetheart. I know,'' Nick said, and Eve didn't know if he was talking to her or to Charley. Maybe it didn't matter. What mattered was the genuine warmth and caring in Nick's voice. He was such a good man. She felt so bad for getting him into this.

''It's nighttime,'' she said. ''You should be out making some beautiful blonde's evening more exciting.'' She couldn't keep the wistfulness from her voice.

But Nick reached out. He brushed back a lock of hair that Charley had pulled forward and that was falling in her eyes. ''I'm fine, Eve. Get that guilt right out of your voice.''

''You're here because of me, because Larry wouldn't have started on this idea if it hadn't been for me.''

''I'm not asking to be anywhere else.''

''You wouldn't. You'd pretend that this was what you wanted to do.''

''How do you know it isn't?''

He had stepped closer to her now, and only her arms holding Charley separated them. Nick slid his hands around the baby's waist and lifted him to lie against his shoulder.

Now they were closer, Charley resting on Nick, chewing on his white shirt. Nick's big hand was splayed against the baby's back. With his other hand he reached out, encircled Eve's waist and drew her to him.

Eve felt his fingers against her, only the thin cotton of her clothing separating his skin from hers. Her heart felt as if it had grown too large for her chest.

"You try to separate your work and your private life." She somehow managed to whisper the words. "You told someone that once. They told me."

"It's the truth," he agreed.

"But it's the best part of the evening. You should be playing, and you're working," she said.

"Am I?"

She hoped so. She had to believe that he was. If he wasn't, then he was merely amusing himself, doing something different. Nick had always been known as an adventurous sort, both in his work and in his play. Perhaps he'd grown bored with his usual regimen. Maybe this cozy domesticity was just an interesting fantasy, a bit of role-playing.

"This is work," she insisted, and she stepped back.

Nick let her go. He brought his free hand up and smoothed it over Charley's back. A small hiccup escaped the baby.

Suddenly Eve didn't care why Nick was here. She was just glad that he was.

"I hate seeing him hurting." Her voice came out weak.

Nick swore beneath his breath. "I'm going to find

Pete. If he hasn't found the gel, I'll go out and get it myself. You'll be fine in no time, little man," he whispered in the baby's ear. "We're going to help you."

Eve knew that Nick was as good as his word. He might play hard, he might prefer his women temporary and his passions quickly taken care of and discarded, but when he said he would get a job done, he always got it done, and he got it done right.

Handing Charley into her care, he gave her a quick nod, then left the room. In minutes, he had returned with a small tube. After carefully reading the instructions, he gently rubbed some on Charley's gums.

"It's not to eat," he warned. "It's just to make you feel better, so that you can sleep."

He stayed with Eve as she paced with Charley and rocked him in her arms. Soon Charley quieted. When Nick bent down to see how he was doing, eye to eye, Charley even smiled.

Immediately Nick grinned up at Eve. "He's back. Charley's okay."

Eve felt embarrassing tears welling up. "Thank goodness, he needs some rest. I'll just put him to bed."

But when she had sung him a song, read him a story and turned out the lights, she settled into a nearby chair.

"Eve?" Nick's voice was worried.

She was a little embarrassed that she was afraid to leave Charley. She wasn't sure if she was more afraid of being away in case something happened to the baby in the night or being alone with Nick when her emotions were so close to the surface.

"I just want to make sure he's really going to rest," she explained somewhat sheepishly. "You go on."

"I'll stay with you."

"No!" She would be self-conscious if he stayed. She might be thinking of him instead of Charley, or she might let her wayward emotions get the best of her and ask him to treat her the way he would treat his usual Friday-night woman.

With a graceful shrug, Nick nodded and let himself out the door. "But you call if you need something or if that tooth bothers Charley again," he ordered.

"I promise." But she knew she was telling a lie. Now that she knew what to do for Charlie, she would do it. All these days of closeness to Nick were having a bad effect on her. She was starting to think of him less as her boss and more as a man.

And that just wasn't the kind of thing a good employee did with a man like Nick Stevens.

Nick watched the minutes on the clock tick by. He'd give her ten, maybe fifteen minutes. Then he was going back in there.

For a woman who usually had it all together, this evening had done a number on her. Another needy baby, another baby she was afraid she would fail. If she thought he was going to let her go through that alone for any length of time, she didn't know him very well.

Or maybe she knew him too well. He was, after all, known for zipping in and out of a relationship. No doubt he missed a lot of tears and anguish that way. A pretty convenient and selfish way for a man to be, even if it was all in the name of self-preservation.

''Ten minutes,'' he muttered, looking down at the clock which seemed not to have advanced at all.

But ten minutes proved to be far too long. After just eight ticks of the minute hand, Nick pushed open the door to Charley's room and let himself in.

He glanced toward the crib and saw that Charley was sawing wood big-time, with Sheila clutched in a headlock. The covers lifted gently with each breath he took. For the first time Nick realized what the term ''little angel'' was all about. Who would have thought this was the same imp who had thrown his milk in the air and showered everyone earlier today?

Nick smiled and finally allowed himself to do what he really wanted to do. He turned and drank his fill of Eve.

She was half seated, half lying in an easy chair that was two feet away from Charley's crib. A fan of her long dark hair covered part of her face; it caught on her lips. He longed to drop to his knees, uncover those lips and kiss her, taste her, have her.

She breathed out slowly and then in, which brought his attention to her lovely breasts. Gently curved under the blue cotton of her blouse, they weren't very large, but they were achingly enticing. Just the right amount of flesh to hold and lift and suckle.

And he was just the right amount of crazy to be having these kinds of thoughts about Eve while she slept innocently unaware. She was his employee, he reminded himself for the umpteenth time. She'd been forcibly trapped into this arrangement with him. She really was not any of those words that Larry had dropped into the script, not his "dearest darling," not his "own heart," not his wife.

Come next weekend when Larry returned and the filming was over, she would go back to being Eve Carpenter, Burnside Baby Foods employee, his right hand. Soon, as soon as her promotion came through, she would take up her new position as director, and most likely their paths would cross less frequently. Oh, they'd still interact, talk business, but they would never work together as closely as they had. He'd certainly never again get to watch her sleep.

That was his problem. She'd worked so hard. She deserved her promotion, not his lust. And she needed her rest.

"You look so damn uncomfortable, angel," he whispered. "Let's fix that."

Without another word or thought, Nick bent down, gently scooped Eve up into his arms and tucked her against his chest. He tried his best not to feel what any man would feel, but her softness made him hard in seconds.

Quickly he marched to her room. With one hand, he peeled back the covers. He started to lower her to the bed, determined to do his duty and leave.

Eve groaned and looped her arm around his neck.

She rested her cheek against his chest and nuzzled closer. Her other arm wrapped around his waist.

He was trapped—albeit in sinner's heaven—and he had to do the honorable thing and free himself.

But when Nick attempted to disengage her arm from his neck, Eve whimpered. She shifted and tightened her hold on him.

"Eve?" he whispered.

She frowned in her sleep. "Is it Charley?" she mumbled. "Charley?" Her voice sounded tearful.

She hadn't gotten enough sleep lately, he was betting. No way would she be able to sleep, for fear she'd miss something important.

"It's all right, angel," he whispered. "Charley's all right. Everything's all right." As if his voice alone had soothed her, she relaxed in his arms.

Nick let out a sigh. That was it. There was no way he was either waking her up or worrying her more by trying to get away from being her night's security blanket. For the moment, it seemed, independent Eve needed a man to hold her. Even a lustful lunk of a man who was going to have to get tough and ignore the tempting messages his passion-slugged body was sending him.

Didn't matter. Not much. He was suddenly just glad that he was the man who had been conveniently near. "I'll hold you," he whispered. "All night long. Sleep well."

Carefully he lowered himself to the bed, with Eve still in his arms. Propped against the headboard, he cradled her as she dreamed.

She was heaven to hold. He was the world's luckiest man tonight, and if he so much as moved a finger over any part of her body, he was going straight to hell.

Chapter 7

"Isn't this going to be confusing for him?" Eve asked Nick the next morning. "I mean, it isn't his birthday, and he isn't even one year old yet."

Today was the day they were staging the How To Throw a Birthday Party for Your Baby footage. Larry had obviously been more than thorough.

"Well, he looks happy enough," Nick concluded, watching Charley surrounded by a circle of brightly wrapped toys that Larry had provided. "Who knows? Maybe Larry and Sandra give him gifts like this all the time. Besides, I have to tell you a secret about males, Eve."

She looked up at him expectantly. "Well, this should be real good. I've always wanted to break the code of how the other half operates. It's usually a total mystery," she teased.

Nick arched a brow. "Yes, we do have our secrets."

His tone was low, and Eve couldn't help remembering how she had awakened in bed this morning draped across Nick, with his arm wrapped firmly around her waist. They had both been fully clothed, but her skirt had bunched up around her thighs, and one of Nick's shirt buttons was missing, as if a grasping woman had ripped it off in her haste to get him out of his shirt.

She'd braced her hands on his chest, felt his warmth, breathed in his masculine scent and forced herself to push up. It was at that moment that she'd realized he was awake and watching her. The blush had raced quickly from her head to her toes, or maybe the other way around. She couldn't be sure; rational thought wasn't even a possibility.

"What are we doing?" she'd asked lamely.

Nick had reached out and brushed her hair back from her forehead, his fingers dragging lightly across her skin. "We're sleeping. Or rather we *were* sleeping."

"Together?" Her voice had been unnaturally high.

"It would appear so." His clear blue eyes had held a trace of amusement. "You fell asleep in a chair," he explained more gently. "I thought it best to put you in a more comfortable place, but you and I...well, let's just say we were better off staying together last night."

"But nothing happened, right?" She barely managed a whisper. She'd been half afraid he would say that something had happened and she just couldn't remember it. Which would have been a shame. If a woman was going to sleep with Nick only once in her life, she should certainly be allowed to retain some memory of the great event.

The rest of her had been afraid that he would say nothing had happened because, then, why were they in bed together?

"Nick, nothing did happen, did it?" she'd asked again, her voice slightly firmer but still squeaky.

He smiled, leaned forward and kissed her forehead. "Eve, my wonderful, talented, intelligent but oh-so-innocent lady, when a man and a woman lie this close through the night, something always happens."

He'd lifted her off of him, slid from the bed and left her room, tall and graceful and very male.

And now here she was, trying to act normal and pretend her body wasn't still throbbing just from the thought of what *might* have happened.

"Eve?"

She looked up, dazed, into Nick's too-perceptive eyes.

He smiled, and she decided that maybe she was wrong. He'd already forgotten last night. She managed to return the smile. "I'm sorry. I was drifting. You were going to tell me a secret about men. I'm all ears."

"You were in a daze."

"Yes, but I really want to know your secrets. And how does this relate to Charley and what we're filming today?"

He shrugged. "It's a party. It doesn't matter if it's really his birthday or not, Eve. He's a male, and I've never met a man yet who wouldn't use any excuse, good or bad, to stage a party. Let him enjoy it."

"Yes," she said. "He does seem to be having a good time, doesn't he?"

Charley reached for one of the bows.

"Not yet, sweetness," Eve cooed, stepping toward him. She suddenly looked down toward her feet. "Nick, why didn't the alarm go off when I stepped into Charley's safety circle? You told me that if he started to crawl out of the circle while we were consulting on the next shot, we'd hear the alarm."

"It's only keyed to Charley. See? He's wearing a little wristband. That's what sets the alarm off if he leaves the barrier. And it's not a scary alarm, either. It chimes. He's perfectly safe."

"Good. Shall we begin?"

No problem. Charley was safe, it seemed, and so was she, for now. She was in the midst of a large group of people, and Nick was behaving like the perfect gentleman. The confusion and desire of this morning in her bedroom was a long way away. Nothing had happened, she was sure of it. Nick had just been talking like...well, like Nick.

He was an incurable flirt. But then, she'd known that. It was what had always protected her.

Today would be no different. She would be fine if only the filming went well.

And, indeed, it did go much better than the previous days' filming had gone. They had finally had one decent shoot.

Nick had been right, it seemed. Every male did love a party.

"Nick, I'm thinking that we need to re-film some of the things we've already shot. Don't you agree? We still have a few days left."

Nick stared down at Eve, who had her arms crossed and was pacing circles on the floor, a look of determination transforming her delicate features into those of the woman he'd known for the past two years.

The party shot over, Charley was napping, and Jenny, the housekeeper, was manning the fort. For now, Eve could let down her guard and be the woman she'd hired on to be, a woman who knew what made the customers happy.

"What parts do you think we need to reshoot?" he asked noncommittally. He had his own ideas, but he wanted to hear hers.

"Almost all of them. The birthday party was fine, but I think that was because it was supposed to be spontaneous and because we were only trying to show the importance of making it an enjoyable experience for the baby. Maybe we can salvage the cookie shoot if we take out all that…um, stuff at the end."

Nick was surprised at how strong his disappointment was, even though he'd known that was what she'd say. "You mean the part where you practically beg me to make you a real woman?" he asked, his tone dry but his senses on full alert. He knew how to tease, but he wasn't completely teasing. Which was a bad thing, he told himself. She had every right to get rid of that part.

''Yes, well, it was probably not really appropriate to the series, and besides, we were just acting.''

Nick chuckled at that, though he couldn't remember when he'd felt more grouchy. Eve reached down and picked up a bit of plastic at her feet. He had a feeling that she was simply ignoring him, which certainly didn't help his disposition.

Greedy, he told himself. You're not used to women ignoring you, and now you want her to notice you and to want you, too.

''Don't you agree?'' she asked, her voice slightly breathy, her eyes darting nervously toward him. She fidgeted with the button on her blouse, and he was lost.

Nick took three long strides toward her. ''It probably wasn't appropriate to the series,'' he said. ''And maybe *you* were acting.''

She swallowed hard, visibly. He closed his eyes to keep himself from groaning out loud, but immediately opened them again. He wanted to see her face, every nuance of her expression. He wanted to touch her very badly. He wondered if she had any idea how much he had not been acting that day.

''We should do it differently this time,'' she said. ''Better.''

She looked up at him with those big green eyes. He wished she would stop being so beautiful.

"Yes," he finally said. "It will be different this time. Better."

"What can we do to make it better?" she asked.

"This time I'm not going to be acting at all," he said. "This time I'm going to kiss you."

And he slid one hand along her waist. He pushed the other up the length of her spine, plunged it into her hair and cupped her head. She waited, but he didn't kiss her.

Eve looked up into Nick's eyes. She had wondered if this was how he seduced women, if he simply overwhelmed them with his presence, if he dazed them so that they would be willing to do anything. Right this moment he could do anything.

But he wasn't. He wasn't kissing her yet, and she suddenly wanted him to kiss her.

"Eve?" he asked, as if he needed her permission, as if he didn't realize that she could not say no.

"Yes," she said on a breath. "That will make it better."

She lifted her lips to his, and he took what she was offering. Over and over his lips met hers, nuzzled softly, nipped, caressed, then moved away.

She moaned, protesting.

"We're not done yet," he responded. "Not nearly done yet."

But they would be soon. Larry would be returning and all of this pretense and passion would be over. She'd only have this once.

She couldn't wait for him to come back to her lips. Eve rose on her toes. She cupped his face in her hands and kissed him with all that she had. For the first time in her life, she did the kissing and the demanding.

"Touch me more," she said, closing her eyes to everything but Nick. "We're almost done. Then we'll be our old selves again."

"We're never going to be that again. That's not going to work."

A pang slipped through her. He was right. This job, this time, this very kiss was going to ruin things. They could never go back.

"Will anything work?" she asked, and she opened her eyes to gaze at him. His eyes were dark and dangerous and not particularly happy, but they were also filled with passion and need.

"Not to go back, but for this moment, this will work," he said. "Only this." And he gathered her closer and kissed her lips, her chin.

She leaned back so that he could touch the most sensitive part of her throat. His lips tracked a warm path down her jaw, to the hollow of her neck, and lower still. He softly nipped the crest of her breast, and her heart began to flutter furiously.

Just as she thought she would stop breathing if he dared to stop, just as she bent back even more, a loud chiming sounded in her ears. Again. Again.

"Hell," Nick said, and he quickly, gently raised her, thrusting her behind him. She glanced down and realized that half of her buttons were undone.

"We about ready to start here?" Pete called, his voice growing nearer.

Eve struggled to close her buttons, but found that

she couldn't manage—and that it was too late. Pete was standing in the doorway.

"Um...sorry. I guess I should have asked for permission to enter."

"My fault, Pete, not yours," Nick said. "And for the record, if anyone asks, this was all me. We'll meet back here tomorrow to re-film a few of the scenes that need the most work. For now, Eve is taking the day off. This stays between you and me and her."

But as Eve peered over Nick's shoulder to see what was going on, she saw that it was already too late to keep this moment between Pete and Nick and herself. A crowd was forming just outside the door. It was clear from some of their faces that they had seen her lost in Nick's embrace.

But Pete gave his word, anyway. He managed to usher everyone out.

"How did they know?" she asked, but she didn't really have to ask. Eve looked down at her hand. She was holding the bracelet that operated Charley's alarm, and she and Nick were standing in the safety circle.

Swinging her hand outside the circle to where it would have been when she lay in Nick's arms, she set off the chimes again.

"I'm sorry," she whispered.

"Don't be. If we'd gone further, you would have had regrets."

He was right, of course. By rights, she should be glad that something had stopped her.

So why was she suddenly envying Nick's girl-friends, the ones she'd always pitied?

No need to scramble for the answer. Those women knew what it was to be completely and totally Nick's, if only for one night.

Chapter 8

"Where are we going? Are you sure Jenny will take care of Charley? You know, she always says she's a housekeeper, not a baby-sitter," Eve asked, and Nick smiled down at her.

He could tell that she was still feeling nervous and embarrassed around him. He intended to do what he could to get rid of that wariness in her expression.

"She's bringing in her daughter who loves babies. And we're going somewhere to keep your mind occupied. The office. I got a fax from Larry this morning. He wants us to start the wheels in motion regarding the film series. Set up some public relations opportunities, talk things up. I thought it would be right up your alley."

"This series must mean a lot to him if he took time

from his second honeymoon to send you a fax about it.''

Eve wore a delicious look of intense concentration. He'd seen it a thousand times. He'd never thought it made her look incredibly sexy, but then, he'd never slept with her in his arms before, either. That changed a man's perspective.

''Well, Larry's son does have a starring role.''

''Yes, which means it might have taken on a larger-than-life meaning. If it doesn't succeed as an ad campaign, he's going to be so disappointed.''

No problem following her train of thought. What she meant was that Larry would be disappointed in *someone*. Her, since she had been the chosen one that sent Larry's mind wandering into film territory in the first place.

''Don't worry, Eve. Larry is going to love anything that has Charley in it.''

''I know. He probably will love it, but if he can't get this film series in the places he wants to, the professional health centers and places like that, it won't matter if he thinks the series is great just because it has Charley in it. If the project fails, Larry's going to want to figure out why, and you and I both *know* why.''

''Because Charley isn't all that cute?'' he teased.

''Nick, Charley is adorable,'' Eve sputtered, and she looked so adorable herself in her indignation that Nick wondered why he hadn't spent more of the past two years teasing her.

''He's the cutest kid on the planet,'' Nick agreed,

and she looked up at him, a suspicious expression on her face.

"Aren't you ever serious?"

"Not often." But, oh yes, sometimes he was serious. He'd been dead serious when he'd kissed her, and that had been a big mistake.

She must have remembered that moment, too, because lovely pink suffused her skin.

"I'm sorry," she said.

"Why?"

"Because I insulted you."

"I'm not insulted."

"But I didn't mean—well, what I *do* mean is that being serious all the time isn't necessarily a good thing. You make me laugh, and I need to do more of that, I think. And you're charming."

"I am, aren't I?" He waggled his brows.

"Too charming," she agreed with a weak smile as he pulled up in front of the office. "We're here for business, Mr. Stevens."

And so they were. He should darn well work harder at remembering that.

A few minutes later they sat down in his office. Nick accessed health-care databases and had an administrative assistant type up an announcement to any companies he thought might be interested in Larry's project. He chatted up the local royalty or what passed for it in Chicago, letting the latest Burnside project slip into the conversation now and then, and he conferred with Eve on an advertisement for a professional journal. Afterward, Eve called on her local media contacts and arranged a brief meeting. Then she began to contact friends, neighbors and loyal Burnside Baby Foods customers, whom she also invited to the meeting. By the time they were done, Nick's tie was undone, the first button on his shirt was open and his hair showed the effects of his having run his fingers through it numerous times.

He turned to Eve, who was looking a bit used herself, but still lovely.

"Hungry?" he asked.

"Famished." Her voice came out on a croak.

"Come on, you. We've got two hours to get you fed, changed and looking as if you're the world's best mom," he said. "Perfect moms never stop smiling, it seems. At least, in the world of sales."

She gave him a look that said, *Yeah, buddy? Drop dead.*

Nick chuckled. "I'll do all the talking if you're too tired."

"Will you hold the babies, too?"

"All at one time," he quipped.

"And what will you tell the media?"

"That Burnside Baby Foods is about to do the world a great service by making a training film for new moms and dads everywhere. The performances are riveting, and the cast members all look...well watered."

Eve chuckled. "I'm sure that will get their attention."

But when Nick and Eve were fed and changed and they wandered down to the lobby to throw open the doors to the media and the parents invited to attend, the sudden flashing of cameras and a crush of questions let Nick know that they weren't going to have to do a thing to get the media's attention.

"Mr. Stevens, is it true that you and your employee, Ms. Carpenter, are having a hot and heavy affair while baby-sitting the president's son?"

"Ms. Carpenter, would you mind twining your arms around Mr. Stevens's neck and giving him another kiss?"

Nick felt Eve stiffen at his side.

"Keep smiling," he told her, but he needn't have spoken. She was a trouper, and for all of Eve's shock at the sudden turn of events, she pasted on the most luminous smile a woman could wear.

"Don't believe everything you read in the papers," she said smoothly to the newspaper reporter who had made the last request. "Yes, Mr. Stevens and I do kiss now and then. We're playing the part of the parents in Mr. Burnside's film series, but that's all there is to the rumors. Now…I didn't come here to discuss boring stuff like kissing. I want some babies to hold."

And once more she had every mother present in the palm of her hand.

It wasn't until a half hour later, when the press had finally filed out, that Nick had the opportunity to turn to her. "Well, I think we got their attention, don't you?"

Eve groaned. "Do you think they'll drop that story about the kiss?"

"Not a chance, sweetheart. America's perfect pretend mom and dad kissing offstage? It's the kind of thing that sells newspapers and magazines. Let's just hope it's the kind of thing that sells baby food.''

"I just wonder what Larry's going to think. Maybe he'll just let it pass.''

"I think it's a pretty clever marketing scheme Eve dreamed up, don't you, Larry?'' Nick was talking into the receiver, Eve had her head down on the desk. Nick thought he'd heard a groan.

It was the kind of thing he might have laughed at in the past, but he knew that Eve was embarrassed, and not only that, she was afraid that she'd messed up her career. All because some fool man had been unable to keep his hands off her.

She had worked hard to get where she was. He knew that. Soon after Eve had started at Burnside, she'd let it slip that she'd been turned down for jobs before because she was too petite and had a high-pitched voice. Not that anyone had ever said she didn't exactly fit their professional image, but it was just something she knew.

She'd been right. He'd heard as much from some of the goofs who had let her slip through their fingers. He hoped Larry wouldn't be as stupid. Didn't the man know that this woman had stayed by his child's bed last night, just to make sure Charley was all right and comfortable? Would he ever have an employee who would do so much without thought of reward?

Nick couldn't help himself. He reached out and

rested his hand on Eve's dark curls. She jerked slightly, then settled like a bird beneath his fingertips.

Gently he stroked. "That's right, Larry," he said. "She did." So Larry had heard about Eve's night with Charley. Nick was glad, but mostly he was concentrating on Eve. She shifted beneath his palm, and he followed the curve of her head down to her cheekbones.

"I hope you know what a treasure you have here, Larry," he said, and his fingertips touched Eve's lips. He felt her smile at his words…or at his touch. Her warmth had him sucking in a deep breath.

"You say you want to know how the filming's going?" Eve's head shook beneath his hand. Violently. She didn't want him to say anything until she was sure she'd re-cut all the problem areas, as she put it. She'd told him so.

"It's going fine, Larry. Just great. Eve turns into a different person behind the camera." Especially when that normally high voice turned low and husky and passionate.

Teeth nipped at his finger and he almost yanked his hand away, but not quite. It had been a gentle nip.

"Don't worry, Larry. We've got things under control." And he brushed his fingers across her lips again. He slid the tip of one finger against the soft flesh and then just inside.

For a second, he thought he felt her tongue against his skin. A low shudder ripped through him. He had no idea what his next words to Larry were.

Eve turned her head slightly. And then he felt it. Her lips very definitely touched his palm.

Nick made a hasty retreat from his conversation with Larry. Somehow he got the telephone receiver back in the cradle.

He turned to Eve, who had raised her head and was looking at him.

"I'm sorry," she whispered. "I didn't mean to do that."

"Didn't you?"

"I don't know, but I shouldn't have done it. We have rules, you and I, rules we're not living by. This has to end."

He studied her, his body on fire. Finally he rose and held out his hand. "Yes, it does. Let's end it."

The warmth of Nick's hand around hers reminded Eve of just how overwhelming he was as a man. She'd always thought of herself as strong and capable, but with his skin touching hers she suddenly felt dizzy, small, needy.

She wanted him touching her. All of him against all of her. She wanted to know what all those other women had known.

And once she knew?

She'd just be another woman to Nick, one more woman he had sampled and savored and finished with. Was that what she wanted?

Her mind started humming as she applied mental brakes. What could she do—or say?

The truth?

"I need to check on Charley," she whispered, tugging on her hand.

Immediately he let go.

"You're right. Of course." He was agreeing with his words, but when she looked into his eyes she saw that she hadn't fooled him a bit. Of course not. She'd only just gotten Charley to sleep when Larry had called Nick. That couldn't have been more than a few minutes ago. There was no need to check on Charley so soon.

Still, as she stood there gazing up at him, the urge to move closer and touch him again was so intense that she knew she should ignore it and make any kind of excuse to get out of there. Anything a person wanted that badly couldn't be good for them.

"I'll just go now," she said, and he smiled slightly.

"You don't have to leave, you know, Eve. I'm not going to force myself on you."

"I didn't think that. I wouldn't. You're not like that."

"You're sure?"

"Why would you need to force yourself on a woman? I know plenty who wish they'd find you under their covers every night."

"Really?" Nick crossed his arms and leaned back against the wall. "Who?"

"Oh, no. I'm not going there. I said you wouldn't force yourself on a woman. I didn't say you wouldn't get an inflated ego under the right circumstances."

Nick pushed off the wall. He moved closer, leaning over her. "How could I possibly get an inflated ego,

Eve, when I want to touch you so badly and you're so clearly reluctant to let me too near?''

"It's not your fault," she said.

"Are you saying that it's yours?"

"I need to be in control of things. I don't like simply allowing things to happen to me. When you let events get away from you, bad things happen."

He reached out and gently ran his fingertips along her jawline. "Those were accidents, Eve. They weren't your fault."

"I know, but still, they were my accidents, and it's best to stay focused. I don't like things that mess with my mind and make me lose my awareness."

Nick bent and replaced his fingertips with his lips. "Are you saying that I make you lose your awareness, Eve?" he whispered between kisses.

She couldn't help it. She tipped her head back. "Yes," she said on a breath. "Oh…yes."

Nick groaned. "Eve, I can't help it. Let me kiss you. More of you."

He had probably said that kind of thing to many women. He was her boss and she had no business kissing him at all.

But she was tired of fighting her own body and her mind. If Nick had been just an attractive man, if he'd been the man she knew just a few days ago, she could have said no, but she'd seen him with Charley and had had him come to her own defense. She'd lain in his arms through the night and he hadn't touched her. She was sure of that now because there was no way she could have made love to Nick and not known it.

"Take me to your room, Nick. I haven't seen it yet."

He stopped kissing her and stared down at her, a question in his eyes.

"You're very sure this is all right with you."

No, she wasn't sure at all, but it was all she could do.

"I think you should know that when all those women were fantasizing around the watercooler, I was fantasizing, too. Only to myself, of course, but still, I've wondered what it would be like to make love with you. Show me."

Chapter 9

Nick took Eve by the hand and led her toward his room. She was right that they shouldn't be doing this. It was against his rules, it would make work difficult, maybe impossible. But nothing would be more impossible than walking away from Eve right now.

He'd been headed this way ever since this project began. He'd been lost long before this day, maybe when he'd first seen her with Charley. There was something incredibly sexy about a woman who could charm a baby.

That was all it was. She was different from the women he usually chose.

This was an oddity, an aberration, a one-time thing.

"We'll make it work," he said. "Somehow."

"What?"

Ah, so she'd been lost in her own thoughts. "Nothing, just…come here,'' he said as he pushed open the door, led her to the king-size bed covered in a plush wine-and-cream-colored spread. ''Come sit with me.''

She chuckled at that. ''You want to sit.''

He raised one brow. ''I want to do much more than that, but I don't intend to simply jump on you the minute I get you in my bed.''

''Hmm, that might be fun.''

''Definitely, but I've waited this long. I don't want things to be over in a rush.''

He guided her to the bed, propped pillows up and helped her lean back against the high mahogany headboard.

She fidgeted with the hem of her charcoal-gray skirt, and he knelt beside her, slipped his hands down her calves and slid her shoes off.

Eve swallowed. ''I suppose you have a system. I'm probably a little out of place here.''

''You belong here, and I don't have a system. With you it's all trial and error. I don't want to scare you.''

''I'm not scared.'' But she looked very nervous.

''I meant what I said, Eve. I want you beyond belief, but I want you willing.''

She nodded. ''Some great assistant I turned out to be. I turn into a ninny the minute I lie down with you.''

''Making love to the boss isn't part of your job requirements. You're the best assistant I've ever had. And I defy anyone to call you a ninny.'' He reached down and unbuttoned her blouse so quickly and efficiently that Eve stared down in shock.

But when she finally raised her lashes, her eyes had gone luminous.

"You're also a woman who knows what to do, who takes command of the situation, Eve," he reminded her. "That's what you're good at, that's why we hired you."

He bent and gently kissed her lips. She had the most captivating lips. Almost immediately he needed to touch her again, and so he brushed his lips over hers once more. He slid her blouse down her arms, his hands tracing silk as his fingers met bare skin.

His breath was coming harsh and fast now, just as hers was. Her breasts rose and fell above the pale blue lace of her bra. He could see the rose of her nipples through the lace, and he just had to taste.

But Eve planted her hands against his chest. She rose to her knees and faced him.

"I'm a woman who takes command of a situation, Nick. That's why you hired me."

And she slowly began to unfasten the buttons of his shirt. Her fingers were somewhat awkward, a fact he found endearing and sexy as hell. When the last button was undone, she shoved his shirt back off his shoulders. It slid and caught on his wrists, and she struggled to unfasten the buttons at his cuffs.

He considered offering to help, but when he opened his mouth, she looked up, her dark hair falling over one eye, her expression mutinous.

"Don't talk," she whispered.

The cuffs finally undone, she freed him from his prison, only to reach out and slide her palms up his chest. The tip of one fingernail lightly nicked his nipple and he gasped.

A predatory look came into Eve's eyes. She might well have been Eve in the garden, planning the downfall of man or the downfall of him. He didn't care.

"Touch me, Eve," he whispered.

She did. He groaned and plunged his fingers into her hair, binding her to him. And then he pulled her away and claimed her mouth.

She was all soft silk and satin, and her mouth was so hot, so pliant.

Eve moaned and opened for him. She swirled her tongue against his and met him kiss for kiss.

"I have to see all of you," he said, and she reached behind herself, her breasts pushing against his chest as she undid the fastenings of her skirt. When he felt the material slip, he slid it down her body, then helped her lift herself free. Now all that kept his gaze from all of her were two little scraps of ice-blue lace.

His head felt as if hot mallets were pounding from the inside, setting him on fire and making his heart lurch from one beat to the next.

"Is this the kind of thing you've had on underneath all those prim little suits you've been wearing for the past two years?"

She lifted a delicate shoulder and the cream of her breast threatened to spill from the cup of her bra. Threatened, but didn't. He swept his hands from her shoulders to her wrists, gritting his teeth and forcing himself to wait.

"There's nothing that says a sensible woman who dresses sensibly has to wear sensible underthings. I like lace and silk," she said.

"So do I. Let's take them off."

She smiled and waited for him as he reached behind her back and unclasped her bra, baring her to his view.

"You are a vision," he breathed, kissing her. He moved against her, and she gasped as his chest grazed her nipples.

"I'm real," she gasped. "And I really want you, Nick." She reached for his belt buckle and pried it open.

He brought her hand to his lips and kissed her palm. Then he quickly removed the rest of his clothing and returned to her.

"Lie back," he whispered, easing her onto the pillows once again. "Let me have you tonight."

"Yes. I want tonight," she said, as he whisked away the last bit of lace that separated them. "Fill me."

"Soon." He kissed her again, then began a path of kisses that led from her lips to her temple, back to her lips and down her chin. He kissed her throat, he swept his hands beneath her as he lifted her, kissing the crest of each breast, her belly and lower still. When she was writhing in his arms, when he was so crazy to have her that he knew he couldn't stop, he raised himself above her and gazed into her eyes.

"Fill me," she said. "Please soon."

"Not soon. Now," he answered, and he slid deep into her. He claimed her, making love to her until her eyes pleaded with him to free her, until his body was slick with sweat and the strain of holding back.

Then, with a low groan, he reached between them, caressed that most sensitive part of her and plunged deep once more. She rose to meet him, and as she cried out and convulsed around him, he gave himself up to an exquisite bliss that rocked him body and soul.

When the world finally slowed down and settled, he knew that something momentous had just happened. Something indescribable.

Too tired to wonder, Nick fell back, pulling Eve into the crook of his arm, against his chest. He slept.

When he came to, she was resting on him, smiling at him.

"You don't have that look of regret in your eyes that I was afraid I might see there," he mused tiredly.

"That's because I don't regret," she said. "Nick?"

"Hmm?"

"I'm not sure—do you think—is it possible to rewind and make that happen again?"

She looked so embarrassed and uncertain, endearing and sweet, he wondered if she knew what a gift her words were.

He pulled her closer and kissed her. "I'm not sure it's possible to do that again, either," he said truthfully. What had happened between them had been unique, possibly a one-to-each-customer experience. "Let's see. Let's try."

They did. They tried, and it *was* possible. The world turned to heat and light and pleasure again.

Nick was just slipping into sleep when the telephone rang. Automatically he picked it up.

"Delavyn Security, Mr. Stevens. Emergency. The baby—"

He didn't wait to hear the rest. Nick ran from the room, praying for a false alarm.

Eve grabbed for Nick's shirt and raced after him.

"Nick, what's wrong?"

"Maybe nothing. Please, God, let it be nothing," he said, but he didn't stop to explain.

When they got to Charley's room, Nick charged through the door and flicked on the light. Eve looked toward the crib. Charley was on the bed, writhing, the blankets tossed aside. His eyes were big and scared, his face was red. He wasn't crying, and his unnatural silence when he was struggling sent terror racing through her.

"Call 9-1-1, Nick. Help him." She rushed to Charley's side. She knew that the paramedics had already been called; it was part of the security company's protocol. But she felt so helpless.

"He looks like he's choking. I've seen it before once. We have to try to dislodge whatever it is," Nick said, his voice tight and thick.

"Yes," she said. Nick's voice cut through her panic and sent a trickle of reason rushing through.

Without another word, she took Charley facedown on her forearm. As gently as she could, trying to restrain her strength so she wouldn't hurt his small frame and yet would provide enough pressure to do the job, she hit him between the shoulders four times, then turned him on his back and pressed on his chest. Who would have thought, when the company insisted that everyone take lessons in CPR, that she'd ever have to do the Heimlich on someone this tiny?

"Nothing, Nick," she cried, and he placed his hand on the small of her back.

"Again," he coached, and she went through the motions again. And again.

Something whooshed out of Charley's mouth. He took a great wheezing breath.

Quickly Nick scooped up the item, then took a howling Charley and grabbed Eve's arm.

"Let's get dressed. If the paramedics don't come in two minutes, we're taking him to the hospital ourselves."

But by the time they got outside, the paramedics were there. They allowed Nick and Eve to climb inside the ambulance and hold Charley's hands as they monitored him.

Later, Eve couldn't remember much of the ride. She couldn't remember much of anything. It was as if her brain had stopped working and she became all emotion until the moment in the hospital emergency room when they took Charley away to check him out, and she and Nick were left alone.

She looked up through eyes that were blurry. "What was it?" she asked in a trembling voice.

Nick fished the item from his pocket where he had put it. A small blue bead not much bigger than the tip of his little finger lay in his hand.

"It's part of his mobile, Nick," she said. "He must have awakened and got up to play. Maybe he even cried out or made some noise. It's not like Charley to be silent. We were close enough that we should have heard him."

But both of them knew why they hadn't heard.

Chapter 10

Nick didn't know who he was more worried about, Charley or Eve. He couldn't begin to deal with the horror that had gone through his mind when he'd seen Charley almost dying before his eyes, or the way the little boy's tiny form had looked stretched out in that big ambulance with people and machines working on him. But Eve, oh, Eve, her sweet face was etched in lines of misery. He could read the self-condemnation in her eyes.

"Don't," he told her. "Don't look like that. You didn't do anything wrong."

"I didn't hear him. I let him get hold of something that could hurt him."

"It was an accident. You didn't put that mobile there. It looked perfectly safe. You couldn't have known."

"You know that's not true."

He did—and yet he didn't. The mobile had been there when they arrived. They had had no reason to doubt its safety. He was willing to go there, to say that, but Eve was clearly miserable, and bound and determined to beat herself up.

"You expect too much of yourself," he said, forging ahead in spite of the fact that he knew she wasn't really listening. Or, at least, she wasn't hearing.

"Nick, no," she said softly, turning to him. "You know what happened."

"Yes, you saved Charley."

"I almost let Charley die because I was too wrapped up in my own passion."

"Eve." He touched her sleeve. "There were two of us in the house, two of us in that bed, two of us caring for Charley."

"You're a man, and one who's never taken care of a child. You couldn't be expected to foresee the problems, but I've taken care of children. I knew what was at risk."

"You couldn't have stopped this from happening. It was only a matter of when you found him, and you found him in time," he insisted. "And if you think I'm letting you take the blame for this alone, then you're wrong, Eve. It's just not going to happen."

She shook her head as if she hadn't even registered half of what he'd said.

"I have to call Larry and Sandra and let them know."

"I've already done that," he said. "They're on the way home."

Swift tears came to her eyes. "They must be so upset."

They had been upset, but he wasn't going to relate that to her—not when she was already being so hard on herself.

"Can we take Charley home?" Her eyes were desperate green ovals, misted with tears and colored with self-recrimination.

Nick jammed his hands into his pants pockets to keep from touching her again, afraid that would only serve to remind her that they'd been touching when Charley had been playing with the mobile. He wasn't going to do anything, not one thing that caused her pain.

"We can't take him home until the morning. The doctor says he's fine, as you know, but they want to keep him overnight, just to make sure."

She bit her lip. "Good, then. He'll be safe."

"Damn it, Eve, don't do this to yourself. Please." *Don't make what happened between us ugly,* he wanted to beg.

But she shook her head. "I already have done it, Nick. Three times with three different children. But it's not exactly me I'm worried about."

He knew. She was worried that she would be forever failing a child.

He wanted to reassure her, make her see reason—

but then, who was he to talk? He'd made it clear that he was never going to attempt parenthood, either.

He couldn't talk. All he could do was pray for a miracle for Eve.

Larry and Sandra swooped into the house in a cloud of expensive perfume, carrying an array of packages.

"Oh, my love. My precious little love," Sandra cried, scooping her son from Eve's arms and hugging him tight, tears in her eyes. "Oh, Charley, my baby, my baby, my baby. Mommy's home. Daddy, too. We're here."

Larry crowded in close and joined in the hugging and kissing. "Are you all right, son? Oh, and to think that you nearly died. He *is* all right, isn't he?" he asked, looking over the baby's head to Nick. "I want the name and phone number of the doctors who were involved, of course. We'll want our own physician to check him out, too."

"It's been done, Larry." Nick's voice was a tad curt, Eve thought, and she knew that he was just protecting her. "He stopped in to examine Charley in the hospital last night."

Larry nodded. "Good, then. If Doc Baines let him go home, then I know that everything is all right. Right, Charley?"

Charley gooed and smiled. He sucked on his fist and looked over his father's head to Eve. He held out his hands to her.

At his side, Nick felt Eve turn in to him, and he wrapped his arm around her.

"Eve?" Sandra's voice was tight.

"I'm so sorry," Eve whispered. "So incredibly sorry. I can't believe I let Charlie get hurt. He's so small. He's such a good baby, such a perfect little angel. You must have gone through hell when you heard."

"Yes," Sandra said on a strangled note, "but...surely you're not blaming yourself for this, Eve?"

"Who else?"

"Who else?" Larry thundered. "Try Charley's parents for one. I hung that blasted mobile myself. Whistled the whole time I was putting it up. If I'd known that someday my boy would almost die because he'd swallowed some little piece of it, I would have thrown it in the garbage, burned it, sued someone—but that wouldn't change things. We chose the blasted thing."

"Yes, and someone irresponsible made it, too. Made it unsafe for innocent babies," Sandra said hotly. "Just to make money. That makes me so angry I could just...well, I could just swear if I knew any good words. I tell you what, too. I'm going to make sure that everyone knows about this product. I intend to make sure that it's taken off the market."

Eve leaned against Nick, and he savored the sensation of having her wrapped against his side. For the past twelve hours, she'd avoided getting close enough to touch him. He'd been cold without her smiles. Not that she was smiling now.

"I appreciate your understanding," Eve said to

Larry and Sandra, "but the fact remains that you left me in charge of your child."

"And we're eternally grateful that we did," Sandra said hotly. "Nick told me how you wanted the security cameras. Without those, no one would have known that Charley was even hurt. If this had happened just two weeks earlier, when Larry and I were here, Charley would have died. Neither of us are light sleepers and there are times when we…well, um, when we get…romantic and I couldn't hear a tornado roaring through the house. We chose you, Eve, because I was so sure that you would step into the fire for my child, that you would risk your life for his, that you would do everything humanly possible to keep him safe. And you did. You did. Look at him. Isn't he beautiful?"

Nick heard a sob escape Eve's lips. He looked down at her, then gently turned her and tipped her head up.

"He's beautiful," she whispered, so low that Nick wasn't sure if anyone else even heard her.

He must have been wrong because Larry and Sandra smiled more broadly, satisfied that their child's value had been acknowledged. But he couldn't help noting that even though Charley's parents hadn't blamed her, Eve didn't seem to have forgiven herself. He wondered if it was possible. After being involved in three incidents when a child had been at risk, she might never be able to bring herself to touch a baby again.

"Hey, little man," Larry was saying. "You go

with your mother now. Nick and Eve and I have business to discuss.'' He turned to face his employees.

"I can't wait to see those tapes. The media's really
playing up our campaign. All kinds of whispers about
what you two have really been doing here. Are they
going to be surprised or what? These new mom and
dad training tapes are going to set Burnside Baby
Foods apart from the rest of the competition. When
people see those, they're going to have a whole new
feeling for what we're all about. I'm going to ask Pete
to do the final editing, and then Friday morning,
bright and early, I'll screen them. I can hardly wait.
We'll have lots to talk about then, so you two go
home and get some rest. Friday is the day of reck-
oning, eh, Nick?''

Nick heard himself agreeing, but all he was regis-
tering was that he and Eve were going their separate
ways today. Right here. Right now.

He was already packed. So was she, their things
placed in separate cars.

Somehow, they both said goodbye to Larry and
Sandra. He gave Charley one last cuddle. Eve gave
Charley one last kiss. Then they were both outside,
in front of their cars.

He looked down into her clear green eyes. "You
okay?''

She nodded slightly. "I'm better,'' she said. "Really. Don't worry.''

Which was like saying, *don't breathe, don't exist.*
"I won't,'' he said because to say anything else
would cause her to worry, too.

"We didn't get around to reshooting those scenes," she said. "Larry's going to be so disappointed. If he should blame you, I—"

He placed two fingers over her lips. "Shh, sweetheart."

She shook her head vehemently. "You know what those tapes were like. You know what Larry's expecting. If he should hold you accountable…"

What was a man to do? Nick gathered Eve in his arms. He kissed her jaw, the tiny spot just beneath her ear. "Go home, Eve," he whispered on a breath. "I'm ordering you to take today and tomorrow off. Larry won't need you until the screening. So I want you to relax. Rest."

She opened her mouth, to protest no doubt, so he just had to cover her soft lips with his own. She tasted of mint. He breathed in the lily-of-the-valley scent of her.

"Drive carefully. I'll see you," he said.

"Drive carefully," she repeated a bit shakily as she climbed into her little car and drove away.

It was only after she was down the road that he realized she hadn't said that she would see him.

He knew what that meant. Larry had pinned all his hopes on her. No question, those hopes had gone unanswered where those tapes were concerned.

Eve wasn't going to get the promotion, but worse than that, he wasn't sure she was even going to care. She considered herself personally responsible for the failure of this venture, and after the incident with Charley, she was going to want to find a place to lick her wounds. Most likely someplace that wouldn't cause her to remember these past few weeks every time she turned around.

That meant she needed a place away from him. And what kind of a man would he be if he couldn't even grant her that much distance?

"Well, you darn well made a mess of things, didn't you," Eve said to herself as she barreled down the road at a speed she hardly ever drove. The truth was that she no longer even cared that she wasn't getting her promotion, or that she was going to be out of a job once Larry saw those tapes. It was Nick she was worried about.

He was so good at what he did, but not many people realized how hard he worked or the hours he put in. When Larry finally viewed those disastrous tapes, he might begin to doubt Nick's abilities. He might start rethinking the business of making Nick his vice president. With the media screaming for something stupendous, Larry would need someone to blame for this fiasco, and Eve knew that she didn't have enough clout to take the fall alone.

"Not fair, Larry. Not right," she whispered as she swerved into her driveway. She had to do something about that.

But as Eve sat down at her computer and began to compose a letter to Larry, she knew this was her farewell to Nick, her love letter to him. He would never know that, of course. She knew those exquisite moments when they'd made love had meant way more to her than they could to him. This was Nick. He made love to women. And when he did, they loved him. *She* loved him, and for her it was special, something she'd never felt before, but she knew that for Nick, their lovemaking had been everyday stuff. She'd become the woman she'd said she never would become—one of Nick's one-night ladies.

She wondered how many of those women really knew him and valued him. She did, and she was going to spend a lifetime missing him. The fact that Larry was going to fire her after he saw those tapes hardly mattered because she would have had to quit, anyway. It wasn't possible to go back and work with Nick, or even near Nick, when she loved him heart and soul. No way could she stick around and watch him move on to the next woman.

But she would do her best to make sure that he didn't suffer any of the fallout from those tapes, and so she began her letter:

Dear Mr. Burnside:

I hope you realize just what a treasure you have in Nick Stevens. Just in case you don't, I thought I'd mention a few of his attributes.

Nick is kind. He looks out for his employees.

Nick never leaves a job until it's done and done right.

He sees the big picture when others only see the details.

Like with me, she thought. He'd known about her fear of babies, even when she seldom admitted it. He'd looked for the woman within.

That woman loved him. That woman was going to miss him forever. Eve felt the sting of tears, but she typed on.

When she finally finished the letter, put it in an envelope and had it ready to mail, she touched it to her lips.

"Be happy, Nick. Please be happy."

She couldn't tell him that she loved him. It would only hurt him to know how much pain loving him had brought her. But she could do this.

She hoped it was enough to save him from Larry's displeasure.

Chapter 11

Nick knew he looked like hell, but then, that should come as no surprise because he felt like hell, too. He'd spent a large percentage of the last two days conferring with Pete, trying to see if the man could make something good out of those tapes that had started out so bad. And when he hadn't been bugging Pete, he'd been missing Eve.

Somehow that prim little woman's soft voice, soft skin and soft ways had crept into his soul. He couldn't even begin to deal with the pain of thinking she just might try slipping out of his life altogether.

Maybe Pete could work a miracle.

"Yeah, and maybe I can turn back time," he said, brushing a frustrated hand across his brow. "Damn it, Eve, don't you know how much you mean to me?"

But how could she? He'd never told her. He'd

never known, and he'd spent a great deal of time explaining how he was not a man to settle down with one woman.

What he was, was a fool. An idiot. A man without the woman he loved.

Was there any way in hell he could convince her of that?

A knock at his door snagged his attention, and he looked up. Larry stood there. He was holding a tape in his hand.

"I couldn't wait," Larry said. "I made Pete show them to me the night I got home."

Nick managed to hide his groan. "Just remember that you gave her no choice, Larry."

"Excuse me?"

"I mean that I don't want Eve blamed for the quality of those tapes. She's a wonder woman, Larry. She's the best you've got. The fact that she was thrown in there with no warning and had to deal with a lug of a nincompoop like me who knows absolutely nothing about babies was a double whammy against her. But she was amazing. She gave it her all. I think she did a damn fine job, considering what she had to work with, and for the record, your son adored her. And she adored him. Have I mentioned that she saved his life?"

Larry gave a slow smile. "You mean after you sent her off and you marched back into the house to tell us that four or five times? We'd already admitted as much, you might remember."

"Just wanted to make sure it was real clear. As for the tapes, you can't expect—"

"For me to hold off on the distribution. You're right. They're too much of a treasure, too hot. I'm getting them out on the market right now."

Nick's brain went fuzzy. Had Pete worked even more of a miracle than he'd asked for? "I thought you said you saw the original tapes."

"Yep."

"The ones that made us look like we didn't know what the heck we were doing?"

"Oh, yeah. I especially liked the one where Charley insisted on having his doll, and so did the test group of pediatricians I rounded up to view the first few tapes on Saturday. And they were rolling in the aisles when Charley...um, watered the plants."

"I don't get it. Aren't these supposed to be training films? Don't you want them to show Burnside Baby Foods in a good light?"

"They do, Nick. They do. You and Eve look like real newbie parents, not some experts who already know it all. And when the two of you pan for the camera and call each other goofy names, it's...well, it's kind of silly and sweet. And the fact that the two of you had a baby and were obviously still so hot for each other was a real plus. That's the problem for lots of new parents. They're afraid they'll lose the spark that helped them make babies in the first place."

"So...you like the way things turned out."

"I love it. This is the greatest thing to happen to Burnside in years. I'm hoping you and Eve can do some follow-up tapes. Maybe the toddler years, maybe the first days of school, maybe..."

"Maybe I'd better find Eve."

That brought Larry up short. "You mean she's not here?"

Nick picked up the letter that lay on his desk. "I have her letter of resignation. She's sorry she let us down."

"Damn. I had a letter from her, too."

Nick bunched his brows. "A copy of this one?"

"A don't-you-dare-hold-this-against-Nick letter."

Nick's throat suddenly hurt. She had cut herself loose and tried to save him. Silly woman. Wonderful woman.

"I guess she thought I might not like the tapes, or maybe she was still feeling bad about Charley. Maybe she doesn't know how much we appreciate her. I'm going to have to do something about that," Larry said.

Nick stood. "No, let me."

She had pulled down the shades, and the house was dark. The television screen showed black and white. The hero was apparently telling the heroine he couldn't settle down to just one woman, but Eve couldn't quite make out the words or the picture. All she could see was Nick's face. All she could remember was how right it had felt to lie beside him, to have him hold her in the dark.

"Never again," she said, as the doorbell rang.

Go away, she thought, although she didn't say the

words out loud. Sooner or later, whoever was there would decide that no one was home and leave.

"Eve! Are you in there? I can hear there's someone there. If you can hear me, let me in."

Eve sat bolt upright at the sound of Nick's voice.

He banged on the door again.

"Eve, please."

A rush of warmth flooded her, but it was quickly swept aside by the realization that he must have received her letter of resignation.

She tried to clear her throat. "I can't come to the door, Nick. I'm busy." Because if she opened the door and he saw her red eyes, he would know instantly that she wasn't nearly as cheerful and breezy and optimistic as she'd tried to make herself sound in the letter.

"With who? Is that a man's voice?"

She turned to look at the television screen where the hero was finally succumbing to the heroine's charms. *"Oh, my darling,"* he said.

"Eve?" Nick's voice sounded less certain now. "If you have a man in there with you and you can't let me in, can you at least come out and talk to me for two seconds. I'll wait...I'll wait if you have to get dressed or something."

But all Eve could think was that Nick was here. He was *here*. She wanted to see him so terribly. But she couldn't see him for fear she'd break down and beg him to love her.

"Eve, it's...it's about Charley. A good thing," he added quickly.

And that was something she couldn't turn away from. She'd worried about her little boy. She hadn't even said goodbye to him properly.

"I'll be right there," she said, rushing into the bathroom to splash cold water on her face. Not good enough but it would have to do. Her eyes were not as red as they had been.

"Nick?" She quickly moved to the door and let him in. She'd been half fearful that he might have gone.

He seemed to hesitate on the doorstep. "Is he gone? Your friend?"

Immediately her eyes slid toward the television set, which she had clicked off.

Nick seemed to collapse against the wall, all six feet of him. "You're alone," he said with a small smile, and then, looking at her more closely, he raked one finger down her cheek. "You've been crying."

She shook her head.

"Oh, damn, darlin'," he said. "Don't worry. Charley's fine, he's completely recovered, and it looks like he's going to be a star. Larry saw the tapes, and what's more he showed them to the people that mattered. They loved them. They loved you."

Eve smiled as much as she was able. He'd come to tell her that their project had been a success. He'd come to reassure her about Charlie.

"Thank you," she said. "I'm so happy for you. I was afraid that Larry would be upset and take it out on you."

"I never worried about that. And if it had happened, it's just a job, anyway, Eve."

"It's your job."

"Yes," he agreed, "and I want my assistant back."

Her heart squeezed tight. "I'm afraid I can't do that." Darn, her throat was closing up, her eyes were turning teary. She quickly looked down and away.

"I've hurt you. You're uncomfortable with me now. I never should have touched you. Hell, I'm such a jerk, Eve."

That brought her head up quick. She didn't even care if he saw the tears. "You're not a jerk. You don't get to say that you're one. I'm an adult, Stevens. I'm responsible for my own emotions."

He took her chin in his hand. "But it looks like someone has messed with your emotions. I thought it was Charley."

She shook her head. "Some very wonderful people explained to me that I helped Charley, and this time, because of a special man whose opinion I trust, I believed them. I'm not a jinx on children. I've just been in the wrong place at the wrong time."

"Or in the right place at the right time. You've saved one or two kids' lives, haven't you?"

She stared silently, then nodded slightly. "I think maybe I have."

"Then, is it Larry and the fear that you had lost the job you loved? Because, if it is, I have to tell you that Larry loves you."

Larry loved her. She was grateful. She was also breaking. And she couldn't speak.

"In fact," Nick continued, his eyes never leaving hers as he shifted position and brought his body closer, "Larry loves you almost as much as I do." His words were low. Eve told herself that she'd heard him wrong, but then Nick reeled her in closer. "It's not even remotely possible that anyone could love you as much as I do, but Larry does love and appreciate you."

Eve's heart began to pound furiously. She almost surged into Nick's arms right then and there, but she stopped herself suddenly. She licked her lips, purposely, and saw his eyes narrow with desire. "I…I take it that you mean 'love' in a casual sense," she said, trying not to hope, steeling herself for what she expected to hear, what other women had heard.

Nick didn't answer. Instead, he bent and kissed her lips. Softly at first and then with fire and hunger. When he finally raised his head, he was breathing hard. "Eve, there is absolutely nothing casual about my feelings for you. You helped me to become the man I didn't think I could be. You helped me realize that I could achieve a balance of play and the tough stuff, as well. I'm so in love with you that I can't even function, and if you'd only tell me what's hurting you, I'm going to spend my life trying to fix it. I'll go after the bad guys for you, even if I'm the bad guy who's caused you to cry."

Eve felt the pain around her heart dissolve. She let the joy rush in as she rose on her toes and brought her lips close to Nick's. "You've already fixed what's wrong. I was just...oh, miserable because I loved you."

Nick smiled down into her eyes. "You're pretty tough on a man's ego."

"Well, then, let me correct myself," she said softly, her lips almost brushing his. "I was miserable because I loved you and couldn't be with you. I know you're marriage shy, and I want you to know that I understand. I won't expect anything of you."

"Well, then, love, I don't think you do understand, but I'm willing to explain the facts to you."

"The facts?"

"Umm," he said as he kissed her, then drew away. "Like the fact that I adore you, and that I want to marry you. And that I want us to have several babies and struggle to raise all of them."

"Will it be a struggle?" she teased.

"It will be a pleasure. Many, many years of pleasure," he said, walking her backward until she was against the arm of the sofa. "Let's start right now."

And he held her as he tipped her back onto the couch and followed her down.

Long minutes later, as they lay in each other's arms, the phone rang. They let it go on, until Larry's voice came through the answering machine.

"Eve, are you there? Is Nick there? I don't know what's happened to the two of you, but I'm coming over."

Eve laughed and Nick groaned. He groped for the receiver. "Don't come over, Larry. I'm making love to Eve, my future wife. We're making more babies so that Charley can have some little co-stars.''

A long silence stretched out. Larry cleared his throat. ''That's good, then. In fact, that's wonderful,'' he said.

''I couldn't agree more,'' Nick said as he hung up the phone and gathered Eve close to his heart.

* * * * *

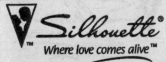